That's right, debutante, quit and run away.

Isn't that what everyone expects you to do? So what if Jeremy dies on your watch? You couldn't be expected to try and save him, could you? You're just a poor little rich girl!

Okay, so I'll quit in the morning.

I crawl forward on my hands and knees, behind the pool pump housing, between the latticework and the bushes that rim the pool. A rustle of leaves a short distance away startles me and I bite back a scream. I see him, ten feet away, slowly rising to peer up over the edge of the pool deck.

I hold my breath, wondering what I'll do when he raises the gun and takes aim, wondering how I'll keep him from shooting Jeremy, or me, or both of us....

Dear Reader,

Porsche Rothschild may be a tad high maintenance, but she's got a heart of gold and perhaps that's why I needed to tell her story. I guess when I start a book I'm just like you, wondering who these new characters are and where their adventures will lead them. I was surprised to find the many hidden mysteries and secrets Porsche's pretty little rich-girl exterior hid. Deep down inside, Porsche needed to find love; she needed to feel that she was making a contribution to the world; and she needed someone and something to believe in. I loved everyone I met as Porsche and I traveled to L.A. Jeremy reminded me of Johnny Depp in *Pirates of the Caribbean*, and Sam, well... What can I say about a man as darkly attractive as that hunk of burning cowboy love? I only hope you have as much fun with my new friends as I had writing about them! Oh, and let's not forget Marlena, the little show-off who just might upstage her mistress now and then!

Please log on to my Web site, www.nancybartholomew.com, and let me know what you think. I love hearing from my readers!

Sincerely,

Nancy Bartholomew

LETHALLY BLONDE

NANCY BARTHOLOMEW

Published by Silhouette Books

America's Publisher of Contemporary Romance

Special thanks and acknowledgment are given to Nancy Bartholomew for her contribution to THE IT GIRLS series.

 SILHOUETTE BOOKS

ISBN 0-373-51380-1

LETHALLY BLONDE

www.SilhouetteBombshell.com

Printed in U.S.A.

NANCY BARTHOLOMEW

didn't seem like the Bombshell type at first. Sure, she grew up in Philadelphia, but she was a gentle minister's daughter. Sometimes, though, true wildness simmers just below the surface. Nancy started singing country music in biker bars before she graduated from high school. And, yes, Dad was there, sitting in the front row, watching over his little girl!

Nancy graduated from college with a degree in psychology and promptly moved into the inner city, where she found work dragging addicted inner-city teenagers into drug and alcohol rehabilitation. She then moved south to Atlanta and worked as the director of a substance-abuse treatment program for court-ordered offenders. Her patients were bikers and strippers and they taught her well…lock picking, exotic dancing, gunplay for beginners and hot-wiring cars.

When the criminal life became less of a challenge, Nancy turned to the final frontier…parenthood. This drove her to writing. While her boys were toddlers, Nancy spent their nap times creating alternate realities. Nancy lives in North Carolina, rides with the police on a regular basis, raises two hooligan teenage boys and tries to keep up with her writing, her psychotherapy practice and her garden. She thanks you from the bottom of her heart for reading this book!

For the "It" Boys! Where would I be without you?

Chapter 1

Emma Bosworth is a manipulative, lying bitch and therefore, my absolute best friend in all the universe, even if she has turned her evil powers against me and Marlena. I can fend for myself, but Marlena's too little to put up much of a fight. I wouldn't be in this complete and total crisis if Emma hadn't convinced me to let Marlena have her nails done *all by herself,* while Emma and I have just the teensiest Cosmopolitan at Bemelmans.

"Now, honey," Emma says, "Marlena will be fine. It's best if her momma doesn't watch and besides, you know how long silk wraps take!" Emma shakes her head slowly, making her long auburn hair shimmer in the shop's light, and smoothes her immaculate Chanel suit impatiently. Emma is not big on public displays of emotion.

I look at my poor, dear sweetie and shudder. Her first silk wraps.

"Are you sure Lisa's good?" I ask.

Emma's already huge green eyes widen and she gives me this look like, "Oh my God, sometimes you are just *so* blonde!"

"Bug," she says. "La Chien is the only salon Vera Wang uses for *her* babies!"

Emma has called me Bug from the first day we met. She said she couldn't stand the name Porsche, even if it is really pronounced like Portia. "It's so nouveau riche," she'd said. "At least be original. Be a red VW convertible with a black leather interior. It's so you—all dark on the inside and flashy on the outside. That's what I'm going to call you, Lady Bug." Only it got shortened to Bug and soon all the girls we hung out with were calling me Bug.

Emma brings me back to reality by taking my arm and pulling me out the salon door. I look back at Marlena and see she is already licking Lisa's fingers; my little ferret, alone for the first time in the big wide world without her mommy!

I am so beside myself that I let Emma drag me away. I drink the first two Cosmos without even realizing what I'm doing and *that's* saying something because Bemelmans' Cosmos are just *so* completely memorable. The third round arrives and I realize an absolutely *sweet* man at the bar is smiling at me.

"Oh, dear God," Emma breathes. "I can't believe it. Why now? Damn!" Then, as if she hadn't said any of that, she says, "Bug, don't you know who that is?"

I'm telling you, all I can see is his black Jack Spade man-bag. I can spot one of those even without my glasses, so if the details of his overall appearance are a little fuzzy, well excuse me. He looks tall, dark and rich. What more do I need to know?

"I have no idea who he is," I tell Emma. "But he fits the profile for 'You Can Smile At Me Anytime.'"

She rolls her eyes. "That's Aldo Huffman," she says, sounding not a little bit impatient.

I squint in his direction and wish I'd put in my contacts, but really, Emma was in such a hurry that I just ran to the limo without putting them in.

"Aldo Huffman? He like, grew up into *that?* He looks so…European. Oh. My. God! He was, like, such a little swine when we debuted! You know he was the kid voted most likely to grow up and face a federal grand jury for embezzling from his own company!" I narrow my eyes into slits and try to make out the details, but it really doesn't matter because he is on his way over to our table.

Five minutes after Aldo joins us, I send a car to pick up my ferret and take her home. Mother love is one thing, but lust is essential to a woman's survival, you know? We have a lovely dinner at La Petit Ennui and decide to hit the Canal Room where Aldo *says* he's meeting a friend. He smiles at Emma and winks, so I figure it's a fix-up.

When Aldo's friend joins us, I have to pinch myself because the man is exquisite. Dark black hair, ultra-Latino, dressed in Armani, with bedroom eyes that make me forget handsome Aldo entirely. Tomorrow the *New York Reporter* will have our faces plastered all over it with "Who's Porsche's New Boy Toy?" captions running below them. Am I lucky or what?

Emma and I hit the ladies' room to freshen up, and I tell her that I think I'm falling in love.

"Don't," she says and the trouble starts.

Something in her voice sends a chill straight through my alcohol-numbed body, sobering me instantly. I mean, don't get me wrong; Emma and I are not fools. We both know I'm not the least bit serious about falling in love. Falling in love, when you're saddled with more money than God, only happens after a thorough investigation of assets, skeletons and criminal backgrounds. So, for Emma to take *The Tone* with me, well, there has to be something seriously wrong.

"Oh, I see, *you* want him."

"Don't be silly, Bug! It's not that. Besides, you're more his type. He likes leggy blondes with big blue eyes, not short, little redheads."

I'm confused. "What then, is he married?"

Emma smiles. "I doubt it." Her face gets that look again though, and she turns away to inspect her lipstick in the mirror. "I know him, not well, but our paths cross now and then and well, I just don't think he's trustworthy, that's all."

I shrug and join her at the mirror. "Oh, well, if that's all…"

Emma won't let it go. "No, Bug, I don't think that's all. God, you and your weakness for the bad boys! I'm serious, Buggie, I don't like him."

I tuck my lipstick back into my beaded Gucci evening bag and turn to stare gravely at my friend.

"Do you want to leave?"

Emma is really getting wiggy on me now. "No, no, not at all! Let's stay. Let's dance. But let's not play favorites, all right? We'll just keep it a group thing, shall we?"

Well, she is my best friend but she is also a very skillful manipulator—this I remember from boarding school. She's not the only one with tricks up her sleeve. I decide right then and there that Emma's not giving me the entire story, so it's up to me to figure it all out on my own.

We walk back out into the club and find Aldo and his

friend already have the best table in the house, right by the dance floor. An ice bucket has materialized by our table. A bottle of Cristal champagne is being opened by a waitress and four champagne flutes sit in the center of the tiny wooden circle.

At least I know the drinks aren't drugged. I slip into the vacant seat next to Aldo's friend and smile as a photographer snaps my picture from the edge of the dance floor. The bouncers rush up to remove him but I wave them away. I'm enjoying this evening too much to waste negative energy on the press.

"Ray, this is Porsche," Aldo says over the noise of the music.

Ray takes my hand, looks deep into my eyes and I feel every nerve ending in my body wanting him. Emma kicks me and I yelp, drop his hand like a hot rock and glower at her. When Aldo introduces Ray to Emma, she smiles knowingly, rises and pulls him up out of his seat and out onto the dance floor.

The scheming bitch! This was her plan all along. She throws me off balance and then runs off with the prize. I remember the way her face changed as she warned me about him. Emma has never been able to lie to me. She doesn't like Ray and yet, there she is, dancing with him.

Aldo slides over, taking Emma's seat, and begins talking about his recent trip to Greece. I listen to him, but the attraction I felt for him is gone. I am distracted, watching Emma and Ray, wondering what in the hell is going on?

When they come back to the table, Aldo stays in Emma's seat and so she takes his and begins laughing and flirting with Ray. I try to kick her and miss. She is too far away. I glare at her when the men are not looking. She ig-

nores me. Many people come up and talk to us, more for
Aldo than anyone, but still, I know people here, too, so for
a while I bide my time and pretend to be fascinated by the
acquaintances who drop by to chat.

At last, I see an opportunity. I pretend to reach for a nap-
kin in the center of the table, let my arm "accidentally"
knock against Ray's almost-full champagne glass and then
gasp as it tips over, falling to spill icy liquid into his lap.
He jumps up, I lean forward as if to help, and with one
smooth movement, slip his billfold out of his suit coat
pocket and slide it down my thigh and into the inside
pocket of my faux chinchilla shrug.

I am so-o-o apologetic! The waitresses come running.
Emma shoots me the evil eye and Aldo misses most of the
moment because he is temporarily distracted by the arrival
of a new bevy of women at the door.

Ray is the only member of our party who is not flus-
tered. He is polite, and affects a very unconcerned manner, but for one brief slice of a second his eyes meet mine
and look straight through to my soul. It is a bone-chilling
search of my intent—at least, this is how it feels—and for
a moment I am worried that he somehow knows what I'm
up to, but then, how could he? I force myself to sit still for
a minute before I excuse myself and wander off toward the
ladies' room again. I am surprised when Emma doesn't
join me.

I dart into a stall, bolt the door and sit down on the toi-
let. I reach for Ray's wallet, feel the smooth soft, leather
and smile as I pull it from my pocket.

"Thank you, Papa," I whisper.

I have one or two very vague memories of my real father. In one, he is a large man, but then, I was but a small

child, and he is laughing as he pulls a quarter from my ear and a flower from my sleeve. My mother and Victor are watching and they are not happy, but Papa is very, very happy. Now I think, perhaps he was drunk, but then, he just seemed happy.

"Leave us alone," I hear my mother say, and she is crying. One day, my father leaves and never returns. When I am older, I buy a magic kit with my own money. I get very, very good at it, but Papa never returns. But when I have magic, he is never very far away.

I open the thin, flat billfold and begin to examine it. There are the usual credit cards. Ray's full name is Octavio Reymundo Estanza and while he lives in Manhattan, I do not recognize the address. His business card is printed on heavy, ivory stock and reads simply "Octagon Enterprises, Inc.," with addresses and phone numbers in New York, Los Angeles and Madrid. I probe further, pulling out a picture of a beautiful dark-haired woman when the door to the ladies' room bursts open. A female voice is speaking in harsh, rapid-fire Spanish.

"Watch the door. If someone wants in, tell them it's broken and they must use the other restrooms."

A second voice, also female, agrees as the door closes behind her. What I hear next turns my stomach and I pull my feet up onto the seat so I won't be seen. It is Emma.

"I don't understand," she says. "What is going on?"

The other woman switches from Spanish to flawless English. "Whore! You know why we are here."

I peek through the crack in the door and see a flash of silver. I think maybe it is a gun. I look at the floor and see three sets of high heels. Shit!

"Listen, if that's your husband," Emma begins again.

She is cut off by the sound of a slap that echoes through the tiled bathroom.

"Shut up, bitch!" the other woman cries. "There is no more time for lies. Tell me who you work for or I'll kill you."

Emma says nothing. She cries out as the woman hits her again, only this time I don't think she has used her hand. What am I going to do? I don't have a weapon. If I try and call for help, they'll shoot us both.

"Who are you working for?" the woman demands. "Who is she? Tell me now and you die quickly—delay and your death will be very painful."

Shit! Victor and Mother were always insisting I hire bodyguards and I was always giving them the slip. Why didn't I listen to them? I draw in a deep, silent breath and think, well, at least it will be an honorable death. I place my feet down onto the floor, flush the commode and slowly open the door.

I can't tell who is more shocked, the two women holding Emma, Emma herself, or me. I step out, just as if nothing whatsoever is happening and smile brightly at them all.

"Hello!" I say. I let my eyes come to rest on the gun and then look at the woman holding the gun. She is the same woman as the one whose picture is in Ray's wallet. Great, the irate spouse.

"Oh, dear me!" I say. "I know you! I just saw your picture! Here, look!"

I shove the small wallet-size picture at her. For a moment she is distracted, and this is all the time it takes. Emma darts around me and does the most amazing kick-thing with her right leg. The gun goes flying in one direction and Emma's attacker is suddenly on the floor staring up at a very irate Emma.

Emma doesn't see the other woman coming for her, but I do. I don't really have any time to think. I just reach out, grab her long, black hair in one hand and yank her backward, hard, into the frame of the metal bathroom stall. Emma springs forward, retrieves the gun from its resting place under a sink and stands up, covering both women with the weapon.

Emma Bosworth has never held a gun in her life, at least as far as I know. Her family is Quaker. They don't believe in it. Yet here's my Emma holding the little silver gun and looking positively *violent!*

She reaches her free hand into her pocket, pulls out a tiny cell phone, hands it to me and says, "Hit one on the speed dial."

So of course I do. A woman answers and says, "Emma?" in a voice I don't recognize.

I look at Emma who says, "Tell her that I need a pickup in the ladies' room."

Now I know the world has turned upside down because Emma Bosworth would never be doing these sorts of things. But I do as I'm told and the woman on the other end says, "Right." But she never asks where we are or what's going on. She just hangs up.

"What about the one guarding the door?" I ask Emma.

Emma looks a little uncertain and appears to be mulling over her options. While I, on the other hand, am completely undone and wish like hell for another Bemelmans Cosmo to settle my nerves. Of course the bathroom door just has to open then, and as I'm standing right by it, I am the one who must deal with the problem.

I grab her arm and pull her forward into the room before she can say or do anything. Emma lifts the gun just slightly so the newcomer can see that someone will surely die if she doesn't behave and says, "Search her."

"Emma," I say, starting to do just as I'm told. "Are you a cop?"

Before she can answer me the door to the ladies' room opens again and the room fills with three very burly men in black camou outfits. The music outside stops and a voice says, "Ladies and Gentlemen, please remain exactly where you are. The Alcohol, Tobacco and Firearms people are only here to perform a routine check for underage patrons. I'm sure no one has a thing to worry about."

Mass panic ensues as nine out of ten patrons begin emptying their pockets of illegal substances and I realize that this is far more than the ATF riding to the rescue. Emma is handing over her prisoners and quietly issuing orders. When she turns to me again, she smiles and takes my arm.

"There's a car waiting for us in the alley," she says.

She reaches for my elbow, but I step back out of her reach. "Emma, who are you and what exactly is going on?"

Emma's lips compress into a flat obstinate line, no longer smiling. "I'll tell you in the car."

"No," I say and shake my head. "Tell me now."

Emma shakes her head. "I can't explain it here, Bug. Come on."

I take another step backward. "I don't think I know you, Emma. Guns? Men in black? ATF? What is all this?"

Emma's features soften. "Bug, honey, I'm still me. I'm just helping with something very important and I'm not allowed to say, at least not here. Trust me, Bug. I'm not a bad guy. I'll take you to meet my boss. You'll see. You'll love her."

It is the pleading look in her eyes that makes me relent and follow her out the back exit of the Canal Room and into the waiting limo, but I promise myself that I'll never again agree to let my poor baby, Marlena, have a silk wrap without mommy.

"You'll love Renee," Emma says as the car pulls out of the alley and accelerates. "But do me a favor, Bug, don't ask any questions. When Renee's ready, she'll tell you about us, but until she is, it's just better if you let it go."

Let it go? Forget women holding guns on Emma and people in black camou outfits swarming the Canal Room like ninjas? *Let it go?* But Emma has that look in her eyes again, and so I figure I'll let it go, for now.

"Oh," I say, digging into the pocket of my shrug again, "here." I hand Emma Ray's wallet. "I don't know if this'll help or not, but I can't keep it."

Emma's eyes widen. "How did you…"

I grin. "You tell me yours and I'll tell you mine," I say, and lean back into the soft cushions of the limousine.

Emma chuckles. "All right, Bug, have it your way!"

We are silent for the rest of the ride, silent as the limo pulls into an underground garage and silent as Emma leads me into an elevator to meet her friend, Renee.

"You're just going to love Renee," Emma gushes again. "We all do."

When I first meet Renee I think she must've watched one too many action-adventure movies. I mean, I know she commands troops of people in black who swoop down to rescue her friends from terrible trouble just in the knick of time, but does she really have to be so incredibly rigid? Don't get me wrong. When I get old like her I want to be powerful enough to have two of *my* friends saved with just one tiny phone call, but I will not lose sight of my femininity.

Renee doesn't look like a man or anything but she's just so formal. I meet her at 3:00 a.m. and she's wearing a Chanel suit and three-inch Ferragamo pumps. Not one auburn hair is out of place. Her makeup is understated and flawless. To make matters worse, she greets me like I'm in a receiving line at the British embassy or something. She's cold, stern and impossibly remote. You'd think she was the Queen of England greeting a commoner.

I look around the room and I realize she's got money, but still, she's not in my financial tier. I try to take some comfort in this. At least I know I'll always be richer than she is, but then, I'll always be richer than almost anyone on the planet. After a point, money is just money. But command, now that's an aphrodisiac. Renee acts as if she is accustomed to the mantle of power; that is what's making me so uncomfortable.

Renee lives in a brownstone and while it is nice, it's no penthouse. And, studying her closely, I'm almost certain there's been work done. I mean, what woman in her forties hasn't had *something* altered? I just can't put my finger on who did her. It looks so natural. Her hair is strikingly auburn. Her complexion fair and unblemished. She's thin, but not anorexic. It's so unfair!

I sit in a wingback chair in Renee's parlor, listening as Renee and Emma talk and wonder why Emma adores Renee. She is about as easy to be around as a porcupine. Still, I haven't been here two hours and Renee has somehow managed to get me to tell her things almost no one knows. I don't mean just the stuff you read in magazines or tabloids, I mean *everything*. She does it so skillfully that I barely realize she's interrogating me while managing not to give away one piece of her own personal information. I've been studying clinical psychology for four years and I still can't do that!

When Renee goes in for the big finish with me she is so good I don't even see it coming.

"So," she says in her clipped, polished voice, "your wealthy stepfather married your mother when you were a toddler. You have never wanted for anything, never worked, never needed and certainly never bothered to exert yourself in any fashion. I suppose you must be wondering who on this planet would miss you if you suddenly disappeared. I mean, if things had somehow gone tragically awry this evening."

We are drinking this amazing white Bordeaux and I admit I'm feeling it. So at first I think she is still speaking to Emma, only she has turned her head in my direction and is still talking.

"No one would miss the 'It' girl," she says. "They would be replaced by the next hot rich thing."

A cold chill sobers me as her words echo in my head. I mean, who would miss me? Paparazzi? My ferret? Emma? Who would remember me for anything but my money? What would my obituary say in *True Style* magazine? Big, fat tears well up in my eyes and I look around for help from Emma, only she has mysteriously vanished. When did she leave the room?

"Emma will miss me," I say, but I sound uncertain, even to myself.

Renee smiles. "Of course she will…for a while. Emma is such a dear girl. I'm sure she'd compose a piece about you—she's such a fabulous pianist. Her life will roll along and eventually, she'll hardly remember to think of you. She won't mean anything by it, but that's just how she is."

Renee sips her wine and stares at the flames dancing in

the fireplace while I just sit there like a lump. I am twenty-four, beautiful, smart, incredibly wealthy and, for all intents and purposes, useless. What am I going to do, endow a building? I swallow, hard, and feel tears threaten to turn into sobs of regret.

"I'm young," I struggle to say at last. "I have lots of time to create a legacy."

Renee turns away from the fire and raises one imperious eyebrow. "Do you? One never knows. Your jet could crash tomorrow. You could wake up with a brain tumor. Does one ever really know how much time one has?"

I chug the last half glass of wine and realize that I am completely sober.

"I'm taking courses in clinical psychology at the New School," I say, and give away the one secret I have left. Against my parents' wishes and without their knowledge, I am going to graduate school. Why do I suddenly feel as if I have to justify my worth to this woman? "I am a semester away from getting my master's, and," I add, "I've almost completed analysis."

"So, you want to be a psychologist, do you?"

"Yes, an analyst."

"And have a private practice or work in a clinic?"

I don't see Renee closing in for the kill until it's too late.

"Oh, private practice, that way I can set my own hours."

Renee nods and smiles her Cheshire cat smile. "So, you'll give up your travels, I suppose. After all, most analysands do require thrice weekly therapy."

I swallow hard. Well, I most *certainly* am not going to do any such thing, but how can I tell her that? And no way was I going to work in a clinic! But if I say any of this, Renee will see me as I'm beginning to see myself, only

Renee and I are both wrong about me. I am a good person, aren't I, even if I don't have much to show for it?

When I don't answer, Renee says, "You're young. You have energy. You know, I run a foundation with women just like yourself."

Oh, a foundation—now *that* was easy. Why didn't Emma tell me Renee ran a foundation? Did she do this in addition to whatever it was she did that involved those commando types? Was she in law enforcement or something?

Maybe Renee will tell all if I express an interest in her charity. All you need to have to join a foundation is money. I can *so* do that.

"I would adore joining your foundation," I gush. But inside, I am secretly disappointed. I suddenly want to join whatever it is that gives you strong, virile men in black SWAT costumes for backup. I want to shoot a gun and flip people over my hip, like Emma did with the Italian woman. It might be fun. I need a thrill in my life. When is Renee going to realize that I am trustworthy and let me in on the *real* deal?

Renee leans back in her wingchair and seems to study me for a moment before she smiles. "I was hoping you'd say that," she says. "The Gotham Roses are a very prestigious group of women. I would guess Emma hasn't spoken much about her work with them, has she?"

I shake my head, genuinely puzzled. She hasn't, and I thought we shared everything!

Renee moves forward in her seat and regards me with a very serious expression. "Porsche, Emma vouched for you. She says you can keep a secret and are not as bubble-headed as your press exploits might lead one to believe."

I start to protest, but something in her eyes stops me.

"Porsche, I would like to tell you about the Gotham Roses, but before I do, I must know that you understand that what I am about to tell you is highly confidential. Lives hang in the balance based on my ability to pick and choose whom I confide in. Would I be making a mistake to tell you about the Roses?"

I have no idea what the woman is talking about but I do know one thing—Porsche Rothschild can carry a secret to the grave. I know things about my friends and their families that would ruin them if I told. Nothing, no amount of liquor or persuasion, has ever gotten one detail past my sealed lips!

"I assure you, I can keep a confidence," I say.

Renee's expression doesn't relax.

"Porsche, if you decide to proceed with this conversation, I will need to tell you something."

I nod, as if she's making sense to me and long for another sip of wine. Somehow I know that this would be the wrong thing to do.

"Porsche, believe me, if I were to learn that one word of what we discuss tonight becomes public knowledge, I could bring forces to bear that would ruin your family and end all possibility of you ever becoming a psychologist. Do you understand me?"

I can hardly believe what I am hearing. Ruin my family? Who the hell is this woman? I know better, but still a frisson of fear ignites deep inside my chest. Do I really want to hear what she has to say?

I swallow, hard. "You have my word," I promise.

Renee nods, reaches into a small wooden box that sits on the end table beside her and withdraws a small, hand-held tape recorder.

"I'll need to make a record of this," she says, and clicks on the tiny machine. "Discussion with Porsche Dewitt Rothschild."

"You know my middle name?"

Renee stops and smiles. "It's not exactly a state secret, Porsche. But, yes, before speaking with you, I had a thorough background investigation completed. As I said, Emma placed your name before me for consideration some months ago. We just didn't have need of your talents until recently."

Talents, what talents?

"The foundation, the Gotham Roses, operates on two levels," Renee begins. "On the lower level, we are a group of talented and wealthy women who do good works in the New York area, promoting worthwhile causes for women. But on another highly exclusive and top secret level, we work to help certain government agencies fight crimes perpetrated against, and sometimes by, the very wealthy."

Renee watches me, to see if I am following her, and so I nod even if I don't fully get it yet.

"Because of our family backgrounds and names, we are sometimes able to gain access to a level of society that regular law enforcement rarely permeates. Because your name is so instantly recognized, Porsche, and because of your reputation as a party girl..." Renee holds up her hand as I begin to protest. "Deserved or not," she adds, "we have a need for your help."

I am thrilled. I am so excited suddenly to be a member of the team that I almost jump out of my seat and kiss the woman, and yet, a little voice inside my head says, *Be careful what you ask for!*

"A situation may be arising," Renee continues, "in

which we could use someone with your skills in the psychological arena. I mean, I know you're by no means a trained psychologist, but you do have a certain understanding of these sorts of issues. And the situation I have in mind requires a certain delicacy and, shall we say, name recognition. We need a very high-profile socialite for this case, an 'It' girl, someone everyone knows and watches and yet, doesn't take seriously."

Doesn't take seriously? Now wait a minute!

Renee ignores the frown on my face and keeps right on going. "We have a little bit of training that you'll need to undertake, as a precaution. You probably won't need it, but it's always nice to have a few tricks up your sleeve just in case. It will certainly be nowhere *near* as risky as the situation Emma was involved with, but still, it's nice to be able to take care of yourself in a pinch."

Of course, I had no idea then what Renee was talking about. And here it is, almost two weeks later and I still feel like Renee hasn't told me everything. However, I'm realizing Emma Bosworth and Renee Dalton-Sinclair had this all mapped out long before I flew in from Paris with Marlena and decided it might be lovely to have my ferret's nails manicured. Renee's investigators have done their homework, too. How else could she know so much about me? That I have an almost photographic memory? Or that I grew up thinking Victor Rothschild was my real father, right up until I found my mother's old marriage certificate saying she'd been married to some man named Lambert Hughes when I was born? How else would she seem to know every secret I've ever told that devious Emma if they hadn't been plotting to get me into Renee's elite little club?

"Why didn't you tell me?" I ask Emma the next afternoon. I am hoping she will think I know more than I actually do and tell me the rest of the story, the real guns-and-ammo part of the story.

She has the nerve to play dumb. "What?"

"The Gotham Roses? How could you be involved in something so secret, so dangerous, so…"

"We try and help others," Emma began, but I cut her off.

"Bullshit! Renee says you work with the FBI, the CIA and God knows who else. And this training, my God—self-defense, secret communication devices, and yet you two just keep saying it's really not dangerous? Renee says it's more of a psychological assessment than a real mission. What are you guys, superspies?"

Emma looks at me like I just don't get it, sighs and shakes her head. "Bug, this is not a game and it's not all glamour. We are not Charlie's Angels. Renee works for a woman she calls the Governess on cases that involve the top layer of society that others just don't have access to because they don't have the right contacts. We do the training because Renee feels it's better to be prepared for anything, even if the danger doesn't materialize."

"Oh, Emma, please!" I say. "Next thing you'll be saying 'It's dirty work but somebody's gotta do it!'"

Emma nods. "Well, it is. It's unfortunate that there's so much crime among the rich and privileged, but that's the way the world is now. The Governess is not without her enemies, either. There is someone she and Renee call 'The Duke,' who is just as determined to bring down the Governess and the Roses as we are to stop his nefarious influence in the top echelon of society. The Gotham Roses are not dilettantes trying on crime-fighting for a hobby."

I don't believe a word of it, but two weeks later, after personal trainers and coaches have done their best to work me over and prepare me for anything, I'm actually relieved to be leaving town. So what if my assignment isn't exactly dangerous? No matter how it turns out, it'll still be better than riding the endless party circuit and listening to dull stories told by dull people. I'll actually have a life, even if I can't tell anyone about it!

The night before I am due to leave Renee calls me into her study and tells me all about my assignment.

"Jeremy Reins, the actor, says someone's trying to kill him," Renee says. "But the evidence indicates it's just another one of his publicity stunts."

She tells me this right after I come in from a grueling sparring match with her self-defense expert, Jimmy "The Heartbreaker" Valentine. I've broken four nails, had half my extensions pulled out and have the beginnings of a nasty bruise forming under my right eye. And here is Renee, telling me she doesn't think it's even a true assignment?

"So, why not blow the idiot off?" I ask. "It's not like he's really *anybody.* Besides, he's been getting himself into a lot of trouble lately. The talk is that he has an attraction for kinky sex with very young men." I shrug. "He's just an actor."

"Just an actor?" she says raising that eyebrow of hers.

"Okay, okay, so he's golden at the box office, but who cares? I mean, if he's faking it, why not just let him hire extra bodyguards?"

Renee shrugs. "The Governess feels he's a national treasure and Jeremy's agent, Mark Lowenstein, is married to a woman who has done us many favors in the past. Andrea Lowenstein is saying she feels a stalker or even a terrorist could be behind these attacks. Reins has done several commando, patriotic, action-adventure films in the past and could be the object of a terrorist vendetta. The Governess feels Andrea Lowenstein's concern is credible. Anyway, it's just not good to ignore such a visible and beloved member of the public. If something really did happen, it would make the rest of the country uneasy. We don't need to take that chance."

She smiles at me, like I'm going to fall for it, and says, "We have you. With your training in clinical psychology, you'll be perfectly capable of discerning the threat level and letting us know if we need to send a team of more seasoned agents out to eliminate the issue."

Seasoned agents, right! I'm sure the entire thing is just a publicity stunt. But I have to admit the idea is somewhat enticing, especially with the rumors I've heard on the circuit that Jeremy is gay. I like knowing the real scoop and this will certainly be the way to find out. Renee doesn't wait for me to accept. She assumes I will do her bidding and continues talking.

"You'll be Jeremy's date for the Oscars and he'll be yours for CeCe Goldberg's post-Oscar charity party. That's your cover, a budding romance and your charity work," she says. "All the Roses have special charities they support. Yours is the Miller Children's Home. CeCe Goldberg, as I'm sure you know, is not only a world renowned investigative reporter, she is also director Spiro Goldberg's wife and quite active with children's charities. You'll be the celebrity co-host of the post-Oscar event for a new children's home attached to Miller Children's Hospital. Andrea Lowenstein will be the only one who knows your true reason for staying at Paradise Ranch. Jeremy will be only too happy to have you as his guest because he doesn't want the rumors about his sexuality spreading and destroying his box office appeal. You have both the name and the, er, reputation to dispel any and all doubts the public may have. I'm sure he'll be only too happy to stick to you like glue and show you all around Paradise Ranch, as well as the rest of L.A."

I ignore the comment about my reputation and instead roll my eyes at the mention of Jeremy's estate—Paradise Ranch, how nouveau riche.

"Has he hired extra security?" I ask.

Renee smiles. "You're catching on, I see. As a matter of fact, he hasn't. He *says* he doesn't want his attacker to think he's scared."

Great. A wild-goose chase. But then, who else would get a shot at analyzing Hollywood's bad boy? Oh, Renee Dalton-Sinclair is good, all right. She doles out just enough information to pique my curiosity and ensure that I am willing to undergo all kinds of crash courses in self-defense and investigation, then turns me loose and says it's probably nothing at all.

"You know," she says, "with your almost photographic memory and your graduate level course work in clinical psychology, you could be most useful to the Gotham Roses, should things go well with this assignment."

Good old Renee, dangling that golden carrot in front of me. I can only become a permanent fixture in her elite undercover organization if I prove to be successful in my mission in Los Angeles. If I wind up blowing it, I'll be useless to the Roses. Of course, I am not about to blow it; sneaking around spying into the secret lives of my fellow rich and famous sure beats attending boring theory courses in psychology at the New School. This is where the real fun is.

"What about the press?" I ask. "I mean, will they accept that Jeremy and I are an item? We've never been seen together in public before now."

Renee smiles. "Oh, but you have. Andrea and I have taken care of that on both coasts. Just read *In The Know*. Rubi Cho's mentioned the two of you at least three times in her gossip column for the *New York Reporter* this week. And Andrea's had Jeremy's publicist vehemently denying any blossoming romance between the two of you. That should be enough right there to spark a paparazzi feeding frenzy."

When I wake up in the morning, I pack and prepare for the long trip to L.A. and my new action-packed life. As I walk out to Renee's waiting limo, her fifteen-year-old daughter, Haley, comes running up behind me.

"Hey!" she calls. Then, when I keep walking, she says it again. "Hey!"

I stop and turn to look back over my shoulder, surprised because the little twit's made a point of ignoring me for the entire time I've been a guest in her home. She's standing there in her school uniform, looking like a runaway Playmate with her long, straight blond hair, her huge, gray eyes and that innocent, pouty mouth older women pay big bucks for at the plastic surgeon's office.

I think she's talking to the driver until she zeroes in on me and says, "Mind if I ride along to the airport?"

I figure it's Marlena who's garnered her interest so I say, "She bites."

"What?"

That's when I realize Haley hasn't even noticed Marlena wrapped around my neck like a fur scarf.

"You need a ride to school?"

Haley shakes her head and starts walking toward the car like she owns it, which I suppose, technically, she does. She breezes past me, clambers into the back seat of the limo and before I can even sit down says, "Are you really Jeremy Reins's girlfriend? So, what's he like in bed?"

"What?"

I look at Renee's princess daughter and know my mouth is hanging open. I reach forward, hit the button to slide the privacy glass up between us and the driver and then turn to give the little twit a piece of my mind.

"Listen, where I come from we don't kiss and tell—and even if I did, I wouldn't tell a kid like you about something like that! What is wrong with you?"

Haley leans back against the seat and looks at me and I realize she's completely unfazed by my attempt to chastise her.

"You're a prude, aren't you?" she says, like it's a matter-of-fact thing and not a slur on my good name.

"No," I say, wishing Marlena would wake up and bite the little shit. "I am just wise enough to know when to keep my mouth shut."

"Oh, come on!" Haley says, pouting.

"Does your mother know where you are?" I say, and immediately want to shoot myself for sounding like my own mother.

"Can I bum a cigarette?"

"I don't smoke," I say, and realize, too late, that Haley is right in the middle of Mahler's separation-individuation process and doesn't really *mean* what she's saying. So I remember my training and attempt to be therapeutic; after all, this is the first day of my new life.

"Haley, in order to break away from your mother and become your own person, it is perfectly normal for you to rebel and do things that your mother would disapprove of," I say. "But smoking will kill you."

"Oh, blow me!" Haley says. Then she sits up and starts rummaging through the drawers of the wet bar until at last she retrieves a pack of cigarettes and a lighter.

"Don't even think about lighting one of those things!" I command. "Marlena is allergic to smoke."

Haley gives Marlena a look, like she's trying to size her up, and finally tosses the pack of unfiltered cigarettes back into the drawer.

"What is he like?" she asks, reverting to Jeremy.

"Spoiled," I answer.

"Does he love you?"

I give up and decide to enjoy my new role as Jeremy Reins's fictitious girlfriend. I smile slyly and raise my eyebrows, and then lean in close, like I'm actually going to share a secret with this hellion.

"He's *mad* for me," I say, and giggle. "He fills my tub every night with champagne heated to a perfect ninety-eight degrees, and then he floats rose petals on the water, and not the red ones, either. He knows I abhor red roses, so he has pale yellow and orange ones flown in from his farm in Florida."

Haley's eyes are practically popping out of her head and I continue, completely into the lie now.

"He once took a slim silver dagger and sliced a thin line down the center of his chest. When it bled he looked at me, with tears in his eyes…."

"Because it hurt?" she says, interrupting.

I shake my head. "No, it was the depth of his emotional attachment to me that made him cry. He said 'I would cut my heart out for you, for our love.'"

Haley sucks in her breath. "But like, wouldn't he be dead then?"

I close my eyes and shake my head slowly back and forth. "No, *idiot,* he meant it as a gesture and as a way of saying that our love would transcend our current earthly incarnations and last for all eternity."

"Oh, man!" Haley sighs. "I want to be loved like that!"

Don't we all, I thought, and am relieved to see the airport come into view. How had Haley learned about my mission anyway? Was her mother careless? What if this had been a really dangerous assignment? But when I ask Haley about it, she shrugs and smiles coyly.

"I'm not the only sneaky person in the family," she says. "I have my ways."

I make a mental note to take this up with Renee upon my return. Perhaps the bond between mother and daughter could be repaired with stricter generational boundaries; at least, that's the family systems theory. I personally think a good smack is in order.

"Please, please, please get his autograph for me," Haley begs as I get out of the limo and start for the private concourse. Then, apparently thinking this uncool, she shakes her head vigorously. "No, don't do that! Bring me a pair of his underwear instead. Used."

I don't think this even warrants a response. I leave her there, staring after me and walk away as fast as I can. I breeze past the security checkpoint and to where a private plane waits for me. For once in my life, I'm glad to be leaving New York. L.A. and Jeremy Reins seem like a vacation compared to the rigorous two weeks I've had training to be a Gotham Rose.

I toy with the idea of calling my mother, but just as quickly decide not to. She and Victor have been in England for three weeks now and I try to forget the argument we had before they left. Parents just have a hard time letting their adult children lead their own lives. Mama was just mad because I bought a penthouse in the West Village instead of living with them.

The flight is so long! It seems to be taking forever to reach L.A. and maybe that's just fine with me because I can't decide if I'm nervous about the next week or just sick of flying.

"Miss Rothschild, we are making our approach to LAX," Tim, the pilot says over the intercom finally. The stewardess emerges from the cockpit, somewhat disheveled from her attempt at keeping her balance while we pitched and rolled, takes her seat and buckles herself in for the landing.

I look out the window and then over at Marlena in the seat beside me. She's curled up, sleeping, looking like a tiny snowdrift of white fur except for the itty-bitty black satin eyeshades I had made for her. She likes them. The moment I put them on, she settles down and goes to sleep. Before the eyeshades, I had to sedate her when we traveled. I figured, what a ferret can't see, a ferret won't worry about, and I was right.

The runway comes up to smack the plane tires and we land with a little bump that shakes Marlena awake. I reach over and take off her blindfold.

"We're here, sleepyhead," I say. Marlena yawns, showing a mouthful of pearly, sharp teeth, and I lean down to kiss her nose. "We're going to Paradise."

I gather up Marlena and my purse, and begin making my way to the front of the plane and stop when I see Tim, the pilot, standing by the doorway. This isn't unusual—in fact, it's expected—but something about Tim is different, and before I can even consciously figure out what is wrong with the picture, I find myself feeling irritated.

He stifles a yawn, tries to cover it with by smiling, and says, "Hope you had a good flight, Miss Rothschild."

I feel a tiny frown wrinkle its way across my forehead and try to smile back, but I'm thinking *Since when have I been Miss Rothschild to you and not Porsche?* And a visual memory cue plays its way across the movie screen inside my head and I see Tim and I clinging to each other and laughing one sweltering hot night on a beach just south of Rio de Janeiro and realize that even months after that mistake of an encounter, I was still Porsche, so what's changed? And then I notice that the zipper on Tim's pants is not quite fully zipped and I see the tiniest smear of pink on Tim's collar. It is the same shade of pink lipstick the new stewardess, Dorothy, is wearing. I feel my face start to color.

I nod to Tim, but it's frosty. I continue on past him, down the steps toward Dorothy, and I am so intent on my mission that I almost fail to notice three people walking across the tarmac toward the plane, two men and a brunette.

Then I see something else, a brief flash of silver glinting in the sunlight of a bright L.A. afternoon. When I glance in that direction, I see two men driving a baggage cart toward the plane, which would be fine if my Hawker jet were a commercial carrier, but completely out of place now, especially as the cart has the words "Amazon Airlines" emblazoned on the front grill.

I start to turn my head back toward Dorothy, and stop

as something distracts me. I squint, narrowing my eyes and trying to force my 20/60 vision to do more with the far-off object I see held in the man's free hand. A gun? Certainly not. But the cart picks up speed and seems not to notice the three people in its path mere yards away.

I'm on the bottom step when something—instinct— takes over and I shove Marlena into Dorothy's surprised arms and take off running.

"Look out!" I yell, not sure if I'm warning the three people in harm's way, or the unaware driver.

I am running faster than I have in years and I have the advantage because I'm closer to my greeting party than the cart is, but it has a motor and I'm wearing Manolo Blahniks with a three-inch heel.

"Look out!" I scream.

The brunette is the only one who hears me. She looks up, sees me running and does a double-take as she sees the baggage cart heading right for her. I am close enough to see the fright in her eyes, to hear the whine of the engine as the maniacal driver stomps on the accelerator and bears down on his waiting victims.

The brunette swings left, stiff arms the man on her right and I see them both fly backward. I launch myself toward the other man and feel my body soar into the path of the oncoming vehicle.

I hit Jeremy Reins midchest, hear the whoosh of breath leaving his body as we fall. I smell hot exhaust fumes and hear the cart's engine rush past us, missing us by inches, it seems. The cart squeals to a stop, backs up and then the guy turns the cart around. He is actually heading back in our direction. At first I assume he is coming to check on us, but with a shock I realize this is not the case.

"He's got a camera!" the brunette cries.

A camera? Not a gun, but a camera?

Two other guys come running out from the concourse building onto the gray tarmac—big, burly men wearing suits and carrying guns. They waste no time. They fire and the driver takes off, circles wide and veers away from us, but his passenger just keeps snapping away, apparently oblivious to the fact that he's being shot at! Beneath me, Jeremy Reins is recovering his composure.

"Hel-lo, darling!" he drawls. "Come to Daddy!"

I look down at him and see dark eyes, black, curly long hair, and realize this fool is smirking at me. I am lying directly on top of him and I realize something else at the same time; contrary to popular belief, Jeremy Reins is not only *not* gay, he is quite happy to meet me.

He brings his hands up, cups my bottom and gives *me*, Porsche Rothschild, a firm double-handed squeeze! I draw back and am about to slap him, when his eyes darken, his grip tightens, and he says through gritted teeth and a completely phony smile, "Watch it, lovey, the press has its eye on us!"

I plaster an equally fake smile on my face, dart a quick glance to the right through my dark Versace sunglasses and see the swell of photographers lining the upper windows of the concourse. My heart is pounding. My hands are shaking, and I am resisting the ridiculous urge to cry—all signs, I'm sure, of my leftover adrenaline rush and the near miss with the baggage cart.

Jeremy pulls me down into a long, slipped-tongue kiss of welcome, which I resist for all I'm worth. "Lovey, now, play along!" he cajoles.

I ignore him and push away just as the two men with

guns arrive, accompanied by the brunette and a man I assume must be Jeremy's agent, Mark Lowenstein.

"Jesus Christ!" Lowenstein gasps, panting for breath and struggling to brush invisible dust off his black suit jacket. "Those assholes could've killed us!" He turns to look at the brunette by his side and his expression takes on an almost worshipful quality. "Thank God, Andrea's got her brown belt. I will never say another word about you taking those classes, Andrea honey. They might've killed us!"

Andrea smiles at her husband indulgently. She is a tall, statuesque brunette in her midforties with long, brunette hair pulled back into a smooth ponytail. Her face is flawlessly made up, just enough to look polished and not enough to look as though she uses anything but the merest trace of mascara. She is wearing a tailored, Anne Klein suit, a cream silk T-shirt beneath it and a massive rock that has to go fifteen carats on the third finger of her left hand. Money without advertisement.

"Mark," she purrs, "you wouldn't say anything to me about my classes even if this hadn't happened. And you were not almost killed—it was just stupid paparazzi trying to get a close-up."

I look at Mark and realize the man is clearly besotted with his wife, even though he is trying to appear in control and unaffected.

"The true credit for your safety should lie with this woman," she says, turning to meet my gaze. "She's the one who warned us. Porsche Rothschild, I believe?" she asks, extending her hand toward me.

I feel like an absolute idiot. I have made a fool of myself over a couple of paparazzi in a baggage cart. There was absolutely no danger and now Andrea, a complete stranger, is trying to help me save face.

Her grip is firm, her blue-gray eyes clear, and her smile honest. My kind of woman. I find myself grinning back at her and making a mental note to keep her around, in case a real threat to our safety materializes and I need help.

In the meantime, Jeremy has dusted himself off and is now standing behind me. When I turn around, I see he still has the same stupid smirk stuck on his face but when I concentrate on his eyes, I think I see fear there. A little frisson of apprehension runs down my spine and hits my stomach. Had he mistaken the paparazzi for a threat, too?

"What the fuck were you two doing while Miss Rothschild here was attempting to save my ass from the over-eager press?" he asks the security guards. His voice is dangerously low and ugly, deceptively so when you take into account that he is still smiling and attempting to fool the paparazzi on the upper level of the concourse.

"Sorry, Mr. Reins," the shorter of the two says. He is bald, his body thick with steroid-improved musculature, his eyes small and deeply set into his puffy, reddened face.

"I'm afraid we were unavoidably detained," the taller one says, his voice deep and gruff, like an ex-military officer. He smiles, his blue eyes twinkle and I realize he is attempting to be charming, but when I take in the flattop haircut and the military bearing, I don't buy the act. His eyes are flat and cold. He is angry at being taken off guard and resentful of me because I'm the "girl" who just did his job for him—at least, that's how I figure he is thinking.

"What is it that you people say, Scott?" Jeremy says. His tone is mocking. "Excuses satisfy only those who make them?" He doesn't wait for the man to answer. "Perhaps you and Dave stopped to bugger each other in the men's room. It really makes no difference to me. What matters is that I was nearly killed and I pay you to prevent that!"

Jeremy's voice had taken on a hysterical quality and I began to wonder if Jeremy's complete personality was just one long acting class. Rage, then hysteria with the body-guards, and cheeky nonchalance with me; what does he really feel about what just happened?

Mark's cell phone rings and he turns away briefly to take the call. Behind us, a door from the concourse building flies open and two uniformed security guards come barreling out onto the concrete, heading at a run toward our little cluster.

"Handle them," Jeremy says to his security guards. He turns his back on the others, blocking my view of them with his body. The smirk has returned as he cocks his head and reaches out with one finger to chuck my chin. "Shall we go to the car?"

"Give me a moment," I say. "I need to collect Marlena."

Jeremy raises an eyebrow. "Oh? You've brought a play-mate along? How delightful! The more the merrier, I always say. Will she be sleeping with us?"

I feel a tiny switch flip somewhere inside myself and I temporarily forget all about Renee Dalton-Sinclair, the Gotham Roses and the salivating paparazzi above us.

I reach out, snatch Jeremy's shirt collar and, before his little pea brain can register what's happening, pull him toward me, so close I can smell the scent of cigarettes and cologne on his small, wiry body.

I smile as I look into his insolent eyes, but the smile is all show. I am well aware that he can read the full intent of my warning in my eyes.

"Listen to me, you little punk," I say. "I am here to cover your ass, not grab a piece of it. You will keep your hands to yourself and your mind out of the gutter where I'm concerned. If you don't, I promise you this, I will cut your balls off while you sleep and stuff them inside your still-beating heart. Are we clear on that point, *lovey?*"

I smile and wait for his answer.

"Why, Lovey," he murmurs. "I didn't know you cared!"

Chapter 2

I don't slap Jeremy. I want to, but I realize this is just what he wants me to do, so I stop myself. Marlena is mad as hell, though, and she starts chittering and hissing at Jeremy, who seems highly amused by her. I watch all this and begin to formulate an opinion about my spoiled charge; he gets off on other people's reactions. I suppose this makes him more of a true director than an actor, but it also fits with Renee's supposition that Jeremy is staging the threats on his life in order to create publicity. I mean, Jeremy Reins is about as well known as any star in Hollywood. He doesn't need more publicity, but now I see he craves it.

Andrea takes my arm as we're walking toward the car, with Jeremy and Mark several yards ahead.

"Porsche, I'm so glad Renee sent you," she says in a low voice. "I was afraid she might not follow through on this."

I am trying to calm Marlena down and so I am not being my most tactful self when I say, "He's full of shit and this is just a big game to him."

To my total surprise, Andrea nods in agreement. "Actually," she says, nodding to the two men ahead of us, "they're both assholes at times, but you need to look past that."

I'm not sure what to say. I mean, I think she's just called her own husband an asshole, which even my mother, faced with her husband's philandering, fails to do when the occasion really calls for it. So I switch to active listening mode and nod sympathetically. "So, you look past their behavior?" I murmur, using her own words to lead her on to her next thought because this is what good therapists do, they open the gate, but never shove the patient through.

"Yes," Andrea says. "Mark is really an overgrown little boy who desperately wants approval, but he needs to feel that he is in charge. He blusters and tells me what I should and shouldn't do, and then I just do as I please. You know what I mean?"

I nod and smile softly, but I'm thinking, why would you do that? We enter a building and as we follow the two men down a long corridor, Marlene falls asleep again—she is not therapist material.

"Jeremy is a lot like Mark, really," Andrea continues. "He comes off like a spoiled brat, but he's really quite insecure. Mark would give you the shirt off his back, but he needs to be praised. Jeremy's the same way—he's really very good-hearted."

I forget therapist mode and fall into my new bodyguard persona. "Then why the threats on his life? Why set up a scenario like that? Why doesn't he just buy a poor family a house or something?"

Andrea laughs and sound makes Mark look back over

his shoulder at her. Andrea's laugh sounds like wind chimes—high, musical and pleasant.

"Jeremy needs the drama and Mark loves to provide it." Andrea's eyes darken and a small frown furrows her forehead. "I think at first it was just to call attention to Jeremy's new project. It's a very dark picture about a religious figure who rises to become the leader of a powerful new nation. I think they wanted to blur the lines between the project and Jeremy the person, but something has gone wrong and Mark won't tell me what it is."

I switched back to therapist. "Mark won't tell you what it is?"

Andrea almost whispers her answer, "no." She takes a deep breath and pushes through double doors that lead to a waiting stretch limo. Jeremy and Mark are just climbing inside the car, and in order to finish her thought, she grips my arm tighter and pulls me aside.

"They don't think I know about all this," she says. "And really, I don't. What I mean is, Mark would be terribly angry if he thought I was interfering with his business. We made an agreement when we got married years ago that I stayed out of his business affairs. He's quite particular about that. I think his first wife nearly ruined him and he needs to feel as if his business is completely under his control now. So I learn what I can by listening when he's talking and piecing things together."

She glances at me, as if trying to gauge my reaction. "I don't mean I intentionally eavesdrop. I just mean that when he says something, or if he's on the phone, I pay attention. I try to look out for him. The entertainment business is ruthless, Porsche. The more I know about Mark's business, the easier it is for me to avoid little pit-

falls and unpleasantness in our social life. Do you understand?"

I am nodding like a bobblehead, but I am totally not sure
at all about what she means. I assume she's trying to tell
me that the world is full of ruthless, dishonest people, but
like, duh, who doesn't know that?

"When these occurrences began with Jeremy, I noticed
that Mark didn't seem nearly as concerned as others were.
Then I realized that Jeremy wasn't just playing at not being frightened, he was genuinely enjoying the attention. I
realized then that they'd concocted this entire scheme for
whatever misguided reason they'd felt it necessary. But two
weeks ago, everything changed. There hadn't been any
threats for almost three weeks and suddenly they started
back up again. This time Mark was almost hysterical and
Jeremy was scared to the point of seeming enraged at
Mark. That's when I knew…"

The limo's rear window slowly slides down and Jeremy
pokes his head out, waggling his finger in our direction.

"Loveys," he calls. "Are you two going to join us, or
must you gossip there on the street like common pigeons?"

His voice has taken on an exaggerated English accent,
and as much as he is trying to keep the tone a gentle tease,
no one is fooled by the act. Jeremy is tense and angry and
working mightily to disguise it.

As we enter the car, Marlena wakes up at the sound of
Jeremy's voice and leers at him from the safety of
Mommy's arms. He stretches out a finger in Marlena's direction and I say, "Watch it, she'll bite you!" But to my
amazement, she doesn't, and Jeremy coos something unintelligible to her and turns his forefinger up right under
her nose, offering her the meatiest part to bite down on. I

suppose it is his way of apologizing for his earlier behavior and I am shocked when my normally suspicious ferret sniffs, but does not chew, the fleshy digit.

"That's a love," Jeremy murmurs and I am reminded that he is rated one of the ten sexiest men on the planet. Of course, I do not find him remotely attractive. To me, Jeremy Reins is a street urchin, thin, unkempt and ill-mannered. The word on him in my circles is that he is quite the slut and not at all discriminating about who he beds, male or female. Recently, all I've heard about Jeremy is that his tastes are now purely reserved for the male gender. Of course, that little rumor was put to rest quite quickly out there on the runway, but I realize I am allowing my mind to drift quite far off the task at hand.

"So, Porsche," Mark says genially, "do you spend much time in L.A.?"

I take the flute of champagne that he hands me and sip it appreciatively before answering.

"No, I'm afraid I find L.A. to be rather tiring," I say, but then I smile at him and hold my glass out in front of me. "However, I've never been treated so graciously."

I hear Jeremy chuckle softly and ignore him as Mark smiles delightedly. "Ah, a connoisseur—I see we will have much to discuss."

But I'm not thinking about champagne. I am thinking instead that I need to shake this man and his manipulative little client until they give up the truth about their little publicity gimmick and tell me how it seems to have gone out of control and taken on a dangerous life of its own.

I am about to ask this when Andrea interrupts her husband.

"Weren't we lucky then, to have Porsche join us for the Oscars?"

She licks her upper lip nervously and I look at her flute and find it nearly empty. What's with her? I wonder.

"I am so glad I called my old college buddy and learned of Porsche's desire to attend the festivities. Of course, Jeremy, I know you'll be glad to return the favor when you escort Porsche to CeCe Goldberg's big do next week."

The three of us are looking at Andrea like she's suddenly sprouted an additional head. She's babbling, talking like this is some elaborate play date she's arranged and not a case of Jeremy's life being on the line and me coming to the rescue, real or imagined…and of course, then I get it. That is exactly what's going on. Jeremy and Mark have no idea why I'm really here, a fact Andrea seems to have omitted in her plea for help to Renee. She is pulling the strings like a puppet master and the three of us were all dancing.

"What?" Jeremy sputters. "Charity party? I hate that old windbag!"

"Oh, now, Jeremy, didn't Mark tell you?" Andrea says, her voice taking on a soothing mother quality.

Mark is looking equally flummoxed. "Charity party? What charity party?"

Andrea manages to look sweetly frustrated with her husband, but I note the beads of sweat that pop out along the ridge of her upper lip.

"Now, honey, remember? You said Jeremy needed to plump up his image and also show his fans that he was not frightened by the threats on his life. You thought the Oscars and the party would be perfect opportunities, and what a coup to be going with Porsche. The press will be all over you two! I mean, Hollywood's bad boy and New York's 'It' girl, what an amazing duo you'll be!"

Jeremy has started scowling and I believe I am seeing his first honest emotion. He is pissed.

"I can get my own date, you know," he snarls.

"Of course you can, honey," she coos. "But Porsche is the current 'It' heiress. Everyone knows her. She is co-hosting the Children's Fantasy Party with CeCe and, well, you know the nasty little rumor mill has been working overtime about you and, well, your love life…. Having such a sexy, well-known, *heterosexual* woman on your arm…"

Andrea skitters to a stop here, her voice dying away as she tips the champagne flute to her mouth and drains the one lone drop at the bottom of her glass.

"I was only trying to help," she says finally, lowering her glass and slowly raising her head to face Jeremy. Her voice is now that of a little girl, pleading for sympathy and understanding. As I watch, making matters even worse, Andrea's eyes actually well up with fat tears that threaten to spill over onto her cheeks.

Jeremy and Mark are just lost and I make a mental note to nominate Andrea for my own "Best Actress in a Manipulation" category.

"Well, I guess if you put it that way," Jeremy says, recovering quickly and turning to give me his standard insolent smirk, "I'd love to escort the little waif. Now tell me again, who you are? An heiress?"

I drain my glass and hold it out to Mark for a refill. It takes everything I have not to slap the patronizing attitude right out of Jeremy's skinny little body. He knows full well who I am; everybody knows who I am! I force a smile and meet his eyes.

"Now, tell me again, *Jason*," I say. "You make commercials?"

Jeremy's eyes glitter dangerously for a split second before he laughs, tilting his champagne flute in my direction. "Touché!" he says softly.

Two hours later, we arrive at Paradise Ranch and I get my first glimpse of what is to be my home for the next week or so. It takes my breath. I am expecting gray and brown desert or something, but instead the green is so lush and verdant that I am tempted to remove my pumps just to feel the cool grass between my toes. Instead I climb out of the limo and stand beside it, breathing in the fresh, salty air of the nearby Pacific Ocean and listening to its dull pounding against the rocky shore somewhere in the nearby distance.

"It's quite something, isn't it?" Jeremy asks, appearing by my side. The ever-present smile is still in place, but in his eyes I see the need for my approval.

"I thought you said this was a working ranch?" I say, remembering that he expects me to be a bitch and not wanting to disappoint him. "Doesn't look like one to me. Where are the horses? Where's the farm equipment? I don't even see a cowboy."

But as I say this, the massive oak front door opens and two people emerge from the mansion, a reed-thin woman with long, curly red hair and, as if summoned by a genie, a genuine cowboy, with boots, hat, mustache—the whole package.

I can't take my eyes off of him and it must be obvious because Jeremy chuckles and says, "Good enough for you?"

Oh, yes. This one is quite good enough, all right. He walks toward us, or should I say, saunters, with this half swagger. His hat is pushed low on his face, shadowing his features, but even so, I can see the thick mustache that almost drips off his chin, and I catch a glimpse of dark, dangerous eyes and a weathered face—not old, but lined enough to give away his occupation. This man lives in the saddle, I think, and immediately picture him riding, first horses, and then, well...never mind!

I force myself to look away because I'm thinking that any fool could read my thoughts about this stranger, and I watch the woman at his side. Zoe Feller is instantly recognizable, even if I hadn't attended the same parties with her, or seen her in almost every Oscar-nominated movie she's ever made. Zoe looks fragile, but don't let that fool you. She is driven by her work, immersing herself in her roles so completely that, for the length of the project, she *is* her character.

I watch her walk beside the cowboy and immediately decide they are most definitely not a couple. In fact, I almost wonder if she is even aware of his presence. She seems, instead, to be totally focused on Jeremy. Her blue eyes burn feverishly as she walks purposefully toward him, slowing to an almost regal pace as she draws closer, then stopping and, if I'm not mistaken, bowing her head and half-genuflecting.

"You're back," she breathes. "I thought you'd never come."

Jeremy's expression doesn't change, but his eyes do. I am learning to read the man now, I think, and it is always the eyes that give him away. He has locked onto Zoe with an intense, cold stare, as if he's daring her to question him. I shiver involuntarily as I watch her flinch and take one tiny step backward.

"Why are you here?" Jeremy asks, but it is not his voice any longer. I hear the words, but still can't believe the change in him. The tone is deep, sonorous and commanding. It is the voice of a much larger, stronger man, but still, it is coming from the actor beside me.

"There are details," Zoe says softly. "I thought we should go over them before we shoot tomorrow's…"

"And I told you that I would summon you when I wanted you. Why are you here?"

Zoe raises her head, and I realize we are watching a scene in progress. Her eyes lock with his, briefly—long enough for me to see anger and pain, defiance that is quickly replaced by submission.

"I. Need. You," she says, each word uttered in a halting gasp, almost forced from her against her will.

Jeremy smiles, and it is the cruelest of his expressions because he is lording it over the poor woman. "Yes," he murmurs. "Indeed you do."

The cowboy makes his move, stepping between them and breaking the mood with his body.

"Can you two knock this shit off a minute? We've got problems."

Zoe tosses her head impatiently, starts to protest, and is silenced by a look from Jeremy.

"Sure, buddy. What's up?" Jeremy says.

How in the hell has he just done this? I wonder. Jeremy's voice has switched from Lord of the Manor to western ranch hand. His tone is two octaves higher and slightly squeaky. I look at his eyes and see nothing but a happy glint. Whoever this cowboy is, Jeremy genuinely likes him.

The cowboy looks in my direction, lets his gaze move to encompass Mark and Andrea, and I hear him say, "We need to talk. Privately."

"Lovely manners," I murmur softly, just loud enough for

Jeremy to overhear but not loud enough to reach the oaf in the cowboy hat.

Jeremy laughs, looks at the cowboy, and says, "I think Miss Rothschild finds you a bit coarse, Sam."

I feel my face start to flush and the cowboy says, "That would be her problem, not mine." He looks at me again, only this time giving me a real thorough up and down. He appears not to like what he's seeing.

"Sorry, ma'am," he says, touching the brim of his hat in a mock salute. "I don't always have time to coddle Jeremy's lady friends. You see, we have real work to do around here and right now, I have business I need to discuss with your boyfriend. So if you'll excuse us, I'll be sure and get one of the maids to show you where you can powder your pretty little nose while you're waiting on lover boy here."

Marlena wakes up, no longer able to sleep with the cosmic energy becoming so disturbed around her, cracks one sleepy eye in the cowboy's direction and hisses.

"Just exactly who died and made you God?" I say, and start to move past Jeremy to plant myself right in front of the overblown bully. "I am not a plaything. I am not a bimbo. I am a guest of Mr. Reins and I do not appreciate rude behavior."

I spin around to look at Jeremy. "If he were my hand, I'd fire him."

"If I were your 'hand' as you call it, I'd quit!" the cowboy says.

"Well?" I say to Jeremy. "Are you going to let him talk to me like that?"

Jeremy seems to be enjoying himself at my expense. He grins and then says, "Aw, now, Porsche, don't mind Sam. He might not come on smooth like you're used to, but his heart is in the right place. He's my manager, and when he says he has a problem, well, believe me, I'd better go hear what it is." He looks back at the cowboy, his grin slowly growing wider. "Sam, this is Porsche Rothschild. I'm helping the poor dear out a bit. She's hosting a charity party and doesn't have a date, so she's here for the week, slumming."

Before I can protest, Jeremy looks at Andrea and inclines his head in my direction. "Lovey, why don't you help Porsche get settled in while I borrow your hubby and try and sort out this mess, all right?"

"But what about me?" Zoe wails. "I need you, too!"

Jeremy looks at Zoe and becomes the king again. "Wait in the library," he says coldly. "I'll come find you when I'm finished."

The men walk away without a backward glance. Zoe appears to have lost herself in her role again because she is following three yards behind Jeremy, head down, pacing slowly back into the mansion.

"What in the hell is going on here?" I manage to ask Andrea.

She shrugs. "Welcome to Hollywood," she says. "Where nothing is real, true or genuine. Everyone is trying to be someone or something else and no one is ever satisfied with things as they are."

"So, do Zoe and Jeremy have a thing or what? I mean, why does she act that way with him?"

Andrea smiles. "It's the project. She's totally immersed herself in it, not just her role, but in the entire project. It's Zoe's concept, after all, and she and Jeremy are co-EP's—executive procedures—on it."

"Oh," I say, nodding but not really understanding at all.

"Apparently Zoe's been spending a lot of time finding

her muse and exploring her spirituality. She's like that, you know. Anyway, somehow in the process of all this, she read about some of the more ancient pagan rituals and religions. That's where the idea came from for the script. She plays the love interest to Jeremy's high priest or something. I think it's a domination theme, you know, she's the subservient follower to his Rasputin."

I am about to say something really awful, like, who in their right mind would adore Jeremy Reins, but stop when I remember the way Jeremy transformed himself into a complete Adonis in the Peloponnesian War epic that got him nominated for an Oscar last year. Before either of us can continue, the security gate at the end of the driveway swings open and a white cargo van begins winding its way toward us with the two bodyguards, Scott and Dave, sitting in the front seats.

"Good," Andrea says, sighing. "I feel better knowing they're here." She looks at me and makes a hasty attempt to retract her statement. "I mean, not that you didn't do a great job of…"

"Listen, you're the one with the brown belt. All I did was yell and shove Jeremy out of the way of a couple of killer paparazzi. I couldn't take on a real threat! I don't think there's a thing wrong with feeling relieved to have a little help, even if we are awesome paragons of female strength and ability."

I grin as I say this last part, because I most certainly do not think I am in any way prepared for real danger in the near future. I know Jimmy "The Heartbreaker" Valentine tried his best with me back at Gotham Roses Central, but practice only goes so far when real life intervenes. What in the world was I thinking, jumping into something like this?

It doesn't matter that the morning's "threat" hadn't been a real attack, the people involved had all been frightened and I sense there is something more sinister going on than I've been told.

Chapter 3

"You will absolutely not believe this," I tell Emma. I am lying on my back, staring up at a huge canopy that covers the antique bed in the guest cottage, pinching myself as I study my surroundings and try to describe them to my friend.

"First of all, the 'ranch' as they call it, is hardly a ranch at all, at least not from what I can see. Remember that time we decided we wanted to get healthy and we went to Canyon Ranch in Tucson? It's like that, only I bet the food's better and the scenery is a definite improvement."

Emma sees right through this. "Who is he?" she demands.

I roll over onto my stomach, look out the floor-length window and watch as Andrea emerges from the house, a frozen margarita in hand, to stroll beside the sparkling blue pool.

"I don't know what you're talking about."

"Bug, there is no way you would be waxing rhapsodic about the Canyon Ranch without there being some sort of specimen of male beauty involved. Remember the cowboy who took us out on that God-awful trail ride? You went on and on about how lovely your ride was for days, and that after your horse tried to run you off a canyon wall and we both came back with saddle sores, stinking to high heaven!"

I close my eyes against the memory. "Em, really, this place is just sweet, that's all. Private and too cute."

"So there's not even one good-looking man, aside from Jeremy Reins that is, on the entire property who meets the criteria?"

"Criteria?" I echo, knowing full well what she means.

"You wouldn't sleep with any man you've seen so far? I mean, excluding Jeremy because he's gay."

"Well, Em, that's what I was going to tell you—Jeremy is not gay, I mean, not totally." I try to distract her with the paparazzi-in-the-baggage-cart story, and for awhile, Emma is at least interested.

"The man had a camera and you *tackled* Jeremy?"

"Well, yeah. What else was I going to do? I thought it was a gun."

"So, you don't think anyone is really after him then?" Emma sounds just a bit relieved.

"Well, I don't know for sure. Jeremy seemed shaken by the episode, as if he expected trouble."

"Hmmm. Bug, are you sure you'll be all right? Have you told Renee about this?"

I roll off the bed and walk over to stare out the window, watching as Jeremy, Sam and Mark walk out onto the pool deck and join Andrea at the cabana bar. I watch Sam's easy, long-legged stride and think he'd be quite something if he'd only been given a personality to match that body of his.

"Bug! Hel-lo! Have you told Renee?"

"Told her what?"

"All right, that's it! What is going on and what is his name?"

I turn my back on the window and focus on Emma. "No, I haven't spoken with Renee. I didn't think I had enough to report about yet, but I'll call her tonight."

"And his name?"

"Sam," I say, miserably. "God, Emma, how do you know me so well? This man is gorgeous, a real cowboy, but he is an absolute jerk. He's rude and overbearing—"

"And has a body to die for, I'll bet," she interrupts.

"Totally."

"Walk away, Bug. You're there to do a job, not get laid."

"I would never!"

Emma laughs. "Yes, you would and we both know it! But really, honey, this is risky business."

I feel myself getting defensive and tell her, "Emma, I was only teasing about the cowboy. I know this is danger-ous and I'm giving it my full attention. Besides, Jeremy's agent's wife, Andrea, says the guy is actually Jeremy's manager. He's from Jeremy's old hometown—so check-ing him out was just part of looking at the whole picture. I mean, the guy could be the one behind all this, although I doubt it. Andrea says he was Jeremy's drama teacher in high school."

"Get out!" she says. "So he's an old guy?"

I laugh. "Older, not old. Experienced is more like it."

A loud knock at the cabin door startles me and I have to hang up quickly with Emma. Dave and Scott are standing there when I open the door, holding Marlena's reassembled cage between them.

"Where do you want this?" Dave asks. The look on his face says, "This is so-o-o not our job!"

"In the corner," I answer, pointing to the living room.

As they work to position it, I decide that I should begin doing some serious investigation, starting with these two. I walk over to them and smile, completely phony and I'm sure they know this, but what else can I do?

"That is so-o-o sweet of you to do this for me," I gush. "I know it's not your job."

Scott ignores me, but Dave looks up briefly and gives me a small smile.

"Jeremy just raves about you two," I say.

Scott raises one eyebrow, and I think I hear him mutter, "Yeah, I bet."

"He says you two are the reason that stalker person hasn't been able to get near him. He told me I shouldn't worry about our safety as long as you're here."

Dave's thick chest seems to puff out even further and I see a flush of red begin to creep up the back of his neck.

"I don't know about that," he says.

"Well, you two were the ones who chased that man off at the airport, weren't you?" I ask. "You saved the day! And to think, I was almost too afraid to come out here. People told me it was dangerous."

"Who told you that?" Scott demands, straightening and looking me in the eye for the first time. He sounds like a drill instructor and for a moment I feel intimidated.

"I...I don't remember who exactly...." I widen my eyes and try to look clueless. "Is it safe? I mean, has he gotten onto the estate?"

"Someone started a fire in Jeremy's downstairs office last week," Dave volunteers, but stops as Scott gives him a warning look.

"A fire? Oh, my God! And the person who set it got away?"

"It was nothing, really. Someone forgot to put out their cigarette and the smoldering butt caught some trash on fire. It was not," Scott says, glaring at Dave, "a stalker."

I cock my head sideways and meet Scott's eyes. "You've had a lot of experience guarding celebrities, haven't you?" I ask. "I mean, I've known a lot of security people and I can tell the ones who've been around and know the business, the good ones."

Scott's eyes narrow warily, but he answers. "About ten years, since I left the military. I guess I know my way around."

I nod, like he's confirming what I thought. "What branch of the military?"

"Army. Special Forces."

"I thought so!" I cry. "I can always tell."

The tiniest beginnings of a smile touch the corners of Scott's lips and I know I've won him.

"So, I guess you've got your ideas about this business with Jeremy," I say, hoping he'll go along with me.

"Scott thinks..." Dave begins, then stops as Scott silences him with another look.

"These things happen all the time to movie people," he begins. "It's no big deal."

I raise an eyebrow. "You know, I heard Jeremy was doing it himself, as a publicity stunt, then someone else started up for real."

Dave gives it away. "Damn," he breathes. "How did you..."

"We'd better get going," Scott says. "We've got to get back. Don't worry, ma'am. I can assure you that you'll be perfectly safe. Enjoy your stay."

With that, the two men hustle out the door and leave me to stare after them. Marlena stirs and lifts her head, sees the cage and begins clicking in my ear, missing her hammock and ready to leave her perch on my shoulders.

"All right, baby," I murmur. "Go play. Mommy has to go talk to the nice people about guns and fire."

Marlena scampers out of my arms and into her cage, sniffing and exploring happily as I leave her to walk out by the pool. I wish my life were as simple as Marlena's. She wasn't worried in the least about rescuing Jeremy Reins from a deranged stalker, or whoever it was that was causing the trouble. Marlena never had to worry about whether or not she was capable of saving someone's life. She certainly never had to worry about choosing bad men or leaving a mark on the universe. No, she wasn't the one paying a therapist to tell her that she pursues unavailable men because her biological father abandoned her and her step-father is too busy to become a real father to her.

As I reach the edge of the poolside deck, I see Andrea break off from her conversation with Mark and turn to smile at me warmly, raising a hand to beckon me over.

"You're just in time," she says as I draw closer. "Maybe you can settle this argument I've been having with him."

"Argument?" I echo.

Before she can speak, Sam the cowboy interrupts. He's behind the bar, still wearing his hat and the scowl that I assume is permanently frozen on his face, but when I look up and our eyes unavoidably lock, I feel an electric current race through my body and settle somewhere deep inside me where it hums like a homing signal.

"What can I get you?" he asks.

"What?" For a moment I am thrown off and can't seem to remember the English language. What is the matter with me? Why isn't it enough to know he's one of *them*, the psychological poison my therapist calls "emotionally unavailable"? Why can't I just know and walk away? But there I stand, stammering like a complete idiot and staring at the man like he's just walked out of an alien spaceship. I'm hopeless.

"Would you like a drink?" he asks, saying each word slowly, like he realizes I've lost the ability to understand him.

"A drink?" Oh, my God, snap out of it! "Yes, yes I would. Thank you!"

When he is still staring at me, I blink and wonder what's wrong *now*.

Jeremy has somehow come into the picture and waves a hand in front of my eyes and says, "I think the man is asking what you want to drink, lovey. You know, like a margarita or a Diet Coke. You know, liquid beverage."

That snaps me to. I give him a sharp look and turn to Sam. "I'm sorry, I was just thinking. I believe I'll have a mar…Diet Coke, please."

I desperately want alcohol but realize that undercover bodyguards most probably don't drink on duty, and undercover bodyguards with no discernible skills should absolutely not drink on duty.

Sam's eyes slowly wander the length of my body and back up to settle on my face. "Diet?" he asks. "Looks like you'd want to put a little meat back on your bones, not deprive yourself. You're too scrawny."

God, he was insufferable!

"Well, Little Joe, where I come from we don't need to carry around a layer of fat for the wintertime. We've got electricity and running water."

I expect him to explode, but instead he laughs. It is a warm chuckle that rumbles up from deep inside his chest and makes him seem suddenly human. I grin back before I can stop myself.

"So, Porsche, help me out here," Andrea says, and I must look blank because she adds, "With my argument, I mean. Do you think Mark's right? He says there can never be too much publicity, even bad publicity, while I say too much publicity sours the public. Look at Paris Hilton, I mean, hasn't she become passé?"

"Well, I don't know…" I begin, but stop as Sam hands me a glass of soda, then lose my train of thought and say, "I'm sorry, would you repeat the question?" Even though I haven't forgotten at all, I just can't seem to think straight whenever I look at the cowboy. It's just so stupid!

"I say the only thing better than publicity for fame is death," Mark pronounces. "Look at Elvis—worth far more dead than alive. That's true of anyone. Death makes you a hot commodity. You know what I'm saying, don't you, kid?" he says, turning to Jeremy. "You think you're hot now, just die tragically in your youth and see how your stock soars! We'd be swimming in money!"

"Mark!" Andrea cries, her expression horrified. "You can't mean that!"

Mark looks at the rest of us, the impact of his words apparently dawning on him as his own expression mirrors his wife's. "Oh, now, you can't think I'm suggesting… Oh, come on!"

I'm thinking either Mark is incredibly insensitive or he's just established his own motive for wanting Jeremy dead. Jeremy, however, seems unaffected, as he slices into wedges.

"Mark's only doing what I pay him to do," he says, not looking up from the cutting board. "Make money off my dazzling good looks and ability." He sets three shot glasses up on the bar, reaches for a bottle of tequila and pours. "Of course," Jeremy adds, handing a shot to Mark, "I would like to benefit from the profits while I'm still alive to do so, but I see no reason why my heirs can't enjoy a little happiness and debauchery after I've gone."

Jeremy hands Sam a shot glass, distributes the limes and salt, and I watch as Sam raises his glass and offers a simple toast.

"To your health," he says, locking eyes with Jeremy. "Your continued good health."

"Here, here!" Mark adds, flushing as Sam turns to give him a very long and dark stare. Andrea steps closer to her husband, as if showing solidarity, and I watch the scene before me and wonder how much of it is genuine and how much is Hollywood.

It's jet lag, I tell myself. It's getting dark and you're imagining things. But it doesn't help and when Zoe walks slowly out of the main house, dressed in a long, flowing black gown, accompanied by another woman dressed identically. Both look like wraiths. Their skin is pale, their eyes dark and rimmed in black, their lips painted a vivid, deep red. Andrea gasps when she looks up and spots them silently walking toward us. Jeremy follows her gaze and I hear him swear under his breath.

"Jesus, will you give it a rest, Zoe!"

Zoe's friend marches right past Jeremy, heading for the bar, and ignoring anything and anyone in her path. She is tiny compared to the lanky Zoe—a blonde with curves and a bad attitude if the scowl on her face is any indication. But when she reaches Sam, the frown is replaced by a wide, toothy grin.

"Hey there, Sam. They got you tending bar now?"

Sam's expression doesn't change. He looks at her, slides a shot glass in her direction and pours tequila into her glass.

"Lime?" he asks.

"And salt," she says, nodding. "I bet you don't even remember my name." Now she's pouting, flirting with the cowboy, and I figure she likes unavailable men, too.

"Bet I do," Sam says, placing the lime and salt shaker in front of her, but he turns away without saying it and walks toward Andrea, who has now moved to a spot beneath a giant hibiscus tree.

I look at the blonde and smile inwardly as I note her following the cowboy with her eyes and practically salivating. Life is so predictable.

Mark edges closer to the blonde, reaches past her for the tequila and pours himself another shot.

"Zoe rope you into dinner, Diane?" he asks the blonde.

Diane gives a little start, turns her back on Sam and gives Mark a thorough appraisal.

"She says it's important for the main characters to bond," she says with an inviting smile.

Mark is looking over Diane's shoulder, past her to the spot where Andrea stands, joined by Sam and a small, dark-haired woman in a white chef's uniform. Sam is watching as Andrea appears to be giving the woman instructions, gesturing with her hands and becoming very animated as she and the chef break into laughter that carries across the lawn.

Mark can't seem to take his eyes off Andrea. I find myself wishing that someone adored me that way and then am startled to see the cowboy studying me.

I turn and walk behind the bar, thinking surely one little drink of wine wouldn't be too bad. The cowboy makes me nervous. I shift my attention to Jeremy and find him deep in a discussion with Zoe. It appears heated, with Zoe shaking her head vigorously and Jeremy glowering at her. I forget about the drink and sidle closer, appearing to be searching behind the bar for something as I go.

"I won't do it!" Zoe says. "It demeans the flavor of the piece. It is antithetical to Belinda's core motivation."

"Bullshit, lovey," Jeremy says, his tone both jocular and dangerous at the same time. "You're only saying that because it's what you want, not what the scene needs."

"Either you believe or you don't!" Zoe says, and this time her voice carries the length of the bar. "You live the truth or you die in darkness!"

Jeremy laughs at her and I cringe, seeing the depth of emotion Zoe so obviously feels and his callous dismissal of her feelings. I wait for her to explode and am not disappointed. A loud stinging crack suddenly echoes off the walls of the surrounding mansion as Zoe strikes Jeremy across the face, tears streaming down her face.

Jeremy slowly raises one hand to his cheek, touching the rapidly reddening imprint of her hand, his eyes glinting dangerously as he works to control himself.

"That was a mistake," he says slowly. "One you had best never repeat."

He is smiling now, looking around at everyone and raising a hand to ward off anyone who might protest or approach.

"The game's afoot," he says gaily. "Just rehearsing! Don't let us disturb you!"

I realize that he doesn't see me there. I am behind the bar, in near total darkness. When he continues, his voice is pitched low so as not to be overheard by the others.

"If you ever lift a hand to me again, Zoe, I will walk off your picture, contract or not. Fuck the money and fuck you. What happened between us on the last project will not be repeated here, do you understand? It's over, Zoe—you and I are working on a movie, nothing more, nothing less."

"But Jeremy, I…"

He lifts his hand to grasp her chin and she winces, letting me know his grip is firm to the point of being painful. He waits until her eyes meet his before he speaks again.

"No buts, Zoe. Either you play by my rules or I walk. If I walk, the picture doesn't get made and you lose millions."

Zoe drops her gaze and I barely hear her say, "Of course. I just wanted you to know that I…"

"Let it go. Concentrate on this project and let everything else go."

"How can I when I know you don't believe?" Zoe asks with one last bit of rebellion.

Jeremy's sardonic smirk is back. "I am your leader whether I believe or not," he says in his regal, commanding tone.

They are back in character and, as I watch, Zoe does her weird genuflection thing and murmurs, "Yes, my Lord."

"Good girl," he answers and walks away from her, calling out to Sam in his ranch hand voice, "Hey, buddy, how about we do a triple shot?"

Diane passes me on her way to slip her arm around Zoe. "Bastard," she says softly to Zoe.

"No. I was wrong," Zoe whispers. "He knows his place, and now, so do I. Everything will be fine, just fine."

I roll my eyes and make a mental note to write a book on pursuing the unavailable male. I'll meet the needs of so many unenlightened women, but of course they won't believe what I have to say. That's the trouble with therapy; the patient never listens until they're ready to hear the truth.

Diane rubs Zoe's shoulders slowly, her strokes gradually deepening into seductive touches that even I can read from where I stand. Zoe seems to welcome Diane's touch.

"Let's go somewhere and…" The rest of Diane's statement is lost as she nuzzles Zoe's ear.

Zoe shakes her head, running one finger slowly down Diane's neck, tracing the bodice of her gown. "Not now," she murmurs. "Later. We both have things to attend to before we can play. Remember why you're here—we'll have our time alone later."

The two women break apart and each returns to a separate end of the bar. I sigh softly and wander out of the shadows to go stand beside the pool. It shimmers as the underwater lights blink on and night falls. I glance at my watch and think it is nearly 10:00 p.m. in New York and the middle of the night in London, where my mother has gone to accompany my stepfather on business. I am remembering the last conversation—make that argument—I had with her. I was once again confronting her about my biological father and she was once again stonewalling me.

"Why won't you tell me more about him?" I asked.

My mother, ever the southern belle, tried tears first.

"Muffin," she sniffed. "It was so painful. I don't want to relive losing your father."

"So he's dead then?" I asked.

"Yes," she sobbed. "It was awful!"

"How did he die? Where is his death certificate?"

I asked these questions and when she wasn't sobbing, she was silent, or saying "I don't know. We were divorced by then. I can't remember. It was all so long ago and I was heartbroken." But she never answered me.

This last time I tell her my therapist says I will never maintain a healthy heterosexual relationship if I don't come to some closure about my father's abandonment.

"Muffin, honey, really, can this not wait until I get back?" She didn't wait for me to answer, just kept on walking toward the door and the car where Victor sat waiting for her.

"No, Mother! It cannot wait another moment! Tell me right now or I'll hire private detectives and find out for myself!"

She whirled on me then, angry and upset. "I told you we will talk about it when I return! Why does it matter so much? Victor is your father! He's raised you. He's sent you to the finest schools, supported you, cared for you! Your father did none of those things and yet you want to search for him and ignore Victor! What kind of gratitude are you showing him with this behavior? Grow up, Porsche!"

With that, my usually mild-mannered mother turned around and stalked off to the waiting limo, without so much as a goodbye, without even looking back in my direction as the limousine pulled away from the drive.

She didn't hear me say, "How can I appreciate Victor as a father when he never gave me the one thing I really needed?" Love. I could count on one hand the times he'd given me hugs, or more like dry, quick embraces. Why was I so unlovable to him? What had I done that made him keep me at arm's length? And how could my mother be grateful to a man we both knew was unfaithful to her?

"You contemplating jumping in, or has the jet lag paralyzed your body now?"

I start, spilling my Diet Coke and nearly toppling into the pool at the unexpected sound of the cowboy's voice. Strong hands grab my arms, pulling me back from the edge, and I am suddenly face-to-face with Sam and way too close for comfort.

"You scared me!"

"Obviously."

I am mesmerized by the darkness I see in his eyes and the pull I feel from them. It is like standing on the edge of an active volcano. Sam is the first one to break the silence, abruptly turning me loose as he does so.

"I didn't think you heard Andrea announce that dinner is being served in the dining room."

"Dinner?" I could slap myself for saying that. It's like every word he says is in some kind of foreign language that I seem incapable of understanding. He must think I'm an idiot.

Jeremy's dining room is a lesson in too much money, too little design taste. I look around and for a moment wonder if Jeremy watched reruns of *Bonanza* as a child. There are, no joke, not one, but three candle-lit wagon-wheel chandeliers above the massive, heavy oak dining table. He has us all drinking out of silver flagons that are set before, I swear, gold-plated chargers. There are black, wrought-iron accents everywhere and a thick, Persian rug on the floor. The only thing missing are pictures of Jeremy's ancestors lining the walls. It is a designer nightmare, and yet, when I take in the accent pieces, I know Jeremy hired the work. I mean, there is nothing personal in the entire room. Every knickknack is professionally placed and that is just the kiss of death as far as I'm concerned. I mean, you either live in a home or you visit a shrine. Jeremy was living on a movie set.

"Consuela has prepared one of her village specialties," he says.

"Shut up!" I say under my breath, wondering if he changed the poor woman's name to fit the tableau.

Sam and I take our places at the long table and I study Jeremy more closely. He's sniffing and talking nonstop. His face is flushed with the alcohol he's been drinking, but the tiny traces of white powder around his nose are a giveaway; Jeremy's been doing cocaine.

I look around the table, searching for his companions in crime and notice two tiny spots of red on Zoe's high cheekbones. Andrea is sitting on one side of me and Sam on the other. Andrea sips steadily on her wine and watches her husband across the table. Mark is flirting with Diane, who seems fascinated by his every word. She lays a beautifully manicured hand on his arm and smiles up at him, and I find myself wondering what she wants from him. I'm learning. Hollywood's a stage and we are but the actors.

I turn to say something to Andrea, anything to distract her from the unfolding scene across the table, but a shrill alarm suddenly emanates from a small panel set into the wall near the French doors leading outside. Everyone stops talking, searching for the noise, but Sam is already in motion, pushing his chair back and crossing the room. He opens the panel, pushes a button and the sound stops. Without another word, he opens one of the doors and vanishes outside.

Jeremy stares stupidly after him and laughs. "Well, loveys," he says, "I suppose my visitor has returned." He's drunk and high. What a combination.

I push my chair back slowly and leave the table to head for the open French door. No one seems to notice. They are all talking at once. Zoe sounds frightened. Diane is still telling Mark stories and Andrea is trying to get Mark's attention. I slip outside and wait for my eyes to adjust to the darkness.

The crackle of a walkie-talkie startles me. I make out Dave standing poolside.

"I got nothing here," he says and moves away.

I start to follow after him, moving quietly around the edge of the pool. A rustle in the bushes to my left sends my heart up into my throat. A high, feminine scream from the dining room chills my blood and I turn to run back inside. I'm a fool, I think. The danger wasn't outside, it was inside.

I start to move and time seems to flow in slow motion. Suddenly there is pain, sharp and nauseating in the back of my skull. I fall forward into darkness.

Chapter 4

Am I dead? Because if I'm not; I'd like to go on record as wanting to be. What in the hell happened? Did I drink too much again? I open my eyes and realize I've gone blind! No, maybe not blind, maybe drunk still, because I see dark shapes and they're moving like fuzzy polka dots. Bushes. They're bushes and I'm by the pool, and, oh, my God, my head aches!

The scream. Someone screamed. Inside. Jeremy! I try to move, struggling to turn over and pull myself up onto my hands and knees. My head is killing me. Someone was trying to kill me! This new thought enters my already crowded head and for a moment I pause, wondering if I'm going to throw up because I am hurt and terrified.

"No, no throwing up. Go find him!" I instruct myself.

The lights from the French doors leading to the patio hurt my eyes. I can hear muffled voices coming from inside but none of them belong to Jeremy. In the distance a siren begins to wail and my heart constricts. What if I'm too late?

Something pings, whistling by my left ear and striking the adobe wall. Another whine and ping and I duck. Someone is shooting at me! I dive into a bush and stifle a scream as sharp thorns tear into my skin. The next shot takes out the French door to my right. I hear someone scream inside.

The sirens are closer now, coming up the drive. I hear footsteps running. It sounds like people are coming from all directions. The shooting seems to have stopped. I stay low behind the bush, tight against the cool adobe as I move toward the open doorway. I will be safer inside, I think.

"That way!" a deep male voice yells in the distance. "He's running toward the beach!"

"He's armed!" another voice adds, closer to the house.

I wait a few minutes before I move, darting through the doorway and into the deserted dining room. The lights are out, leaving only the glow from the candles that line the long table to illuminate the scene before me.

The plates and silverware lie neatly placed just as they had been before I'd left, but a few of the wine goblets are overturned and several are missing, as if the guests had taken them as they ran. I am approaching the table, heading for the doorway into the main hall, when I hear the first moan and rustle of movement.

Low and husky, I can't distinguish whether it is a male or female groaning, but I freeze, listening. Have I imagined it? No. Someone is breathing hard, panting—struggling, it sounds like. Soft mewling sounds, a cry, and this time there is no doubt. A woman is lying hurt under the dining room table.

I duck down, my headache intensifying, and pull back the long white tablecloth. There is no way to prepare myself for what I see. I stop, rooted to the spot, telling my hand to release the cloth and run away, but I can't move. I am watching a train wreck in progress. Zoe's actress friend, Diane, is lying prone on the floor, gasping, eyes closed, grimacing, her mouth opening and closing as she emits the low keening sound that first alerted me. Sitting astride her, naked from the waist down with his nether part obviously implanted, is Andrea's husband, Mark.

"Oh, my God!" I gasp, unable to stop myself.

Mark turns his head in slow motion; eyes dazed and glassy, startled at the intrusion. He tries to remove himself from Diane, but she stops him, clutching at his waist and grinding her pelvis against him.

"Not yet!" she whispers. "I'm almost there!" She glares at me. "Go away!"

"Let me go!" Mark cries, his voice slurring slightly. Panic is etched all over his face.

"Oh, God!" I drop the starched linen, feeling sick, and back away from the table. I lurch toward the doorway and step out into the hall just as Andrea comes flying toward me.

"I can't find Mark," she cries. "Is he still in the dining room? I was in the restroom when I heard the first shot. Jeremy said someone was shooting into the house!"

She makes a move to push past me and I stop her.

"No! He's not in there! You can't go in there—the gunman might still be outside. I came in from the patio. There's no one left in the dining room." The lies come fast and furious and I can't seem to stop them. "I think I saw him outside. He was directing the police. Let's go into the living room and wait for them."

Andrea turns to come with me, the anxiety for her slime-ball husband clearly shaking her normal composure. The sound of a door opening behind us stops her. Mark lurches out into the hallway. His hair is tousled. A shirt button is missing. His trousers are horribly wrinkled. Still, I think he might pass himself off as having pursued the gunman into the night until I see his lips are smeared bright red from Diane's lipstick. A thin trickle of blood is running down his neck from a bite to his lower right earlobe and below that is an angry purple passion mark.

Andrea's face pales as she stands there studying her husband. It feels like an eternity but is, in all actuality, only a moment. The hurt in her eyes is palpable. Her gaze moves to me, branding me a betrayer as well, before looking at Mark for one final moment. Her body stiffens as she draws herself up, ramrod straight, and then spins on her heel to walk away from us.

"Oh, shit!" Mark mutters. "Oh, God! Andrea, baby, wait!"

She stops, spins on her heel and turns, her face a frozen, unreadable mask as she stands waiting for Mark to say something, anything that will undo this horrible pain.

He stops, perhaps knowing that approaching his wife will break the very thin thread that holds her there. "Andrea, I…"

But the door to the dining room opens again and this time Diane is standing there framed in the dim glow from the candlelight. Her long, blond hair hangs in messy waves that crowd her face and the skin around her eyes is rimmed with smudged mascara. She isn't even attempting to hide what has happened beneath the table. Instead, she flaunts it, giving Andrea a triumphant little smirk and slowly letting her fingers slide toward the ripped bodice of her black satin dress.

But Andrea is gone, vanishing around a corner, her heels clacking against the terrazzo tile floor.

"I need another glass of wine," Diane says, her voice a whining, childish plea. "Go get me one, would you, sugar?"

"Fuck you," Mark says, but his voice sounds dead and lacks conviction.

"Why, honey, I believe we've already covered that territory," she purrs. "Now I want a drink." She moves past us to follow Andrea down the chilly corridor.

Mark's shoulders slump as he stands staring after her. He's aged ten years in the past few minutes, but I don't feel sorry for him. Instead, I move away from the man and head toward the others, at the front of the house.

Scott, Dave, Sam and two uniformed police officers have just arrived, and the others—Jeremy, Zoe, Diane and Andrea—have turned their attention to the men.

"Did you catch the bugger?" Jeremy asks casually. He seems to have sobered up some and there is no longer a powder ring around his nose.

Sam frowns. "No. I don't know how the guy does it. We were running along the cliff, almost on him, when he just disappeared."

The police officers are clearly impressed by their surroundings so it takes them a minute to fall back into their professional demeanor and begin to ask Scott and Dave questions. I see Sam's attention hone in on Andrea as he notes the flush that creeps down her neck and across her chest, takes in the reddened eyes, the dark pupils, the hum of agitation that makes her appear barely able to stand still.

He searches the room slowly, inspects Zoe and Diane standing next to her, whispering in the redhead's ear and giggling softly, moves on, noting me, meeting my gaze, then shifting as Mark slowly walks to stand at the edge of the great room, the outsider.

I watch Sam put it together, note what little time it takes him to get the full picture, and realize this is probably nothing new to him. I reflect back on the adoring look Mark had given Andrea earlier and wonder if I was completely wrong about him. I'd assumed he loved Andrea. But to slide beneath the dining room table and stay there, even when bullets start flying, just to take advantage of a cheap lay? That didn't make any sense to me, and I had to know what caused a seemingly faithful husband to act so out of character from his normal behavior.

My head aches horribly and I work really hard to concentrate on Scott's story. I squint a little, trying to bring the small group of men into focus, and realize that I'm seeing one and a half of everyone. What in the hell hit me out there? Who hit me?

"The security sensors on the west side of the property alerted us to an intruder at 7:36," Scott says. "We released the dogs, trained the infrared cameras on that sector, and responded to the area."

One of the officers, a clean-cut, young guy about my age, looks up from his notepad. "Did you get a good look at the guy?" he asks.

Scott shakes his head and exchanges a quick look with Dave. "We thought we had him, but the bastard's slippery. He just vanished."

Across the room, I hear Zoe gasp slightly and her face seems to grow even paler than it already is.

"Perhaps it wasn't a human being," she murmurs. "There are many who are not of this world yet walk amongst us."

Diane is nodding her head vigorously, her expression almost worshipful as she stares up at Zoe. "Of course," she says. "It is the season."

Sam ignores them and moves so that he's blocking the cops' view of the two women. "I saw him run across the lawn. I'd say he's a little under six feet tall, thin, and he was wearing a black outfit with a hood, maybe a wet suit. If he came in from the ocean side of the property, a wet suit would make sense."

The other cop shakes his head and frowns. He's older than his partner, who I guess is maybe my age. He's maybe in his late 30s and he looks like he has the attitude cops get after a few years on the street. Everybody is guilty until proven innocent.

"How would the guy get a high-powered rifle in if he swam in from the ocean?"

Sam shrugs. "I don't see how the guy got in at all."

"Yeah," Dave adds. "One minute the guy's on the west sector, the next he's shooting out windows on the east side of the house. That's impossible."

"Maybe there was more than one," the young cop says.

"Reymundo," I hear Zoe whisper to Diane.

"Who's Ray?" I ask, coming up behind her.

Zoe turns and gives me this hollow-eyed stare. Her pupils are pinpoints and I know she's flying high on cocaine.

"He is a spirit warrior in the Compali religion," she says, like this makes sense to me and she is not a complete head case. "The Book says that Reymundo comes on the wind to lessen the pain of his earthly followers."

Diane is still giving the nut this adoring look, like maybe she's a goddess instead of a complete whack job, and I have the urge to tromp on her fat little foot with the sharp heel of my stiletto Prada. Surely Zoe doesn't believe some spirit warrior is shooting out the windows of Jeremy's dining room in an attempt to relieve pain and suffering!

"So, what?" I say to Zoe. "You think some spirit guy drops down onto Jeremy's lawn in a wet suit with a rifle so he can bring us to a higher astral plane?"

"Our earthly bodies are mere manifestations of our benign existence in this time and space. The earth is a depot and we are but passengers waiting for our transportation to a better place."

I want to roll my eyes and tell her what a fool she sounds like, but I can't. "Well, if the goal is to reduce our suffering, why did he hit me on the back of the head?"

I must've said this a little too loudly because Sam picks up on it. "Are you hurt?" he asks.

Before I can answer him, I feel this little gyroscope start in my head, spinning the room around on a crazy axis. I don't know if it's my reaction to the cowboy or the hit I took outside, but it makes focusing on Sam's face even more difficult.

"I'm fine now," I say. "I went outside after you did and somebody clobbered me. I guess he knocked me out for a few seconds. When I came to and tried to go back inside, the idiot started shooting at me."

Now I have everyone's attention. Like a flock of geese they walk toward the spot where I'm standing with Zoe and Diane, and I see a fuzzy crowd approaching me. I almost start laughing because they all seem to have three eyes and their bodies waver and take on the swimmy qualities of a mirage seen through the desert heat.

"Lovey," I hear Jeremy say from somewhere just behind my left shoulder. "Where did he hit you? Here?"

I shriek as his fingers touch the back of my head and jump forward, almost bumping into Sam, who stares at me with dark concern in all three eyes.

"How soon after I left did you start to follow me?" Sam asks.

"I guess I waited about a minute and then I got curious."

The older cop steps in and asks, "Where were you when you were hit?"

"I was right by the pool, I think."

"And when you came to, the guy started shooting at you? Wonder why he didn't just shoot you when you were down?" the younger cop says.

Jeremy tries to touch my head again and I turn on him. "Listen, touch me again and so help me I'll…"

"What, lovey?" he asks. "Sic your ferret on me? I'm only trying to see if you're badly injured. We might need to call a doctor or something."

"I'm fine!" I say, but my head is hurting so badly now I think I might throw up.

"Close your eyes, balance on one foot and touch your nose with your left index finger," the young cop instructs.

"I'm not drunk and even if I were, I'm not driving!" I snap. I think he wants to give me a field sobriety test and this seems completely ridiculous.

Sam is peering intently into my eyes. "Got a flashlight?" he asks the older cop. When the man says he doesn't have one, Sam places one finger under my chin and tilts my head up toward an overhead light.

"Nah, her pupils are equal and reactive," he says. "It's not a skull fracture, but I'm betting she has a concussion."

"Will you guys knock it off?" I say, backing away from them. "I told you I'm fine. Can we get back to business here?"

"We're just trying to make sure you're all right," Sam says, his voice is taking on a patronizing tone. "I think you were out longer than just a few seconds."

"Oh, well, it doesn't matter how long it was. I'm fine." I look up and see that Mark is still leaning against the doorway at the edge of the great room watching Andrea, who is making a great show out of watching all of us. I'd left the dining room thinking that everyone was drunk or high or both, and returned to find the room empty except for Mark and Diane. What had happened inside while I was outside?

The Santa Jacinta police are very thorough. They quiz Sam, Scott and Dave in great detail about their movements, their perceptions of the intruder's invasion and the time-line of events. After this they begin asking questions of everyone else who'd been inside the house when the shooting started.

"Well, I wasn't actually in the dining room when the shooting started," Jeremy says. "I was showing Zoe a piece of artwork I'd purchased in Thailand. We were in my study."

I'm sure the "artwork" Jeremy is referring to is another line of cocaine.

When it's Andrea's turn she looks straight ahead at the cops, ignoring the rest of us as she answers their question.

"No, I wasn't there, either. I'm afraid I felt sick and went to the restroom to splash water on my face."

I figure this is code for "My husband was drunk and flirting so blatantly with another woman that it made me sick. I left the room rather than let him rub my face in his betrayal."

Mark colors as she says this. He tells the two officers

that when the first bullet hit the window, he ducked down under the table with Diane and that the two of them stayed there until they heard the sirens and felt they were safe to leave the room.

Diane giggles and pokes Zoe. When the cops ask Diane if she saw anything she gives the young cop a big smile, pauses, probably waiting to insure that everyone is listening, and then answers in a loud, clear voice.

"My eyes were closed," she says. "Mark was shielding me with his body." She lets her gaze wander the room until she locks eyes with Andrea. "He did such a good job that I just about forgot all about the danger."

Andrea stands there, locking eyes with Diane, two high spots of color darkening her cheekbones as she refuses to let Diane goad her into responding. She just stares at her, looking like a queen without a crown, until at last Diane looks away. Only then does Andrea allow herself to turn and leave the room.

I can't stand it. I go after her, only I don't know what I'll do when I find her because I know she hates me for lying to her about Mark. But I can't stand to see her hurting and alone. I cross the room and start down the hallway, remembering the pained look in her eyes when Mark stepped out of the dining room, followed by Diane. It was the look of an animal, trapped in the jaws of a hunter's trap, innocent and unsuspecting, trusting until betrayed and overwhelmed by the grief and loss of the world as it had been and would never be again.

Andrea is walking swiftly down the driveway, rounding the house and heading for a dark green Jaguar parked in front of the five-car garage.

"Andrea, please, wait!" I call. I am not surprised when she ignores me.

I reach her just as she is opening the driver's side door. When I grab her forearm she turns on me, eyes flashing, tears streaming down her cheeks.

"Leave me alone!" she snaps.

"Andrea, I didn't know what to do. When I saw them I...and then you were there and I didn't..."

"You should've been honest," she says. "I knew that woman was throwing herself at him. He was lapping it up and I was disgusted. That's why I left the room, but when the shooting started, I had to know he was all right. He is my husband after all. I didn't think he'd take it that far with her, but I guess I was wrong."

Her voice trails to a stop and she stares at a spot on the car door, as if she's watching something other than green metallic paint.

"He'd had too much to drink," I say.

Andrea snorts. "As if that excuses it! If your husband did that to you, would you feel better knowing he was drunk at the time?"

Of course not, I think, and feel so sorry for her. "No," I say softly.

"We go out five nights a week. It's Mark's job. Sometimes he goes out without me, entertaining clients, wooing important deal-makers, and I have never questioned his devotion to me. Then, tonight, he throws it in my face. He's slobbering all over that two-bit whore and doesn't even care I'm in the room, across the table from them!"

"Why didn't you kick his ass, or hers?" I ask. "I would've grabbed him by the hair, said 'You're drunk!' and then hauled him out the door. Maybe I would've kicked her ass first."

Andrea starts to sob softly and without thinking, I pull her close and wrap my arms around her. I stand there, letting her cry it out, and wondering how in the world something so wonderful and solid just falls to shit in a single moment.

The sky is brilliant with stars. The ocean is pounding against the rocky shore below the house and the air smells of frangipani and gardenias. But Jeremy's beautiful estate is no different than Andrea's marriage, a lovely illusion that seems to be crumbling as I watch.

"Come on," I say, dragging her away from the car and across the lawn to my guest house. "Let's go have a hot cup of tea and talk about this. It'll make you feel better and then we can make a plan. You're in no state to drive anyway."

My voice has taken on the sing-song, falsely cheerful quality that sounds ridiculously stupid to me, but I can't help myself, it's just what comes bubbling out. Andrea starts to say no, but I ignore her. I don't for a minute believe that a hot cup of tea will erase the horrible events of the evening, but I'm on autopilot, remembering the times when my nanny would say those same words to me. Sometimes it did make the world look a little brighter and it certainly couldn't make things worse.

Marlena greets us with noisy chatter, demanding that I let her out. I lead Andrea to a table in the kitchen, find a teakettle, fill it with water and set it on the stove to boil before tending to Marlena's bruised ego.

"I'm sorry, precious," I whisper as I undo the cage door. "We have a bit of a crisis here."

Marlena looks over at Andrea, who's snuffling into a tissue, and seems to get it because she climbs up onto my shoulder, settles around my neck and watches Andrea with a thoughtful ferret gaze.

I make the tea, put out some crackers and settle down

across from Andrea. It is always better to let the patient begin the session. The therapist sits in silence until the patient's anxiety reaches the level where they feel bound to speak. I know this is an older approach, a more psychoanalytic, rather than cognitive, technique, but it works for me, and it works with Andrea, who I know is not my patient, but might as well be. She's in a hell of a mess and just maybe her mess is connected to the catastrophe I'm trying to prevent from happening to Jeremy.

"I don't understand," Andrea says finally. "This isn't like him. Oh, maybe it was once, when I first met him, but that was almost twelve years ago. He's changed."

"Changed?" I prompt. Marlena nibbles on my natural pearl choker, bored with the lack of attention and I try to ignore her.

"When I met him, Mark was a jerk, a real asshole who chased anything that moved. But after we had been together for just a few months, he changed. I think he began to trust me not to hurt him as his ex-wife had. I know I certainly trusted him."

Andrea is struggling, trying hard not to cry. The tears threaten, but she sips her tea too quickly and swallows hard. Marlena says something soft, almost like a human "Awww" sound, and slowly edges down my arm and onto the table. Andrea offers her a cracker and without hesitation, Marlena takes it and munches, all the while studying our new friend and cooing softly to her.

I let the two of them bond while I think about the evening's events. Somehow, in my gut, I know the shooting and Mark's lapse with Diane are connected. I can't prove it, of course, but I feel it. I am so deep in thought that it shocks me to hear Andrea begin talking again.

"I told him I didn't like this project. There are too many variables, all of them risky, I said, but he wouldn't listen." Andrea looks at me, as if she really needs me to understand and agree with her, so I nod, but it's Marlena who chatters in vehement approval.

"It was Zoe's idea," she says, "and while she is a brilliant actress, she's never produced a movie. Then Jeremy jumped on board and came to Mark saying it was the opportunity of a lifetime and that he should invest, too. I thought Mark had lost his mind. Jeremy is a lunatic! He uses drugs, he drinks. He has two illegitimate children and doesn't seem to give a damn about them or their mothers. And now he's taken up with men. The only thing that boy does well is act. But Mark didn't listen to my opinion and nothing's gone right with us since."

I lean my elbows on the table, cradle my teacup and wait for the rest. Andrea has been talking to a spot between us on the table, as if I'm not even present, and that's good because I know that whatever she's saying is something that's built up inside her for a long time and needs to be said aloud. People feel so much better after they "empty their cup" of troubles.

"There's no chemistry between Jeremy and Zoe," she says. "How can there be? Jeremy's too busy chasing any cute boy toy that enters his line of vision. Zoe lives her part, so she's just following him around, mooning like the devoted disciple. It's ridiculous! No one's providing the leadership for this project. This movie is supposed to be an erotic thriller. At this rate, the audience will all die of boredom! Mark will be ruined. His career will be over. And he can't see it—all he sees is that slut being dangled in front of his dick!"

Marlena picks this moment to show Andrea her favorite trick. She utters a shrill ferret shriek, clutches her chest and falls to the table, playing dead. This, of course, does not bring about the desired result. Instead of rewarding Marlena with a treat, Andrea screams, frightened, and leaps up from the table.

"Oh, good job, Marlena!" I say, scowling. "Just scare the poor woman to death!" But I slip her a piece of cracker anyway because I know she's only trying to help.

The expression on Andrea's face tells me she thinks we're both nuts, and I'm about ready to agree with her.

"I'm sorry," I say, trying to restore some sense of order to things. "Marlena just wanted to make you laugh. She was worried about you."

Andrea gives Marlena a look like she's wondering how a rodent could be capable of empathy and smiles weakly at her anyway.

"Okay, really, the tea was nice but don't you have anything stronger in this place? I could really use a drink!"

I walk to the small refrigerator and am surprised to find a lovely Bordeaux blend that simply screams "Drink me!" I open the bottle and find glasses while Andrea sits quietly, lost in thought.

We are about to take the first swallow when we hear an engine roar to life and take off down the driveway.

"That was Mark," Andrea says, jumping to her feet. "He's left without me!"

She runs to the door, flings it open and stands staring after the car as it races away from the estate.

"Son of a bitch!" she swears softly.

Marlena, sensing the tension, screams and falls dead on the table again. This time no one gives her a cracker. Andrea is watching her husband leave while I am distracted by a dark shape that is moving silently across the lawn. The form keeps close to the bushes that ring the pool deck and then disappears from view. I hear a splash as someone jumps into the water, then two male voices, one Jeremy's, carry across to the guest cottage.

"Come here," he says. "I've got something for you."

The other voice answers but I can't make out the words. When I step out a few feet from the house and stand listening in the darkness I see the shape again, this time edging toward the pool house. Something glints in the moonlight and my heart jumps to my throat. The figure in the darkness is carrying a gun.

Chapter 5

Behind me, Marlena screeches again and the sound echoes through the open doorway, out into the cool night air. Andrea isn't paying any attention to Marlena. She is walking toward the driveway like a zombie, stiff and unsteady on her feet.

"Did you hear someone scream?" I hear Jeremy ask, his voice coming from somewhere inside the pool area. His companion says something and the two men laugh, oblivious to the danger that surrounds them.

Why am I the only one left to deal with an armed intruder? I am not a Marine or a martial arts expert. Even Renee thought Jeremy was making up this business about a death-threatening stalker.

I think all of this as I begin to move into the shadows and toward the pool. My brain comes up with a million and one possibilities. Maybe it was only my imagination. Perhaps it was Scott. No, the figure was too short; or Dave, or Sam, making their rounds and watching out for Jeremy. Could the police still be roaming the grounds? When I scan the driveway, I see that all the police cars, marked and unmarked, are long gone.

I trip over a tree root, fall with a heavy thud, then roll beneath a bush in an attempt to hide. My heart is pounding against my rib cage and I make a mental note to quit this job, if I don't get killed in the next few minutes, that is. I will quit and leave with Marlena as soon as I can hire a car to come get us.

A tiny voice inside my head starts talking. *That's right, debutante, quit and run away! Isn't that what everyone expects you to do? So what if Jeremy dies on your watch? You couldn't be expected to try and save him, could you? You're just a poor, little rich girl!*

Okay, so I'll quit in the morning.

I crawl forward on my hands and knees, behind the pool pump housing, between the latticework and the bushes that rim the pool. A rustle of leaves a short distance away startles me and I bite back a scream. I see him, ten feet away, slowly rising to peer up over the edge of the pool decking.

I hold my breath, wondering what I'll do when he raises the gun and takes aim; wondering how I'll keep him from shooting Jeremy, or me, or both of us. I try and remember what The Heartbreaker taught me about self-defense, but the blood is pounding so loud in my ears, I'm having trouble remembering to breathe.

The guy slowly pushes the vine aside and for the first time I have a clear glimpse of his face. Oh. My. God! What a fool I am. It's Dave, the security guard. I feel so stupid!

There I was planning my big rescue of Jeremy and it's only his bodyguard...*spying* on his employer! I hate when people do that. I'm about to say something when I think, no, let's just wait and see what he's up to.

Dave is watching the pool with an expression that doesn't look like professional interest to me. He looks angry. I see the gun in his hand and watch his index finger slide onto the trigger, then off, then back on. I see his lips tighten and his eyes shine as he stares without blinking at Jeremy and his male friend.

Classic homophobia, I think, and turn toward the pool to confirm my suspicions; only I can't quite see from my vantage point behind the latticework wall. I wedge one foot into a thin, wooden slat, grasp a thick vine and begin laboriously and quietly inching up the side of the pool decking.

I sigh silently and shake my head as I climb. Why are men so archaic? I mean, people love who they love. Just because some people love others of their gender, it doesn't mean those who know them are suddenly going to "catch" homosexuality! Wake up and smell the coffee, Dave, I think, and then as my head pops up over the top of the wall, I follow Dave's gaze and see what's upset him. Jeremy is in the pool, locked in a very intimate clinch with Dave's co-bodyguard, Scott!

The two men are in the pool and Jeremy has Scott wedged up against the wall by the diving board. I turn my head to look at Dave and feel the earth begin to give way beneath me. Dave is raising the gun up level with the pool. He's taking aim!

"No-o-o!" I yell and forget all about being undercover or spying. The latticework has given way from the posts that hold it. The vines are ripping and I am falling! "Help!" I scream.

I land hard, on my back, and lie there with my eyes closed. This has so-o-o not happened to me. There is splashing in the pool as Scott and Jeremy climb out, confused and too high to do much more than fumble for towels and run to my side of the terrace. What I hear next is the sound I dread most of all. Dave is making his way toward me, crashing through the bushes and greenery, swearing mightily and yes, I think, sniffling a bit, as though fighting back sobs.

Men are so emotionally labile and impulsive. Dave is liable to shoot me in a display of misplaced aggression. He wants to shoot Scott and Jeremy, but finds this task too threatening to his well-being; so he makes me the negative object and transfers his ill will onto my poor, uncoordinated body.

Dave is standing over me, eyes wide, biting his lower lip in a fruitless attempt to keep his chin from dissolving into quivers of grief. The gun is still in his right hand and his finger caresses the trigger.

I must do the right thing, say the proper words to calm this madman before he strikes.

"What you're feeling is perfectly normal," I say in a squished, breathy whisper. The air has been knocked out of me by my fall, so my voice sounds like the Wicked Witch of the West after the house has fallen on her.

"Huh?" Dave looks like I'm speaking in a foreign language.

Denial is the first obstacle to insight, I remind myself, and try again.

"You have a right to your feelings," I say cautiously. "Name them and claim them."

"Bloody hell, lovey!" Jeremy says, rounding the side of the terrace. He is wearing a towel wrapped around his waist and beneath that; it looks like he's hidden a roll of quarters. He grins when my gaze becomes fixed on his midsection.

"What the hell?" Scott says, but he isn't talking to me. He's spotted Dave. The two men are staring at each other like wary animals.

Jeremy is blustering about, making joking remarks and trying to dance past the tension that any moron would acknowledge as potentially lethal. I shoot him a frowning headshake which he totally ignores. I have seen the male ruffled grouse affect this same sad behavior when he perceives a threat to his mate's nest. He attempts to distract the prey away from the brooding hen by puffing out his chest feathers and putting on quite a show. Sometimes it works, but Scott and Dave are no ordinary birds.

The two bodyguards are locked in silent, mortal battle. Scott is taking the belligerent, "I've got nothing to hide" posture while Dave seems to be adopting the "How could you do this to me?" attitude.

"Okay, okay, this is actually good," I say, getting up and stepping into the fray. "The issue is out on the table, so to speak, and we can move forward from here. How about we all go sit by the pool and talk about this. You know, it may look bad now, but affairs are seldom what they seem…"

"Shut up!" the three men say, in unison.

"Okay, good, anger. I can deal with anger. It's a healthy expression of…"

"How could you do this to me?" Dave says.

Scott bristles, looking more like a porcupine, and looks down on Dave.

"Oh, that!" Jeremy interrupts. "That was actually nothing. Scott was helping me go over my lines and…" He stops here, regrouping, and switches persona, adopting his more strident, firm-boss character. "Actually, I believe it's none of your business what I was doing or with whom!"

"Now, look here!" Dave says, raising his right hand. "Scott and I have an arrangement."

For the first time, Jeremy notices Dave's gun. The response is immediate.

"Well, I didn't know," Jeremy says, taking two steps back.

"Dave, maybe she's right," Scott says. "Maybe we should talk about this. It wasn't what you thought."

Dave and I think they're lying. I can tell Dave is thinking this because his finger is still slipping in and out of the trigger guard and a tiny vein is pulsing near his right temple. But unlike me, Dave wants to believe them.

"Why not use Zoe?" he asks Jeremy. "Scott don't know nothing about acting."

Scott shakes his head slowly from side to side, reading Dave's desperate hope, and begins to smile.

"Dave, Dave, Dave," he says. "Don't you remember me telling you I was the lead in the school play my junior year?"

Dave's eraser-pink skull wrinkles as he frowns and tries hard to remember.

"West Side Story," Scott prompts.

A fine bead of sweat breaks out across Jeremy's forehead and I bet he's praying.

"And," Scott continues, "in case you didn't notice, there was a lot of excitement around here tonight. Zoe went home and the others are in no shape to rehearse. I was only helping Mr. Reins, here, out. He's got a scene to do in the morning."

"That's right," Jeremy interjects. "The camera waits for no man!"

Dave's finger has eased off the trigger.

"I am sure," I say tentatively, "that Mr. Reins respects the *sanctity* of your relationship and would wish no harm to come to it, *would* you, Jeremy?" I give him a quick scowl, like he'd better get his lines right now because this is no dress rehearsal.

"Oh, absolutely!" Jeremy says. "Let's go have a drink and forget about all this nonsense." Reverting to his party boy personality, Jeremy steps between the two men, ignoring Dave's gun, and slides his arms around Scott's waist and across Dave's burly shoulders.

We all have to celebrate, but no one asks either. Instead we all walk back around to the pool bar where Jeremy cranks up the music and begins pouring shots of tequila with maniacal abandon.

Less than a minute later, Andrea appears, still looking like a wild-eyed zombie, and heads straight for the bottle of tequila sitting out on the counter. She isn't waiting for the nicety of a glass. No. She picks up the bottle and slugs down a good inch or two of the harsh-tasting stuff before Jeremy reaches over to take it from her.

"That won't do, honey," he says gently. He pulls her into his arms and cradles her against him. It is the first time I have genuinely found something to like about Jeremy Reins. He is tender and warm with Andrea. He strokes her hair, whispers to her when she starts to cry and is utterly believable in his role as comforting friend.

"Why?" I hear her wail.

Jeremy raises his head slightly and our eyes meet for a moment. "I don't know, babe. Hollywood? Stress? Midlife crisis? You name it, we all do it. We're all assholes, babe. You know that better than anyone."

I can't hear her reply because her head is buried in Jeremy's shirtfront. He bends his head to listen to her, then chuckles. "No, now, lovey… We can't have you talking like that! You're going to drink a little more tequila, spend the night in one of my guest rooms and get a fresh start at all of this in the morning."

He sounds optimistic and I want to believe that everything truly will be better for Andrea in the morning, but how can it be? Her husband has just boffed a local "B" grade actress under the dining room table at dinner! How does that look any better in sunlight?

I fade farther back into the shadows, find a chaise lounge and sink down onto it, content to be an invisible observer for now. A deep weariness seeps into my body and I realize that if I were in New York it would be almost 2:00 a.m.

I close my eyes and start thinking about the Oscars, realizing I have not one gown with me that would be at all appropriate. I mentally review the possibilities—Armani, Vera, Gucci… No, none of those are just the "right" thing. No, I think I need something vintage. Something blue to match my eyes, or perhaps brown, to match Marlena's because she will, of course, be attending. I make a mental note to call Kristy Burke, Renee's stylist for the Roses, in the morning. She'll find just what I need. I make another mental note to have Kristy find something for Marlena, too.

I smile to myself as I imagine Marlena in vintage couture, and then frown as my imagination brings Sam the cowboy into the picture. He is wearing a Western-cut tux and black, snakeskin boots, and he is walking toward me, his hand extended. He wants to dance!

I shake my head "no" but he insists and moments later I am in his arms, waltzing. His scent intoxicates me and I find myself molding into his strong embrace. I want this man more than I have ever wanted any man in my life. I am about to tell him this when the dance floor suddenly opens up into a large fountain. A dolphin splashes loudly as it jumps high in the air and falls back beneath the surface. A man chuckles softly. I open my eyes with a start and realize I have been dreaming.

The splashing sound is coming from the pool area where Jeremy stands, attempting to skim rocks from the flower beds across the surface of the water. The bottle of tequila on the bar is empty. A mirror lies along the edge of the pool and on it rests a razor, two short straws and a small pile of white powder. Andrea is nowhere in sight and the candles on nearby tables have burned down to nubs of red wax. How long have I been sleeping?

I sit up, struggling to clear my brain, and see Sam strolling slowly toward the side of the pool where Jeremy is standing.

"All right, partner," I hear him say. "You've got an early call in the morning."

Jeremy looks up at him, smiles drunkenly and says, "Sod off! I haven't even been in the water yet!"

Sam looks Jeremy in the eye and says nothing.

"Aw, come on, Sam! Live a little. Have a drink with me." The British accent is gone; in its place I hear the western twang return.

When he turns and lurches off toward the bar, Sam reaches out, grabs Jeremy's elbow and firmly steers him off toward the house.

Scott and Dave, in the meantime, wander to the edge of

the pool and Dave steps up onto the diving board and grins back at Scott.

"What d'ya wanna bet I can get those five rocks down there in one dive?" he asks. "I was a lifeguard in high school, you know."

Scott raises a skeptical eyebrow. "They had pools in south Georgia?"

Without another word, Dave walks to the end of the diving board and drops the towel around his waist. He is completely naked, and while I try not to look, it is like turning away from the scene of an accident. I shrink back against my chaise and try to remain forgotten and invisible as I watch Dave prepare to jump into the pool.

He bounces twice on the edge of the board, a naked, pink-skinned doughboy, and flies up into the still night air. He jackknifes and hits the water with almost no splash. His execution is flawless, but when he surfaces, I realize something is terribly wrong. His eyes are wild and he screams through clenched jaws.

"Help! Shh…shhh!"

His body jerks like a marionette connected to invisible strings, and Scott, without thinking, reaches out to grab his partner. He, too, begins the macabre dance as I realize they are being electrocuted.

Sam and Jeremy have just reached the doorway into the house, but Dave's cries stop them. I am on my feet and running. Remembering my Girl Guide first-aid training from summer camp, I grab a towel as I go. Never touch a person who is in contact with a live wire. Break the conduction between you with something inert.

I reach Scott and throw the towel across his broad forearm, grab both ends and tug, breaking his hold on Dave.

I hear Sam running toward me and I yell, "Don't touch Dave. We've got to cut the power first! Jeremy, hit the circuit breaker! We've got to get Dave out of the water!" But Jeremy is too stupid with chemicals to be of any help. It's Sam who dashes for the pool house and seconds later all the lights in the pool go out and the pump falls silent.

I lean down, trying to grab Dave and pull him to safety, but Sam reaches us, pushes me aside and pulls the unconscious man from the water. Scott is conscious and struggling to control his still-quivering body. He reaches Dave's side and watches as my fingers find Dave's carotid artery and press to feel for a pulse.

Behind me I hear Sam on the phone, calling 9-1-1 and giving them information in a strong, calm voice.

"Is he breathing?" Scott asks.

"Yes, but it's irregular and shallow." I continue to work with Dave, frantically grabbing up towels from a stack by the bar and trying to cover him as best I can. "We don't need to do CPR but let's get the two of you covered up and warm." I turn to hand Scott two towels and find him staring at Dave and almost unaware of my presence. "An ambulance is on the way," I say. "Are you all right?"

Scott nods briefly, but his eyes never leave Dave's face.

"What happened? You were just in the pool earlier. What happened?" I grab Scott's arm and shake him, but all I get is a puzzled look in return.

In the distance, I hear sirens and breathe a sigh of relief. Sam has come up to stand behind Scott, but when he hears the sirens I see him turn to look for Jeremy. He spots him leaning in the doorway, watching the scene before him with a dazed expression.

"Stay there when the ambulance arrives," Sam says quietly. "I don't think they should see you in your condition."

"Is he?" Jeremy starts to ask, clearly shaken to the core.

"He's going to be fine."

Jeremy nods and sinks into a lounge chair as the front gates slowly swing open and the ambulance pulls into the courtyard, red lights flashing.

Sam meets the emergency techs, leads them around the house to the pool and stands by as they take over. As the EMTs tend to the two bodyguards, I walk over to the side of the pool and bend down to look for anything that might've caused the problem. I am squatting there, using the full moon for light, when a shadow falls across my shoulder.

"Find anything?" Sam asks. He leans closer, bending to peer into the water.

"See that?" I say, pointing. A slender wire dangles from beneath the diving board. "I don't know what it is, but I bet it doesn't belong there. I think it fell down into the water when Dave jumped on the board."

Behind us I hear the sound of the gurney being lifted as the EMTs prepare to roll Dave out to the ambulance. Sam straightens and says, "I'll be right back." He crosses the patio again and escorts Scott and Dave to the waiting ambulance.

Scott hangs back as the doors swing shut on Dave. I see him shake his head when Sam asks a question and hear, "No, as long as I know he's all right. We have a job to do here and that's what Dave would want."

Sam says something else that I don't hear because he's got his back to me, and the two men turn and start walking toward me. As Sam passes the bar I see him stop for a moment and grab something from beneath the counter, a flashlight that he switches on as the two approach.

"Show Scott what you showed me," Sam says, but he doesn't wait for me to do as he's asked. Instead he points the beam of bright light at the diving board and follows the slender wire to the water where it disappears behind the underwater light fixture. I rise to my feet and move back so Scott can replace me at the water's edge.

When he does, his lips tighten and his expression grows grim as he nods. "Electrical Sabotage 101," he mutters. "Lucky it didn't kill Dave. Sorry son of a bitch!"

I sink down onto a nearby lounge chair and watch the two of them figure out how the wiring has been rigged. Of course they don't include me. I'm just the wealthy heiress visiting the bad boy actor.

"What was that police detective's name?" Sam mutters. "I need to call him."

Scott shrugs and turns his attention back to the wire. "Not much point in doing that," he says. "There won't be any prints on the ground wire. Far as I can tell, the police have done a piss-poor job of assisting us. Santa Jacinta's a small town. They don't know dick about forensics."

This gets my attention. It doesn't matter what Scott thinks about the police force, this is certainly a police matter. Someone could've been killed. We were just lucky. I look over at Jeremy. He seems to have drifted off to sleep. There's no way he could've done this. He's too high to pull off a stunt like this one.

"I'm calling. They need to be notified."

I close my eyes for a brief second as the back of my skull begins to pound in earnest. I am having a mental conversation with Renee, a rehearsal for the talk I plan to have with her as soon as Sam and Scott finish their inspection of the pool light.

"Renee," I will say, "send in your team of camou-fighters. This is the real deal. Jeremy's not playing and I want to come home."

Oh, and I'm just sure she'll want to use you *again real soon!* the little voice in my head says. *Finally, someone believes in you and you give up without a fight!*

I hate my inner voice, especially when it could be right. I was sent to discover whether the threat to Jeremy Reins was real or not. What sort of proof did I have that Jeremy, or a hireling, hadn't shot up the estate or booby-trapped the swimming pool? After all, Jeremy wasn't injured in any way. I felt my heart sink all the way to the pit of my stomach. I couldn't go home; not yet.

I make a mental note to get a new internal voice and open my eyes in time to see Sam walking toward me.

"Listen, Scott and I are going to make a thorough search of the property. The police are on their way, but on the off chance someone's still on the grounds, we'd better take a look around." Before I can say anything, he hands me a walkie-talkie. "We'll be nearby, so if you see anything or get scared…"

"Don't worry about me," I say. But my head is pounding and I feel sick to my stomach. I wish someone *would* worry about me.

Sam grins, but the smile doesn't reach his eyes. "If Jeremy wakes up, try and keep him out of the house until I give the all clear, okay?"

I nod and watch as Sam and Scott disappear in opposite directions. Scott is moving stiffly and I wonder at his ability to recover so quickly from what had to be a strong dose of electrical current. This leads me to wonder further about his reluctance to call in the police. Does he know something we don't? His partner was the one injured. You'd think he'd want to call the cops.

I wander over to the edge of the pool again and look down into the water by the diving board. The slender wire still dangles beneath the board and as I follow it back along the board I discover its path back to a junction box at the base of the diving board.

"Lovey, an electrician, are we?"

Jeremy's sleep-slurred voice startles me and I adjust to find he's come up behind me silently.

"Well, aren't you curious?" I ask. "Someone sabotaged your pool. It almost killed Dave. That could've been you, or hadn't you considered the possibility?"

Jeremy's mocking expression vanishes. "Of course I know that, lovey, but showing fear only lets the enemy know you can be rattled. No chinks in the armor, lovey, no soft spots here!"

His voice has dropped to a whisper and he looks over his shoulder into the darkened shadowy stillness behind the pool walls. Without meaning to, I shiver. When the headlights of the arriving police car play across the courtyard it is all I can do not to run toward it.

"There now, see?" Jeremy says, sounding suddenly cheerful. "There's no need to worry. The police will track down our intruder and we can go on about our lives."

I stare at him. What line from which movie is he quoting now, because surely Jeremy can't be naive enough to think the solution to his threatening saboteur is going to be this easy?

Sam and Scott emerge from the darkened grounds into the light of the courtyard and walk quickly to meet the cruiser. As I watch, the older detective who investigated the

earlier incident steps out from behind the wheel and the
three men consult before turning to walk in our direction.

"Has anyone checked on Andrea?" Jeremy asks. He is
halfway across the slate patio before I can stop him.

"Wait, Sam said you should stay out here. He and
Scott were going to search the house. We shouldn't go in
until they…"

Jeremy isn't listening to me at all. He breaks into a
sprint, forcing me to run after him.

"Jeremy!"

I step into the house, following the echo of Jeremy's
footsteps as best I can, but the place is totally dark. Did
Sam cut the power to the entire estate? Where is Andrea?
My skin prickles as my nerve endings tingle with alarm.
Why hadn't I remembered that Jeremy had insisted Andrea
stay the night?

I close my eyes for a moment and stand still, listening.
When I open them again, my eyes have adjusted to my inky
surroundings. I follow the distant sound of Jeremy's footsteps and follow him up a staircase to the second floor.

"Andrea!" Jeremy's voice is unexpectedly nearby, his
tone anxious. "Andrea!"

I follow the sound to the entrance of a bedroom and almost run into him. Jeremy is holding a cigarette lighter
high above his head and staring at an empty bed.

"She was here," he says, turning to look at me. "She was
right here! I brought her upstairs, saw she had what she
needed and then I went back downstairs to my room. She
was right here!"

A low rumble, like a jet passing overhead, startles us.
The light in the hallway suddenly flickers as power returns
to the house. Jeremy reaches over my shoulder to flip the

light switch and the room is filled with bright, white light. The bed is empty and from all appearances, undisturbed.

"Where the hell is she?"

Jeremy spins away, pushing past me as he darts back out into the hallway, rushing toward the staircase. Just as suddenly, the lights go out, leaving me disoriented and in total darkness again. I move in what I think is the direction of the staircase and hear Jeremy cry out sharply, as if in pain.

"Jeremy, where are you?"

I reach the top of the stairs unexpectedly and almost pitch forward, but grab the railing. A low moan comes from somewhere below me.

"Jeremy?"

I rush down the steps and fumble my way around the hallway, listening for any sound that will help me find him. I reach the edge of the hallway and hesitate at the edge of what I remember as the great room, trying to reorient myself. When I hear another low moan, I move forward and collide with a fast-moving body, running past me.

"Jeremy?"

The dark figure shoves me hard into the opposite wall and I feel myself falling. Someone snickers and I hear a terrified scream—my terrified scream. Shouts erupt out on the lawn and I hear people calling out in a chaotic frenzy. The lights flicker again but this time they come on and stay on. Across the room, Jeremy is attempting to rise to his feet; an ugly bruise colors the skin above his left eyebrow.

Chapter 6

Marlena is singing. It is the first thing I hear as I come swimming up from the depths of a deep sleep. Okay, other people might not consider the sounds Marlena makes as singing exactly, but I know my baby and she is singing. It is her morning song, her "Why haven't you fed me? Oh, I don't mind!" tune that gently awakens me each day. To the untrained ear, it sounds like little bird chitters and clucks, but I know better.

I roll over and, for a moment, forget where I am. I lie on my stomach, facedown, breathing sweetly scented sheets and feeling warm sunlight on my hair and shoulders. The world is a wonderful place, until my pink rhinestone cell phone starts ringing and reality once again invades my serenity.

I sit up, searching for the cell as the events of the evening rush back to me in a fast-forward collage of mental images. Dave and the pool electrocution; Jeremy with a huge bruise over his eye, caused by an encounter in the dark with the same intruder I bumped into; Scott and the police, chasing across the south pasture, pursuing someone who abruptly vanishes; Andrea, missing.

I grab the phone, hoping for news, alarmed that I could've fallen asleep when I intended to stay awake to monitor my possible concussion.

I flip open the phone, hoping for news. "Hello?"

"Muffin?"

I cradle the phone against my ear and roll over. I so do not need this.

"Mummy?"

"Muffin, where are you?"

I open my eyes and look around the guest bedroom, bringing the brightly lit room into focus. I need to get her off the phone, but I can't let her know I'm in trouble.

"San Jacinta, California."

My mother is not pleased to hear this. I can feel her stiffen, even though I cannot see her. It's just her way.

"What are you doing in California?"

I sigh silently, roll out of bed and go in search of coffee.

"Finding myself," I say, even though I know flip is the wrong attitude to take when Mummy is in one of her moods.

"I don't believe you!" she cries, and I suddenly realize this is no normal disapproving attitude—my mother is truly angry.

"Mummy, what is wrong? Am I supposed to be somewhere else? I agreed to host a…"

She cuts me off. "Porsche Dewitt Rothschild, I told you to wait and we would talk about it when I returned. Instead, what do you do? You hire a private investigator and go off after him!"

Now I am completely thrown. There isn't enough coffee in all of California to wake me up enough to deal with
my mother on the rampage.

"Mother, what are you talking about?"

"Don't try and snow me, young lady! I know exactly
what you're doing in California and I forbid it! That man
is no good! Furthermore, he could be dangerous!"

I hold the phone out away from my ear and stare at it.
How in the hell has my mother found out about Jeremy
Reins and the Gotham Roses? Just as quickly I realize she
could not possibly know about the Roses, but any paper in
the world could and would carry a picture of my arrival
yesterday. Mummy was probably holding a newspaper
with a picture of Jeremy and me rolling around on the
L.A. airport runway.

"Now, Mother, it isn't at all what you think. He's really very…"

She stops me again. "He is a liar and a con artist. He's
mentally unbalanced and has been ever since Vietnam."

Vietnam? Did Jeremy make a film in Vietnam? I search
my memory and can't think of any, but then, I wouldn't
watch a desert movie anyway.

"Well, he drinks a bit much, but that goes with the territory," I start to say. She interrupts again.

"How did you find out he was still alive?" she demands.

Suddenly my world goes still as the impact of what
she's saying hits me. We are not talking about Jeremy "Bad
Boy" Reins. We are talking about my father.

I don't say a word. I can't. My father is alive and she
has lied to me about it for years. Why? Why hasn't she let
me see him? What does she mean he's emotionally unsta-
ble and possibly dangerous? Where is he?

"Why didn't you tell me he was still alive?" I say, working to keep my voice calm but wanting to scream the words at her.

Mummy's voice changes when she answers. She sounds broken and uncertain. "We thought it best," she says finally.

"Who thought it best, you and Victor, or was it just Victor?"

I am sick to my stomach because I know the answer even if she denies it. Victor Rothschild owns my mother. She dances at the end of his string and has for as long as I've been able to consciously observe them.

"Your father was never the same after the Special Forces," Mummy says quietly. "He came home addicted to morphine and liquor. He ran through my trust fund in one year and left us broke and almost homeless. If Victor hadn't come along, I don't know what we would've done."

She's lying. The voice in my head is strong this morning, on my side. *Remember the magician who wouldn't go away? He was your father. He said it. He told you so. He didn't want to leave!*

"You're lying, Mother," I say. "He didn't leave us. I remember him. I remember you sending him away."

"You remember nothing!" she cries. "You were a baby! You didn't know what he was like! It was awful! He had flashbacks. He urinated on the Persian rug in my mother's living room because he was so high he couldn't remember where he was. He hit me and sometimes I thought he would kill me! You know nothing about that, Porsche, because I protected you!"

The coffeepot hisses, finishing its brewing cycle, and despite the sunny day, I feel chilled to the bone.

"Why did you tell me he was dead?" I ask in a monotone.

"Because to me, he is! The man I loved and married is dead and gone. I got a monster in return."

She inhales deeply and I suspect she is smoking. She thinks I don't know she still smokes, even after her breast cancer three years ago, even after Victor and I both pleaded with her to stop. It is the one thing my stepfather and I ever agreed on, my mother's smoking.

She exhales and says, "I suppose you'll be going to Carlito." It is not even a question. She states it like fact.

"I don't know," I say cautiously, hoping she will give me more and just not sure what I will do with my sudden windfall of information.

"It won't be pretty, Porsche, if that's what you're thinking. The man lives in a trailer. He has dogs. He doesn't like people. If you're expecting him to welcome his baby daughter with open arms, think again. The years have not been kind to your father."

"How do you know this, Mother?" I feel a cold, hard anger growing in my chest, a bitterness that erects a thick, icy wall between me and her.

"Victor and I felt it best to keep an eye on him," she says. "We were worried that he might try and harm you."

A tiny bubble of rage rises to the surface and pops as I say, "Were you afraid he would hurt me or were you more afraid he would try and see me, maybe tell me that you and Victor were keeping him away."

"He signed over his parental rights, Porsche," she says, and the words bite into my heart. "How else could Victor have adopted you?"

I close my eyes and see the funny man, laughing and pulling coins from my ears and flowers from my sleeve. He didn't want me?

Don't listen to her! the voice inside me screams.

"How much did you pay him?" I ask coldly.

"That doesn't matter…" my mother says, and I snap the cell phone shut.

Almost immediately it rings again. I ignore it. I pour coffee into a brilliant blue pottery mug and listen to the phone ring over and over again. I leave it on the table as I feed Marlena and let her out of her cage to play. I hear it as I walk into the huge master bath and turn on the shower, finally stopping the sound of my mother's voice, echoing all the way from England. *He signed over his parental rights, Porsche.* He didn't want me.

I stand in the steaming shower until the water finally runs cold, crying and thinking, feeling years of loss that tumble around me in an avalanche of emotion. By the time I grab a thick, white towel and emerge from the huge shower stall, I know that I will have to find him and ask my questions for myself.

The phone is still ringing, but I answer it this time. I need to make her to tell me where he is exactly. I pick up the phone, flip it open and say, "What is his first name and what is his address. You owe me that."

"I beg your pardon? Porsche, is that you?"

It is Renee's cool, crisp voice that startles me. I look at the clock on the stovetop and realize that it is almost noon in L.A. midafternoon in New York.

"Oh, Renee, sorry! I thought you were someone else."

"Is everything all right there? You sound upset."

I take a deep cleansing breath, remember my yoga breathing and try to relax.

"Couldn't be better here," I lie.

But immediately after I finish, I panic because I realize

I have absolutely no idea where Andrea is and I have some-how forgotten or lost the past ten hours of my life. Bits and pieces of memory suddenly flood my brain with images. Jeremy, bruised and dazed. Dark figures running.

"Well then?" Renee says. "What do you have to report?"

More deep breathing on my part.

"Actually, Renee, if you wouldn't mind, could I call you right back? I'm right in the middle of something and well, it might be better if I finished that first."

Renee doesn't hesitate. "Oh, I see. You're okay, but you've got someone there and you can't talk?"

I look at Marlena. "Yes, that would be correct."

"All right then," Renee says briskly. "Just call me when you can."

She severs the connection and I exhale loudly.

"What kind of Rose am I, baby?" I ask the ferret. "I don't even know what's going on!"

Marlena chuckles happily while I struggle into a pair of my favorite Lucky jeans and throw a stretchy James Perse T-shirt on before running out the door and heading for the main house.

Workmen in white coveralls are repairing the French doors leading into the dining room. They talk in rapid-fire Spanish, laughing as the shorter one teases his partner about his pregnant wife. A few yards away Sam is stand-ing next to an older man wearing jeans and a T-shirt that reads "Robins Electrical."

I slow to a more unhurried pace and try to be less obvi-ous about my curiosity. I stop to inspect bougainvillea, sniff a nearby climbing rose and listen.

"You see this?" the man is saying to Sam. "It's your ground wire. It runs all around the pool. You gotta ground your ladders, your diving board, your lights, your pump and anything that might carry current. Looks to me like your wire got frayed right about here." The electrician is pointing to a spot on the wire he's removed. Sam inspects it, looks up as he notices me, and nods in greeting.

"Have they found Andrea?" I ask.

Sam gives me a grim smile. "Turns out she borrowed one of Jeremy's cars and drove into L.A. Said she couldn't sleep. She checked into the Beverly Wilshire and didn't think to tell anyone until just a few hours ago when she woke up, watched the news and discovered she was allegedly missing."

Sam's facial expression and tone are deliberately casual, probably because of the electrician standing next to him, so I don't press him about Andrea.

"Where's everyone else?"

"Well, Jeremy's at the studio. Scott drove him in and then he was going to go see Dave at the hospital. Now, if it's breakfast you're after," he says, making a big show of looking at his watch, "well, you missed that by a good two hours, but maybe Consuela will rustle you up a couple of eggs and a big, fat burrito."

I ignore his sarcastic suggestion, but only because he is currently my only tie to Jeremy and I need to be where he is.

"I was really hoping to watch Jeremy work," I say. "He was supposed to take me with him but he didn't call. I suppose I overslept."

Sam has turned back to the electrician and seems to be ignoring me. "Normal wear and tear, faulty installation, or did somebody cut the wire?"

"I was wondering about that myself," he says slowly. "It hasn't been cut, that much is true, so near as I can tell, it's either human error on the installation end or somebody messed with it so it'd come loose." He looks up at Sam, shoving the wire toward him. "I'm not saying it was done on purpose. Could be people was just not taking the care they ought and by being rough, things started coming loose. I guess all it took was for somebody to jump on the diving board and the wire just wore through."

The electrician doesn't say what I guess he's thinking, that rich people don't take care of their belongings, but Sam apparently sees what he's thinking.

"Well, I'd have to say that pool's fairly new and Mr. Reins hasn't been in it more than three or four times that I can think of in the past year, so…"

The electrician nods his head vigorously. "Like I thought—installation error then."

But Sam doesn't buy this. He shakes his head. "No, so far there's never been a problem."

What Sam doesn't say is what I'm thinking, that someone deliberately tampered with the ground wire so that anyone jumping on the diving board would dislodge the live wire causing it to fall into the water, where it would give the diver, or anyone unlucky enough to be in the water at the time, a nasty dose of electricity.

"Well, I'm sorry for your troubles," the electrician says, taking the wire back from Sam. "But don't you all worry. I can get it fixed right in about thirty minutes. I just gotta get something out of the truck and we'll be good to go."

He doesn't wait for Sam's dismissal. He scuttles away, reminding me of a hermit crab. I walk over to the spot where Sam stands and ask, "What do the police think?"

Sam frowns. "It's fairly obvious. Jeremy seems to have a stalker intent on being a nuisance at the very least. The amount of current probably wouldn't have killed anyone, but it came too damned close. The police are doing criminal history checks on all the employees and delivery people. We know someone's been getting onto the grounds, we just don't know how they're doing it."

I nod. "Who's watching Jeremy now?"

"The studio has sent extra security people to cover Jeremy until the police get to the bottom of all this."

"Will you be going in to meet Jeremy?"

"I'll take you in, don't worry," he says, sounding weary and put-upon. Sam is suddenly back to the sulky, rude man he was before last night's crisis.

"Never mind," I tell him. "I can call a cab. I wouldn't want you to knock yourself out on my account!" I put my hands on my hips and square off in front of him, barely aware that I am unconsciously mimicking the stance my nanny always took when she was heading into a confrontation with me. "Have I done something to offend you, or is it just my mere presence on the planet that irritates you?"

Sam studies me for a long moment before answering, apparently unruffled by my outburst.

"I just don't have much use for unemployed princesses who have nothing better to do than shop, lunch or skinny-dip in Italian fountains," he says. "It's kinda like having a Chihuahua on a working ranch when you really need a herd dog." He lifts his shoulders and lets them drop, punctuating his comment with his body. "However, what I think isn't what matters here. You're Jeremy's guest, so I reckon I can drive you into town. I'll have the car out front in five minutes. Be there."

He leaves before I can set him straight, before I can even formulate a snappy comeback. I realize that the workers repairing the French doors have fallen silent, only too happy to have overheard Sam's opinion of my overall worth.

We ride for a full hour without saying a word and I stare out the window at the miles of highway that initially rise up away from the beach and hug its contours as we travel south toward Hollywood. I tell off the sullen cowboy in my head but don't waste my time saying the insults aloud. I am thinking of him as a small gnat and trying my best to ignore him, but he has rented too much space in my head. I am in, I realize, a state of cognitive dissonance.

I have a psychological conflict arising from the inconsistency in my feelings about Sam. On the one hand, I find him intensely attractive, and I do believe that there is more to him than this current manifestation of ill temper belies. I feel he is hiding behind his gruff exterior and that the flashes of kindness and levelheaded thinking are glimpses of what lies inside the inner man. But on the other hand, he has pissed me off! I will not, cannot, and have *never* allowed anyone to treat me the way Sam does. I don't need to take verbal abuse or callous disregard. I am a worthwhile human being and deserve to be treated with respect at the very least. Unemployed princess, my ass!

Marlena is curled up at the bottom of my lime-green leather carryall, oblivious to the conflict going on above her, but when Sam finally speaks, she pokes her head out of the bag and clucks twice. I feel she disapproves of him just as I do. "Listen, I'm sorry I was short with you earlier," he begins.

"You weren't short," I say in my best haughty diva voice. "You were quite long-winded."

"Yeah, well, it was uncalled for and I apologize if I hurt your feelings."

I am staring straight ahead at the road, but sneak a side-long peek at him. He is also keeping his eyes on the road, but a tiny muscle in his square jaw twitches with the effort to make up to me.

"Apology accepted," I say, sniffing slightly. He hasn't said he didn't *mean* the things he said, only that he is sorry he said them. "You know, I may not need to work for a living, but I do work. I mean, my life does have meaning. I'm not exactly a bubblehead with no purpose in life."

"I'm sure you aren't," he says, but the way he says it makes me think he doesn't believe that. Really, I shouldn't let this bother me, but for some reason the fact that this cowboy-used-to-be-drama-coach-turned-personal-manager thinks I'm shallow and purposeless has absolutely worked its way under my skin.

"I donate money to many worthy causes," I begin.

Sam is silent.

"Go on, say it! It's all over your face—just tell me what you're thinking." When he remains quiet, I can't help myself. "You're thinking, well that's an easy thing to do, give money, but you don't actually *do* anything. How hard can it be to write a check, huh? Well, people need money and I have it. I have something not everybody has and I try and use it to better the lives of others."

He looks at me, eyebrow raised.

"What?" I demand. "What?"

"Donating money to the Weasel House? Last year you gave half a million dollars to a group of tree-huggers who want to save abandoned rodents." Sam held up a hand to ward off my protests. "Oh, yeah, and you gave money to the usual and standard charities, but you threw away a half a million dollars building a home for oversized rats! How is that doing something meaningful?"

"How do you know about No Ferret Unloved?" I ask, shocked that he knows so much about me.

"I make it my business to know all I can about the man I work for and the people who come into his life," Sam says. "When I heard you were coming to stay for a couple of weeks, I wondered what was in it for you, so I checked you out. I figure you must be slumming. I mean, I know why Jeremy needs you. His reputation has gone through a bit of a shredder lately, but why does New York's hottest socialite need him?"

"The Miller Children's Home is an important project," I say. "Jeremy has agreed to attend the event I'm cohosting. He'll bring friends with deep pockets and the children will benefit."

"Oh, yeah, right," Sam says. "Your good work extends not just to homeless wharf rats but to *their* friends, the little homeless children."

I bite down on the inside of my cheek, trying as hard as I can to remember that while I may hate this man in the moment, he is key to staying close to Jeremy Reins.

"You and I have an obvious clash of moral and ethical values," I say and hear myself sounding like a prim Sunday school teacher.

"What, because I think saving homeless children is more valuable than spending millions on weasels and designer clothing?"

That's it! I turn in my seat and glare at him. "I give away millions every year. For your information, the event that I am cohosting will raise over five million dollars just because my name is on the ticket. That's what socialites *do!*

And, for your additional information, my friend, I do have a job, a real job, and it's important and dangerous and…"

Oh, dear God, what have I said? I shut my mouth, appalled, and look down at my hands, trying to gather my wits enough to do damage control. But Sam beats me to it.

"You have an important and dangerous job?" he says, clearly not believing me but curious nonetheless. "Do tell."

I sniff and become the Diva. "You wouldn't understand," I say.

"Yeah, I probably wouldn't, but why don't you try me anyway?"

Oh, great. Now what?

"You know," I say, "I don't think I owe you any explanations. Like you said, I'm here as Jeremy's guest."

"What is it you do that's so dangerous and do you use that megawatt brain of yours while you're doing it?"

He is mocking me. The cowboy is mocking me! Well, whatever! At least I've taken his mind off my stupid comment about having a dangerous job.

"Is this our exit?" I say, overexcitedly pointing out the Studio City exit sign. "You know, I have never been on a movie set before!"

The Cowboy shakes his head slowly, clearly not impressed by my sudden starstruck enthusiasm.

We drive through the gates, barely stopping as the guard waves to Sam and writes something down on a clipboard. I make a big show of being amazed by the city of studios and trailers, but I am not actually new to the movie world. When you're a household name, the club gets small and sooner or later you know everyone who's anyone. I know my share of actors. I've played around in their world just as they've hobnobbed with my society set. After a while you realize people are just people and, other than money, not much separates us from our basic common denominators.

I know, I didn't say this to Sam, but deep down inside, it's how I truly feel. Money buys all the trappings and it does buy a good measure of happiness, I don't care what anybody says. But when I sit in my therapist's office I have the same issues as any other woman; they're just gilded a bit by my good fortune.

Sam parks outside of what looks like an airplane hangar and when we step inside we are suddenly transported back two hundred years, to what appears to be a cross between a Brazilian jungle and the Salem witch trials.

Jeremy stands in the center of a clearing, dressed in a flowing black robe not unlike the dresses Zoe and Diane wore to dinner the evening before. He is surrounded by women who also wear black, but some of them are so scantily clad it's really not worth mentioning. They are wearing little strips of fabric that sway as they walk, revealing almost every inch of their bodies. It seems to be a ritual sacrifice that Jeremy is conducting because he has a woman tied to a tree and is approaching her with a knife.

They are rehearsing. The red light that indicates filming is not on and around us there is the quiet murmur of conversation. Zoe sits next to a cameraman, leaning in to instruct him as Jeremy closes in on his victim.

When he reaches the young woman, her eyes widen in fear as he raises the knife. With a single movement his left hand shoots forward. The woman screams and faints, and Zoe calls quietly, "Perfect!"

She stands up, leaving the cameraman's side and I realize she is dressed identically to the woman tied to the tree.

Jeremy steps back. His intended victim leaves and Zoe replaces her against the tree trunk. The look she gives him sends shivers of anticipation through my body. She wets her lips with her slick, pink tongue and seems to issue a challenge with that one simple flicker. There is a chemistry between the two of them that wasn't there with the stand-in.

"Quiet on the set," someone calls.

"And…action!"

The red light is on. The cameras are rolling and I forget that the figures before us are actors. The energy between Jeremy and Zoe is intense and strangely violent as he approaches her. Zoe does not play the scene as her stand-in did. She tilts her chin defiantly, thrusts her breasts out in invitation and, just as he reaches her, turns her head to offer her neck to his knife.

The other women standing around the clearing in a circle begin to chant and drums play. Diane emerges from the cult, slinking forward to come up behind Jeremy and it is obvious that she is about to do something when we hear "Cut!" There is a brief freeze and then everyone dissipates, vanishing to their various trailers and resting places.

Jeremy sees Sam and makes his way toward us, Zoe trailing like a vapor behind him. I think he doesn't know she's following him, because when he gets within earshot of Sam he says, "Load of crap, huh? Where's the believability?"

Zoe's eyes blaze and she veers off toward a small group of people clustered around a table and equipment. I see a few extras gesture in my direction, excitedly tapping others and know I have been recognized as a visiting celebrity.

When Jeremy sees me, he breaks into a wide grin and becomes the genial host.

"What do you think?" he says, sweeping one arm to include the set and everything around it.

I smile. "Quite nice," I say. "Sort of like a giant topiary."

Jeremy shrugs. "It's a living."

He seems full of energy, as if the events of last night had never taken place. It is amazing, really, to see him portray the casual, happy attitude of a Hollywood star leading a charmed life.

"Listen, I thought I might take you with us tonight," he says. "You know, to see the town and all that. I've an apartment in Beverly Hills so we don't have to make the trip back to the ranch tonight."

"But I don't have my things…" I begin.

Jeremy lifts his hand in a dismissive gesture. "I'll have someone bring in what you need. It's no big deal, but you will need an outfit."

I look at him and wonder what he's got planned.

Jeremy smiles at me. "You coming here was Andrea's idea and I don't know what favor she called in to do it, but I figure she'll feel just a little bit responsible for you, and Mark will have to watch out for me. You know, I am a bit of a wild boy!" He says this with an overly exaggerated wink to me and then laughs as if it's some kind of huge joke. "I've told Andrea she simply has to come along, you know, duty and all, and that she doesn't even have to talk to Mark if she doesn't want to."

"She won't come," I say, but I am really hoping Jeremy holds the magic card and can force her into it. I want to hear her version of last night's events. I suddenly find myself trusting no one, not even the woman who had called Renee and begged for her help.

Jeremy smiles like he knows a big secret and says, "Oh,

I think Andrea will come!" He leans closer to me. "Mark sent her an absolutely fabulous room full of flowers this morning and a long letter of apology."

I shake my head and look to see Sam apparently having the same reaction.

"Who sent the flowers and letter, Jeremy—you?" I ask.

Jeremy feigns mock dismay. "Of course not! I may be an asshole with plenty of experience in these sorts of predicaments, but I would never…"

"Spare me," I say.

Jeremy drops the act. "Okay, I helped but I didn't write it. They're my friends and in a way, it's probably my fault that bitch Diane got her claws into him. I owe them a little help. Come on, Porsche, I'm not heartless!"

I realize Jeremy really does appear to mean what he's saying. Every now and then a flash of sincerity seems to bubble up from the depths of Jeremy's personality. I look at my watch and realize it's already midafternoon. My stomach growls and I think it has to be a long time before dinner.

"I'll take her to the condo," Sam says, which makes me feel like luggage, but grateful luggage.

"Maybe Porsche would like to see Rodeo Drive, Sam," Jeremy says, gleefully baiting his friend while tantalizing me.

I am so distracted by the shopping possibilities that I don't notice Zoe and Diane approaching until they are almost upon us. Zoe has a clipboard in hand and is glancing at it nervously, while Diane eyes Sam and Jeremy with a speculative glint. I figure she's planning her next conquest. They arrive just in time to hear Jeremy tell Sam where to make reservations for dinner and when to order the limousine's arrival.

"Oh, goodie!" Diane coos. "Wolfie's!"

Jeremy ignores her and lets Zoe take him over. The two walk off, consulting the notepad and discussing what I assume is the next scene. Sam turns his back on Diane and leads me back to his SUV. He doesn't say a word, just starts up the car and takes off, the sullen scowl back in place. It's going to be a lovely evening.

"You don't have to take me to Rodeo Drive," I say, attempting to make peace. "I've been before. It's nothing new and the paparazzi in this town are too damned voracious."

Sam continues to stare straight ahead as we drive away from the studio. "Didn't intend to take you," he says.

"Well, good. I didn't think you were much of a shopper."

I take a moment to fantasize a suitable punishment for his transgressions and feel much better when I imagine him trotting behind me, toting hundreds of bags from every boutique shop in Beverly Hills.

"Where are we going to party tonight?" I ask.

"Don't know, don't particularly care."

"You know, you're about as friendly as a cactus," I say, finally losing my temper.

This draws a glare from him. "Why, princess, should you care about a hired hand's attitude?"

I sit there across from him, stewing, and am surprised when I feel a sudden sting of tears behind my eyelids and my throat tightens dangerously. For some reason I find myself flashing back to my conversation with Renee. "Who would miss the poor little rich girl if she suddenly vanished from the planet?"

Why do people see me as such a superficial playgirl? I have feelings. I have a mind. I'll show them. I'll show them all, I vow silently.

Chapter 7

It is long past midnight and I itch in all the wrong places. Perspiration trickles in rivulets between my breasts and joins the creeks and rivers of sweat that are running downhill beneath my absurd costume. I stomp my foot, open my mouth and scream from the sheer frustration of it all, but no one hears me. The band is too loud, and anyway, everyone else is screaming, too.

My only pleasure comes in knowing that Sam the cowboy is more miserable than me. He is wearing the same thing he always wears, a ten-gallon Stetson, tight jeans and a white, cotton dress shirt. His discomfort comes from Jeremy's choice of entertainment. Venue doesn't play country music. It is a tightly packed, ultrahot dance club and Sam the cowboy doesn't fit in with its young, chic clientele.

I fit right in. I am wearing Stella McCartney shiny black pants, paired with a white, handkerchief peasant top and Manolo Blahnik stiletto sandals. I am almost as tall as Sam and I positively tower over Jeremy and the other two women. Mark, however, is about my height, or would be if he'd stop standing with his shoulders slumped in a pitiful display of affected humility and remorse. I don't know why he bothers; Andrea has not so much as looked his way.

She is wearing a black Kevin Johnn pantsuit. Her brunette hair is swept back in a ponytail and she wears almost no makeup, probably because she has spent all day and most of the evening crying. At dinner, she left the table at least five times only to return with less makeup and a slightly redder nose.

For the occasion Mark has chosen a long, black leather trench coat and matching fedora. He would look sinister if he weren't so pathetic.

Scott has accompanied us, along with two extra bodyguards hired for the evening to fill in for Dave. Scott stands a short distance away from Jeremy, shadowing his every move, but the other two are nowhere in sight, well-hidden but easily summoned should the occasion warrant their presence. Scott isn't wearing a designer suit but his regular dark suit and grim expression make him fit right in.

At the beginning of the evening, Jeremy stayed stuck to my side, fawning over me at dinner and almost vacuuming my lips off outside the Geisha House as we waited for the others to board the limo. The man smells a photo op and is more of a ham than anyone I know. I mean, I am not averse to having my picture taken, but I certainly don't make a spectacle of myself! All right, so there was the Italian fountain incident…and maybe one or two more…and yes, perhaps a video with an early and somewhat *older* boyfriend: but it's not as if we actually *did* anything in it! I am not Paris Hilton, for God's sake!

Anyway, Jeremy certainly seems to have forgotten me. Zoe, accompanied by the obviously unwelcome Diane, has somehow materialized at the restaurant where we are to eat dinner, and now seems to have monopolized his attention. She is wearing black leather, too, but her getup makes Andrea's tastefully sexy outfit seem ultraconservative. For one thing, the seams of Zoe's floral silk pants are ripped straight up the sides, almost to her waistband. She was wearing a long tunic top at dinner, so no one noticed, but once we entered the club, she stripped the blouse off to reveal a sheer rose-colored, silk bra.

Of course, Zoe and Diane have brought a little added enticement. I see them slip off with Jeremy to a secluded private booth and I can tell from the way they're sniffing when they return that Zoe brought nose candy along with her.

A few yards away from where I'm watching the action, Andrea stands beside Sam. I've tried to talk to her, but she just stands there like a statue, and doesn't appear to hear a word I say. Sam has not left her side all evening. So, of course, that leaves me stuck with the only other person in our group, Mark.

"Wild scene, huh?" he screams over the music. He nods his head, like he thinks the music has a beat he can follow, like he's hip and into the whole scene.

I look at him, frown and cup my hand to my ear. Let him think I can't hear him and maybe he'll wander off. Idiot! But he doesn't leave. Instead he stands next to me, pathetically watching his wife ignore him.

"I don't know what happened," he says, speaking right into my ear so there's no drowning the words with techno-bop. "I think she must've put something in my wine. One minute I was fine, the next I was drunk on my ass and floating above the table, you know?"

No, I did not know. I like control too much to lose it on a chemical.

"Everything felt so good," he says. "It was like my nerve endings were supersensitive. Everything tasted better, sounded better, felt… Well, you know."

I have been leaning against the wall, watching the crowd as Mark talks, but suddenly the air is too close and I feel as if I just have to get outside and breathe.

"Be right back," I say, not caring if he hears me, and start through the crowd toward the exit.

The bouncer stamps my hand and attempts to kiss it, but I pull away from him and half run through the doors to the cool evening air. I hate L.A. I hate everything about it, the phony people, the lies, the lights, the glitz that only seems cheap after a while. The town is dirty and sleazy, even the good sections, and yes, even Beverly Hills. I look up at the night sky, the stars obscured by the dull orange glow of street lights, and wish I were anywhere but here.

I walk off a few steps, aware of a photographer across the street who is following my every move with his zoom lens. I notice one of Jeremy's security people heading in the man's direction, know the press won't be a problem and pull my cell phone out of my tiny Gucci bag to dial Renee's number. By my watch, it must be close to 6:00 a.m. in New York—time for her to be up anyway. She'll be mad that I haven't called back sooner, but may be too groggy to give me much hell about it.

"Hello, Porsche," she says, her voice as cool and crisp as ever. Damn caller ID.

"I'm sorry. It's been a rather hectic day and this is my first chance to get back to you," I begin, but Renee isn't interested in excuses.

"I was getting a little worried," she says, and I am sure I hear annoyance in her tone.

I walk a little farther away and lean against the side of a car. Without further delay, I tell her everything that's happened since my arrival. She listens with very few interruptions.

"So, Reins couldn't possibly be behind the failed attempt at the pool?" she asks.

"It wouldn't be impossible," I answer slowly. "And the shooting incident could've been done by one of his bodyguards or his manager or even Andrea, but I don't really get the feeling that's the case. The police have recovered the slugs and are running an analysis of all the staff weapons to compare them with the bullets so they should know definitively within a day, I'd guess."

Renee sighs softly. "I don't like the way this sounds," she says. "The Oscar party is in three days. I'm sending Emma."

"What?" Why send Emma, not that I wouldn't be glad to see her, but why? Surely she wasn't going to send me home?

"I'm sending Emma because her father's corporation, as you well know, owns a large chain of office supply stores. She'll be bringing a large check and the promise of school supplies for the students. No one will question why she's there with you for the party."

"Except for me," I say. "Why are you sending her?"

A tiny twinge of jealously gnaws at my stomach. This is my job. I'm handling it. I don't need a babysitter.

"Now, Porsche," Renee says, her voice set to soothe. "Two sets of eyes have got to be better than one. Besides, it sounds as if things could escalate and if they do you'll be glad of the help."

Only I'm not glad. I'm pissed. I mean, I love Emma, but this is *my* first job. I want to do it by myself! I know what I'm feeling isn't rational. Yesterday all I wanted was to come home, but somewhere along the line something changed inside me. I have something to prove now, to myself.

Renee isn't interested in my wounded pride. She wants the job done with the least amount of risk to her Roses. I know this and that's why I don't argue further with her.

"I'll talk to Emma," she says. "I should be able to get her there by tomorrow night or the day after at the latest. I trust you and Andrea can work out the details so no one wonders at her arrival."

Oh, what am I supposed to say to that? No? Of course not. "Okay, we'll be ready," I say, and hang up. I turn away from the sidewalk, sheltered by the SUV I've been leaning against and consider bashing my head into its metal frame until I am knocked senseless. I am a failure. Why else would Renee send backup? She doesn't trust me to discern the real story here. She's sending someone to look over my shoulder.

I stand there, feeling sorry for myself for a long minute, and then my self-respect gene kicks in. I don't know where this gene comes from because I don't know my real father and I don't think my mother has it. It's this well of icy cool that overcomes me in times of extreme stress. It just surges up through me and takes over. I'll just up my timetable and find out the real score before Emma can make it to L.A.

I straighten up, turn, and find Sam the Cowboy standing three feet away, arms crossed, watching me.

"I wondered where you went," he says.

I know I've been crying, not much, but enough that there could be a stray tear or two on my cheeks or my mascara could have run. I hastily wipe my cheeks and shove my cell phone back in my purse before I step away from the car and approach him.

"Is something wrong?" he asks. He's looking at me with this expression of what, pity? Compassion? No, I vote pity.

"No, nothing's wrong."

He's not buying it. "Bad news from home?"

I choke off a snicker. What other kind of news would there be from my home? But Sam doesn't know this and I have the feeling he won't let the matter rest until I give him something, anything, that explains my minimeltdown.

"Okay," I say, with a deep sigh. "I guess I've had a bit of bad news." I hang my head wondering what in the world I'm going to come up with, and hear myself say, "It's about my father. He's um…missing."

The look on Sam's face inspires me. He's hooked. Humans are inexorably drawn to the turmoil of others. That is why soap operas have such an attraction. We love to hang on to another's tragedy.

"Your father is missing? Victor Rothschild, missing?"

Oh, this is too good. I hang my head and am surprised to find tears forming in my eyes, choking my throat, and threatening to overtake my little melodrama.

"No. You see, Victor Rothschild is not my real father." I meet his concerned gaze. "I thought my biological father was dead, but it turns out he's alive and living in California."

Sam's eyes widen. "Really? So that's why you're really here. The Oscar party, this thing with Jeremy…"

I nod slowly. "It's all a sham so the press won't get wind of it. I came here to find him, but now...now..."

I choke, for real this time. I have no idea what to say next!

"What happened?"

I hold up my hand, head down, apparently overwrought. "I can't," I whisper.

Sam is by my side now. He puts an arm around my shoulder and offers me his clean white handkerchief. He smells good—spicy and masculine—and his arm is firm with work-hardened muscle that makes me feel suddenly safer than Jeremy's well-armed bodyguard could. And there is definite chemistry between us, something that jumps like a current between our two bodies, but I have to ignore this. I have work to do.

"We were so close," I say, raising my head as the answer comes to me. "I know his name is Lambert Hughes and he lived in Carlito at one time, but the private investigator says that's all he can come up with. He knows he was living in a trailer a few years ago, but that's where the trail ends. Now I'll never know him!" I wail, and collapse onto his shoulder. I am beginning to think I could have a future as an actor.

Sam pats my shoulder and for a moment I feel guilty.

"Porsche, this is the job you wouldn't talk about on the trip down here, isn't it?" he says softly.

What? For a moment I have forgotten all about my blunder in the car. Without even realizing it, I have covered up my past mistake. I'm so brilliant. I can take care of my problems without even using my *conscious* brain! I do a mental victory dance. Sam the cowboy is off my tail!

"Yes," I answer softly. "That's my secret, only I suppose I've hit a dead end. I'll never know my real father."

I sigh and square my shoulders bravely. "I guess we should go back inside."

"Wait," he begins, but it's too late. I've turned and when he follows, we both see a sudden eruption by the front door. The bouncer opens the door, grabs the burly doorman and the two disappear inside, leaving only a man with a clipboard to keep the anxious line outside from surging ahead into the club.

Sam breaks into a run with me right behind him, a gnawing flame of uneasiness churning in my stomach. He reaches the doorway, pulls it open, and the two of us plunge inside the darkened club.

The band is playing. People are still screaming so, at first, nothing seems to be wrong, until my gaze hits a spot near the back of the dance floor. A group of women, all dressed in long flowing black gowns, have surrounded Jeremy and Zoe. They form an impenetrable wall and as I watch, they close in and Jeremy disappears. I see Zoe's mouth open in a silent scream before she, too, is absorbed into the sea of black.

The club erupts into a frenzy of motion as the club bouncers, Jeremy's security people, and Sam and I try to reach the movie star. I watch, realizing there are too many people to break through to Jeremy. As I watch, an all-out battle begins to take place between the black-clad women and the men trying to rescue Jeremy Reins. I haven't seen Mark or Andrea anywhere, but when I begin edging along the wall toward the stage, I find Andrea. She is standing in a small alcove, chewing her bottom lip and staring out at the dance floor, mesmerized by the action.

"Come on," I say, grabbing her hand. "I have an idea and I'm going to need some help."

This seems to snap her out of her stupor, because she nods, more alert than I've seen her since the night before.

"We need a couple of those black robes," I say, "and a hat or some sort of headpiece."

Andrea doesn't ask why. Without another word, she wades into the fray, seizes a woman at random, and rips the robe off her body. The woman, about Andrea's size, starts to fight back but Andrea pitches her on her ass easily and tosses the robe to me. The woman on the floor looks up at Andrea, smiles and sticks her tongue out, making a licking motion and running her hands over her scantily clad body. I recognize her. She was the stand-in for Zoe's sacrificial scene with Jeremy.

I pull on the robe and, while Andrea is scoring her second gown, I reach out and pluck a peacock-feathered headpiece from a passing transvestite. The women around us are chanting something over and over. "Reymundo!" they cry. "Reymundo!" They move now, in a horde, and seem to be carrying a swell of people with them, toward the exit of the club. If something doesn't happen, and fast, they will leave taking Jeremy and Zoe with them.

The band has stopped playing. The house has realized something has gone wrong, something unplanned and not part of the normal course of abnormal club behavior.

I look at Andrea and signal to her to join me on the stage. Together the two of us make our way up the narrow steps and into the middle of the platform.

"Do you have a cigarette?" I ask her.

"What?"

"A cigarette. Do you have a cigarette?"

Andrea stares at me like I'm crazy, but finally nods. "Yeah."

"Light it, please."

"There's a smoking ban…" she starts, but when she sees me grab a roll of duct tape and a microphone stand, she seems to see a plan forming and does as I tell her. When the cigarette is lit, I grab it from her, tape it to the end of the mike stand, lit end up, and raise the pole above my head. It is inches from a sprinkler and within moments the system works as it is supposed to, showering the club and its patrons with a sudden burst of cold, cold water.

From where I stand, I can see the group of women trying to move toward a side exit with their captives, but the shower has momentarily disoriented them.

"Come on!" I cry, and grab startled Andrea. "There they are!"

The two of us blend into the group of black-hooded women and while Andrea uses her martial arts skills to carve a path, I use the sharp spikes of my stilettos to kick, poke and pierce my way through the human barrier.

Soaked by the sprinklers and startled by the sudden painful attacks, the hooded women trip over each other, falling in their attempt to avoid my heels and Andrea's violent moves. We reach Jeremy and Zoe just as I hear the shrill piercing sound of police whistles coming from the entrance to the club.

Scott and his men appear, finally able to locate their boss by following the path Andrea and I have cleared. They surround us and we move, fast, toward the back of the stage. The police waste no time surrounding and securing the dance floor, sealing off access to the stage.

"Jeremy, what in the hell is going on?" I ask once we are safe behind the curtain of LAPD's finest.

"I don't know," he says. "They seem to think I'm

Reymundo. What a bunch of crackpots! That was three years ago!"

"Let's keep moving, folks," Scott says. "We're taking the back exit."

We don't have much of a choice in the matter. The LAPD is behind us and Scott and his two men are corralling us forward. In less than a minute we are outside the club in an alley where Sam is leaning against the open door of our limousine.

Andrea and I throw off our ridiculous robes and leave them lying in the street. We clamber into the back of the car and in seconds are on the road. Jeremy is the only one speaking. The rest of us seem to be in various states of shock.

"We need tequila," he cries. "Come on! Everybody!"

With maniacal abandon, Jeremy pours tequila into shot glasses and starts handing them out like tonics. For the first time I realize Diane has followed the others into the limousine and is sitting next to a very uncomfortable Mark. Andrea is sitting as far away from them as possible, against the far side of the car, next to Scott, who shields her with his sheer bulk. She has retreated back into her still, trancelike state and I wonder if she's taken tranquilizers or is merely overwhelmed.

I set the shot Jeremy hands me aside, sink back against the overstuffed seat cushions and close my eyes. I have to think. Since landing at LAX, all I've done is react rather than act. A good psychologist carries a mental map in her head, outlining her patient's strengths, weaknesses and issues. She always has a plan of intervention. The problem with me is, I have no plan. Hell, I don't even have a map. I have not done a thorough assessment of Jeremy, nor have I assessed the cast of characters who surround him. I have no hope of making a determination about the threat to my client until I have completed the basic groundwork. I've been too busy putting out fires and dealing with every crisis to even put one together.

I take a deep breath and let my body relax. In the background I hear Jeremy's voice above the others, coaxing them into a second shot, probably in an attempt to keep everyone from feeling the amount of anxiety he feels. I open my eyes for a moment and watch him in action. I know by now not to watch his body language or listen to the content of his speech. Jeremy Reins carries his true feelings in his eyes. Right now, his eyes dart everywhere, but they land on Scott and Sam with the most frequency. He is scared.

So far, Jeremy has not been harmed, not seriously. Why, then, is he scared? Was it just the lack of control over the group of women or was it more than that? I close my eyes again and think back over everything I have learned about the man. I mentally review every piece of gossip I've heard, every article I've read, and the background report thoughtfully provided for me by Renee's staff the morning I left New York.

He is 28, never been married, was raised in Montana by a single mother with two other, older, siblings. The baby of the family, according to the Adlerian theory, is often protected and may become spoiled. They want to be bigger and may have huge plans for their future that may or may not work out. But Jeremy's career has panned out. He is quite successful. Why go to the trouble to "create" more publicity. Was he not voted *People's* Sexiest Man Alive this year? What else could he need or want by generating more publicity? Would he not be in danger of becoming overexposed to media attention and thus become yesterday's news?

I open my eyes again and survey the occupants of Jeremy's limousine. If Jeremy doesn't stand to gain from this publicity, then does someone genuinely want to hurt him? This option seems more viable, but I wonder why and who? Could it be someone riding along with us tonight, or a total stranger? I study the current pool of suspects and wonder if any of them would have a motive for wanting to hurt the star.

Zoe is sitting next to Jeremy, so I think about her first. She and Jeremy are working on a project together, Zoe's first as executive producer. If she hurts—or worse, kills off—the leading man, wouldn't that mean her project would fail? Of course, she and Jeremy do seem to have shared a past and there is always an undercurrent of animosity between the two. Hmm. Doubtful, but it bears further investigation.

Diane is sitting next to Zoe. As far as I can tell, she has very little to do with Jeremy. She has no history with him that I know of. She doesn't seem to be angry with him, and she was too busy entertaining Jeremy's agent under the dining room table last night to have been the one shooting out the French doors and leading the others on a merry chase.

Her alibi, Mark, sits beside her. Ditto, his alibi, but wasn't he the one who said Jeremy would be worth far more dead and immortalized than living? Mark would still earn his 15 percent agent's fee whether Jeremy was alive or dead. He could be a wealthier man if Jeremy suddenly became the James Dean of his generation.

Any of these people could've hired someone to do the actual shooting, I think. Greed is a superior motive for murder, but only if the attacks on Jeremy were meant to kill him. So far, I wasn't sure at all of the attacker's true intent.

I felt rather certain I could discount Mark's wife, Andrea. After all, wasn't she the one who called Renee and wanted the additional help? If she wanted to hurt or frighten Jeremy, she wouldn't have summoned help in protecting him, would she? But then, she wasn't in the dining room when intruders were spotted on the estate property and she was nowhere to be found when Dave was electrocuted and Jeremy hit in the head. If she stayed married to Mark and Jeremy indeed brought in more money as a dead idol, then she'd gain from his death as well. Still, my gut feeling was that she was innocent.

I looked at Scott next. He was hired to protect Jeremy, but he certainly hadn't done a very good job so far. Tonight was another perfect example. When Jeremy had needed help, Scott and his "crack" team hadn't been able to protect him. Why hadn't Jeremy fired him? After all, fans mob stars all the time. Scott should've handled this little "Occurrence" without any trouble.

The relationship between the two seemed to have taken on a new dimension last night as the two men cavorted around in the pool. Was Jeremy too besotted with the man to realize he wasn't doing his job?

While Scott might not have a reason to want Jeremy frightened or hurt, Dave certainly would. He stood to lose Scott to Jeremy. Yet, if that were the case, then why sabotage a pool and jump into it? He had to know he was risking serious injury or death by doing that, if he was the one responsible for booby-trapping the pool.

I considered Sam last. The Great Unknown. The man who followed Jeremy to Hollywood after introducing him to drama in high school. The man who functioned as a quasi-parent, shepherding his charge off to bed when he has an early call the next morning and, in general, watching over the bad boy actor. Would he want Jeremy hurt or worse, killed? What motive would he have? Was there some secret from his past that drew the two men together?

Sam suddenly looks away from Jeremy and catches me staring at him. He meets my gaze and holds it, not in a challenging manner but as if he is curious to find me studying him so intently.

"Jeremy, I'd like to go home," Andrea says quietly.

Sam's attention turns instantly to Andrea.

"Yeah," Mark adds. His eyes are pathetically hopeful. "We'd better call it a night."

Andrea ignores him, keeping her gaze on Jeremy's face. "I'm at the Wilshire," she says, and I watch Mark's shoulders slump.

"I want to go home, too," Zoe says. "My nerves are shot."

When we return to Jeremy's penthouse condominium, Sam, Jeremy and I ride up in the elevator with Scott and his two auxiliary security guards. We ride to the top floor in silence and step out into a gleaming marble-tiled foyer. Two LAPD police detectives are waiting for us. They step forward, flash badges and introduce themselves.

"We need to ask some questions about what happened at the nightclub," one says. He is tall and skinny with no discernable chin. "We got a request from the local boys in Sam Jacinta. They want us to follow up—just in case the incident at the club is somehow tied to the trouble out at your estate."

Jeremy smiles pleasantly, but defers to Sam and Scott. "Gentlemen, if you would give me a few moments to rejuvenate myself and make sure that Miss Rothschild is comfortable, I'll be glad to answer questions later. Perhaps my manager and security consultant can answer some of the preliminary questions?"

Jeremy isn't taking no for an answer. He walks off into the penthouse without waiting for a response. Thick cream carpeting cushions our steps as I follow him into the living room, drawn by the bank of glass that completely encloses the room with a wall-to-wall view of downtown L.A. the Hollywood hills and surrounding Beverly Hills. I catch my breath at the sheer beauty of it all and hear Jeremy chuckle by my side.

"It's quite something, isn't it, lovey?" he says quietly.

I say nothing. I am drawn to the vista before me, suddenly homesick for a home I've never had. My life has been filled with sumptuous suites, palatial condos and estates, but never a home. The lights twinkling on the nearby hills are a winking reminder that some people live in regular homes—comfortable, lived-in nests where things stay the same and memories accumulate because of the steady, reliable routines of the families that live inside.

"You're a thousand miles away, lovey," Jeremy observes. "What are you thinking?"

I pull back from my selfish longings and turn to meet his gaze. His eyes show me nothing other than genuine curiosity and a softness that I have not seen before.

"In the past two days intruders have broken into your estate, people have been hurt, including you, and tonight…God, I have no idea what tonight was about! Do you enjoy this?" I ask. "Because you certainly don't seem upset by all of it. Do you enjoy the attention, the endless stream of paparazzi following your every move, tracking your ups and downs? Is this what being a movie star means to you? Do you not get that someone out there could really want you killed? Or is this all part of the Hollywood 'spin' game?"

Jeremy frowns, probably surprised by the sudden turn I've taken, and looks a bit longingly at the granite-topped bar behind us. We are all alone, so he can't play off Sam, or distract me by luring others into the conversation.

"Lovey, I had nothing to do with that fiasco at the club. As for the movie star business, it gets old after awhile," he says. "Once you realize the lifestyle comes at the cost of your privacy, yeah, I guess it feels like a golden cage. Certainly I'm not enjoying being stalked, but Porsche, once they see fear in your eyes, they own you. I won't give them that victory, lovey!"

He practically sprints to the bar, opens the wine refrigerator and pulls out a bottle.

I walk over to take a seat in the high-backed chairs rimming the opulent counter. I run the tips of my fingers across the cool surface and see our reflections in its high sheen.

"Why, lovey, it's getting to you, isn't it? Darling, are you scared?"

"I've ever known, but I've never had my life threatened," I say. "I don't have people sabotaging my estate or trying to kidnap me. I don't let myself get into those types of situations. I'm high-profile, but I'm not stupid. Jeremy, I don't think your security people are doing a good job of protecting you. And the police do what they can, but you need more."

Jeremy seems uncomfortable with what I'm saying and I truly don't understand, so I go into therapist mode.

"Jeremy, didn't you grow up on a farm or something? This must be quite a switch from home. I mean, do you ever get lonesome for your family? Do you get back to see them much?"

"My, my, lovey," Jeremy says. "So curious!" He has lost his battle with his better judgment and is uncorking a bottle of sauvignon blanc. I idly note the year and vintner, Peter Michael, with approval.

"I get back now and then," he says. "My mom lives outside Butte, Montana, on a little ranch she and my dad bought when they were first married. It's just her now, so I try and keep an eye on her."

"No brothers or sisters?" I ask, knowing the answer but wanting to hear his take on it.

Jeremy pours two glasses of wine, hands me one, and takes a sip of his own before answering.

"A sister and a brother, both older, but we're not as close as I am to my mom. There's a five-year gap between me and the next oldest, so I guess I was always a pain in the ass to them."

A look crosses his face quickly—pain, perhaps? I can't tell because it is gone and replaced almost instantly by Jeremy the Host.

"Sam tells me Scott brought your ferret and her cage down for the evening, said you insisted?"

I bristle just slightly, even though I know he's trying to divert me off the subject of his childhood.

"Marlena and I go everywhere together. Besides, she needs human contact and your estate is not her home."

"Now, lovey," Jeremy remonstrates. "Consuela would've been only too happy to tend to your precious pet."

I smile. "Now, Jeremy," I parrot back. "You wouldn't leave your best friend behind. I don't see Sam sitting home tending to the ranch."

Jeremy smiles. "Lovey, Sam's human and he's my personal manager. I could hardly leave him behind!"

It is my turn to appear puzzled. "I don't get it," I say slowly. "But then again, perhaps I do. Sam is from your hometown, right? I believe Andrea told me he was your drama teacher? Did you bring him out to Hollywood because he was someone you trusted?"

Jeremy looks toward the door, as if expecting Sam to materialize, or making sure that he didn't before answering my question. When he speaks, his voice is so low I almost have to strain to hear the words.

"I guess I owe Sam a lot," he says. "I was heading for trouble when he met me. I hated school, didn't have any use for it. I hated the rules, hated the routine and most of all hated the busywork they handed out to keep us quiet and complacent. I got into Sam's class when I shouldn't have—I changed my schedule card from a ridiculous lifestyle skills class to introduction to theater arts. The rest, as we say in Hollywood, was history."

Jeremy stares out at the hills behind me for a long moment and I know he's not seeing them. He is drifting on a tide of long-ago memories and I capitalize on it.

"So drama wasn't boring?" I ask softly.

"No," he says, still staring out the window. "It was fucking amazing. I could be anyone, anywhere, in any time period. I could become someone else, live their life, and dream their dreams."

"So it wasn't Sam, per se, it was acting that saved you."

Jeremy glances back at me sharply. "No, it was Sam." He pronounces this flatly. It is fact in his mind. Sam saved him.

"How?"

Jeremy pours more wine into his almost empty glass and gives me an appraising look. "You're really interested?"

"Absolutely. I find it amazing that someone can go from,

shall we say, rags to riches, and still remember the folks back home."

Jeremy laughs, but it is a short, sarcastic bark of a laugh and not at all gleeful.

"You had to know Sam back then," he says. "He's nothing like the man he was then. Ten years ago, Sam was on fire with teaching. He brought the world into the classroom, made us taste it, and taught us to believe in our various acting roles. He made it seem easy and I, for one, loved him for it. You don't forget someone like that, no matter how big you get, or how far you travel."

I stretch and push my glass forward for a refill.

"I would think it would be rather difficult to get a man like that to leave the classroom and move to Hollywood."

Jeremy fills my glass and shakes his head softly. "I don't think Sam cared where he was or who he was with when I went to get him," he whispers. "His wife and daughter had been killed in a car accident the year before and Sam had pretty much been livin' inside a bottle ever since their funeral."

"So you went back and got him?"

Jeremy hunches his shoulders in a self-deprecating shrug and grins. "Come on, lovey," he says. "Look at me. I need Sam far more than he needs me!"

As if on cue, Sam walks back into the room, shirt sleeves rolled up, hat and Western-cut suit jacket gone, clearly determined to have his say with his charge.

"I can't hold them off any longer," he says, removing the wineglass from Jeremy's hand. "They're waiting in the den with Scott. Go get it over with."

Jeremy grins. "All right, Pa," he says, in his country-hick voice. "I know—there's cows need milkin' and horses need

feedin'. I'm a goin'!" He starts off, walking out from behind the bar and taking a half step away, then ducks back
suddenly, plucking the glass back up from the bar where
Sam has placed it and drains it in one fast gulp. "Jest
needed a little fortification, that's all!"

He grins, cackles manically, and practically dances from
the room, leaving me alone with the cowboy.

Chapter 8

Sam and I are silent for a long moment after Jeremy leaves the room. The cowboy is busying himself cleaning up after his charge, while I stare out the window, secretly watching Sam's reflection and trying to reconcile Jeremy's portrayal of Sam with the bits and pieces of his personality I've been able to pick up on in the past two days. He is moody and compassionate; kind to those in pain, like Andrea, and distant to the rest of us. In fact, I realize as I stand there, that Sam has only been truly nice to me since learning of my father's disappearance. Does this somehow make me "safe"? Am I a member of his club now, the grievously wounded by life's capricious whims club?

"I suppose you'd like to see your guest suite?" Sam says.

I realize I have allowed myself to become swept up in the events of Jeremy's hectic, rapid-paced life and have forgotten all about Marlena. Scott supposedly brought her down from the ranch in case we spent a few days in L.A. but I hadn't remembered to even check on her!

Sam turns and I follow him down another long carpeted hallway, watching the slight slump of his shoulders that makes me think he is as tired as I am. I am trying to think up something nice to say, something that doesn't let on that I know now all about him and feel sorry for him, but he stops in front of a doorway before I can muster up anything other than, "Oh, here?"

"I've been meaning to ask you something," he says. He is leaning his arm up against the door frame and I realize he towers over me, even when I'm wearing four-inch heels.

"What is that?" I ask, aware of the ridiculous beating of my heart against my rib cage. Why does the man make me feel so nervous?

"That thing you did, walking up on the stage and grabbing the microphone—how did you come up with that?"

I laugh. "I don't know," I say finally. "I suppose I was desperate. I didn't know who those women were and I knew we needed to get to Jeremy and Zoe. I didn't know if it was a real emergency or not, but I've studied crowd behavior and I know how dangerous they can become. I guess I just decided to err on the side of caution and try and help out. I thought they'd take Jeremy out of the club if I didn't come up with a distraction. I figured if I stopped even a few of them, the rest of you might be able to get to him."

Sam nods slowly. "It was bizarre in there," he says. "I don't get this Hollywood bullshit. I saw the look on Jeremy's face and I realized he was clearly terrified. He was calling out to Scott and Zoe was screaming her guts out. Scott couldn't get through all those women and he couldn't overreact and hurt one of them. It was just chaos. It got out of hand pretty quickly."

"Sam," I ask, looking directly into his eyes, "you think someone really is trying to hurt Jeremy, don't you? You don't think this is all part of the publicity sideshow do you?"

Sam doesn't look away. For a moment he just looks at me, as if deciding something, and then he lets me in. "This isn't a game, Porsche. Jeremy's a rash, impulsive idiot at the best of times and self-destructive at worst, but he's straight-forward about it. If he'd set this up, he'd have told us."

I nod. "I didn't think he did," I say softly. "But I wasn't entirely sure."

I am about to ask more questions but he preempts me.

"Better get your beauty sleep," he says, pushing away from the door frame. "Leave the worrying to us profession-als. Jeremy and you will both be safe. Your little visit is go-ing to go off without another hitch, I promise. Nothing but happy trails ahead, ma'am. Good night!"

As I watch, his face becomes the impersonal mask of the courteous employee. Gone is the accessible moment, the connection between two like-minded individuals. I watch him walk away from me before turning the door han-dle and stepping into my suite for the night.

Marlena has been waiting for me and she is in a hell of a mood, shrieking, chattering and in general going on about how mistreated she's been.

"Baby," I croon, opening the cage door and pulling her out and up onto my shoulder. "Mommy is so-o-o sorry! I have missed you so-o-o much!"

Marlena is only slightly mollified by this. I must pro-vide treats and kisses, which I do with tired abandon. Then I step into the bedroom and find myself smiling with approval. An antique four-poster canopy bed provides the focal point, with rich, brocade tapestry curtains draped to encase the regal bower of soft down pillows, velvet quilts and layers of sweetly scented, cotton sheets and fluffy blankets.

"Oh, Marlena, look!" I whisper.

On the bedside table there are all my favorite magazines—*Paris Vogue, Vanity Fair* and even the *London Times* newspaper. A tray is set with cookies and chocolates, bottled water and a carafe that, upon investigation, I find holds hot chocolate. It is perfect.

Along the wall, in a perfect line, are all of my suitcases. In the marble and brass bathroom I find my toiletries and lavender-scented towels warming on their rack beside the freshly filled and somehow still-hot tub.

"Oh, Marlena," I purr. "Mommy thinks this job is maybe not so bad!"

Marlena isn't at all sure the fuss is worth it. She scampers down onto the bed and curls into a little ball, content to watch me as I undress and slip into my bath.

I lean back, rest my head on the cushioned bath pillow, and begin to plot tomorrow's course of action. The celebrity event and, of course, the Oscars and all the celebrations surrounding it, require that I make sure Kristy Burke back at Gotham Central will be sending the appropriate gowns and accessories, immediately. Jeremy's situation demands that I start narrowing down the field of suspects, so I make a mental note to call Andrea and ask her to come to lunch with me. I have quite a few questions for her, and there is no longer any time to waste.

I now believe, as does Sam, that Jeremy is not trying to stage these attacks as a cry for attention. I think someone really wants to hurt Jeremy and I am beginning to think

Emma's presence will be more helpful than I was willing to admit to myself earlier.

I step out of the bath and prepare for bed. A sense of re-lief washes over me as I begin to think about how well Emma and I will work together. But I must have a plan. For a start, I will begin looking for people who might wish Jeremy harm. I am thinking it may be someone who knows him, knows his schedule and might have access to the es-tate. This feels like the easiest answer and it's always best to start with the simple scenarios and work outward. I po-sition Marlena's tiny sleep mask over her eyes before ly-ing back and slipping on my own. I fall asleep smiling and don't awaken until the shrill ringing of my cell phone in-terrupts a lovely dream I am having about Valentino and Ralph Lauren. They are fighting over which gown I will wear to the Oscars.

"What? Hello?" I mumble into the phone.

I hear squeaking, realize I am holding it upside down, and quickly reverse the phone to fit my ear. I do not remove my sleep mask because I am seriously hoping it is all a dream. Surely I haven't been asleep for more than twenty minutes.

"Porsche? Wake up!"

It is Renee and she sounds uncharacteristically stressed.

"What time is it?"

"Sorry, darling, it's eight a.m., my time, so that's five a.m. yours."

"No-o-o! Let me sleep!"

"This is important, dear," she says firmly, and I push the eye shades up onto my forehead.

"All right. Talk."

Marlena whines in her sleep, burrows deeper into the

covers beside me and snores on, her eye mask untouched, her beauty rest undisturbed.

"I've spoken with Emma and there's a problem."

I sit up in bed, wide-awake now. "Problem? What sort of problem?"

"Well, she's in the middle of something and can't break away for another two or three days. She may be able to make it in time for CeCe's party, but that depends on some very fluid factors."

"Fluid factors?" I echo, confused.

Renee is clearly not going to tell me any more than she already has about Emma's situation because she goes right on as if I hadn't asked. "So, I suppose you'll get your wish. You'll get to press on without her for a couple of days. I'd send someone else, but I'm afraid at the moment we're all a bit jammed with this...situation. Will you be all right, dear?"

I'll show Renee she can count on me. I'll do my job and Emma's, too. I'll know who's threatening Jeremy and perhaps even eliminate the risk. Of course, this is getting a little carried away and I realize the fact before I speak.

"Renee, don't worry about me. I am fairly certain that Jeremy isn't behind the events of the past few weeks and has probably just provoked someone who wants to get his attention, that's all. I mean, none of the attempts has actually hurt him, and he's added additional security personnel, so I think we can relax a little bit."

Renee expels a sigh of relief. "Good! Now, of course, if the situation changes, call me and I'll work something out. Remember, you are there to assess the level of danger to Mr. Reins, nothing more. I do not, under any circumstances, want you placing yourself in jeopardy nor taking any unnecessary risks, do you understand?"

What am I going to say? I reassure her every which way I can that I would never *dream* of doing any such thing and hang up. Then I lie awake for another two hours, making out my virtual will and planning my funeral because of course, I do exactly intend to move heaven and earth to find out who is after Jeremy and then take care of the problem. I'll show that cowboy and everybody else who thinks socialites can't do anything except dole out money. I think I will make a spectacular Gotham Rose!

I roll over and fall back into a dreamless sleep, only awakening when Marlena insists, hours later, that I feed her. Marlena only has her best interests at heart, I know, but she is a lifesaver.

"Baby, how did it get so late?" I ask, pouring her favorite kitty kibble into a china saucer. It is almost 10:00 a.m., California time. Jeremy will be long gone to the studio, probably Sam in tow to keep an eye on him.

I walk into the living area of my suite and find a tray with a carafe of coffee, fresh fruit and an assortment of breakfast pastries and yogurt, along with a note.

"Andrea will be by to pick you up for lunch," it reads. "She'll bring you back out to the ranch later. I'll take care of your bags and the overgrown rodent." Sam, displaying his moronic sense of humor, I suppose. Rodent! Really!

I don't have time to think about the cowboy, I tell myself, and rush about getting ready for a day of hard physical labor. Shopping really takes it out of a woman. There are so many decisions, so many…issues; like accessories and borrowed jewelry and coordination. I mean, one must be original and smashing and, above all else, gorgeous. My hand flies to my head and I moan—my hair, who will Kristy find to do my hair? Does she have someone in L.A.? What if I have to take care of these arrangements myself?

Given Andrea's recent emotional trauma I am expecting no back-up support from her, but to my surprise, when she arrives to pick me up, Andrea is back to her normal self. In fact, she seems almost serene. What is this?

"Okay, whatever drugs they're giving you, I want some," I say when we're seated on the outdoor patio at The Ivy.

Andrea smiles, letting her gaze wander around the patio of the small cottage restaurant and nodding to a few people who wave and seem happy to see her. I lean back in my seat, sheltered by the cozy white umbrella overhead, and wait for her attention to turn back to me.

"Mark's drug test results came back," she murmurs. "It was positive."

"Andrea," I say, leaning forward, "what are you talking about? What drug test?"

The waiter appears beside the table and it is all I can do not to scream because I want to know so badly and will now have to wait.

"Two juleps," Andrea says softly, and the waiter disappears, but reappears almost as quickly with two mint-sprigged drinks.

"House specialty," Andrea says, indicating the drinks, and I want to strangle her.

"Who cares about the drinks?" I hiss across the table. "What drug test?"

"The other night, when Mark drove off and left, after…well, you know. He went straight to his doctor, called him on the way back into town, and demanded that he meet him at his office and do a drug test. It was positive for Ecstasy."

I felt one skeptical eyebrow shoot up involuntarily.

Andrea sips her drink and holds up one well-manicured hand, warding off what we both know is the obvious barrage of questions I'm just dying to unleash.

"I know—you want to know how he could've been that high and still driven, let alone had the forethought to call his doctor."

"Well?" I demand.

She shrugs. "He says by the time the police left, he was feeling more alert. Apparently Mark realized Diane must have slipped him something."

I am frowning harder now. "So, is he going to press charges?"

Andrea shakes her head. "No, but I wouldn't try getting a job in the business if I were Diane," she says. "Mark's word is golden in the business. No one will work with her."

I lean back against the soft cushioned back of my chair and study the woman across the table from me. If I found myself in her situation, would I be as cool and forgiving? I can't imagine it. I can't imagine not wanting to personally exact revenge, on someone, either my husband or the woman involved.

"So, Mark says 'Hey, she slipped me something,' and that's it? You forgive him and go on just like that?"

Andrea shrugs. "Pretty much." She meets my gaze, her wide blue eyes darkening with intensity. "Porsche, it's different in Hollywood. The rules are different, the entire game is different. You can't understand and I wouldn't expect you to unless you lived and worked here. Besides," she says with a tight-lipped smile, "what goes around comes around. Diane'll get hers, don't you worry."

Andrea laughs and it sounds genuine, which makes me laugh along with her before I remember that I am panicked.

"Andrea, I haven't heard a word from Kristy in New York. Renee assured me that she would be taking care of my gowns and accessories, but I don't know if that means she'll be arranging for me to have my hair and makeup done or…"

She interrupts me with a reassuring pat of the hand. "Porsche, darling, don't worry. I forgot to tell you, Kristy called. We're meeting my stylist today at three. She's already talked with Kristy and the two of them picked out some lovely gowns for you to try. Someone from Harry's is coming, too, you know, for the jewelry. Don't worry. It's all taken care of."

"But, my hair and my…"

Andrea smiles. "Like I said, Porsche, this is Hollywood. We do things differently here. Relax, everything has been taken care of. Trust me!"

And I do because I like Andrea, I really do, but I still can't rule her out as a suspect. And what had she meant that Diane would "get hers?"

When we arrive back at the Paradise Ranch, exhausted but triumphant, I find a short note taped to Marlena's cage. It is in Sam's handwriting and reads, "I need to see you alone. I have something for you. S."

Something for me? I open the cage doorway and Marlena scampers into my arms and up onto my shoulders. "What does the cowboy have for Mommy?" I ask the disgruntled ferret. But if Marlena knows, she's not telling.

"Come on, baby," I whisper. "Let's go see the nice man who has something for Mommy. If Mommy doesn't like her present, I promise, you may bite him."

When I find him, Sam is sitting out by the pool, reading. He looks up as I approach and indicates a chair next to him.

"I hope you don't mind," he says, when Marlena and I sit down. "I took the liberty of following up on our talk last night." I must look puzzled because he prompts me. "You know, about losing your father?"

A sudden sense of dread overwhelms me. "What have you done?" I ask quietly, fighting to control my voice.

"Well, you seemed pretty upset about not being able to find your Dad and that P.I. of yours coming to a dead end, so I called a buddy of mine up that way. He's retired state patrol." Sam frowns. "You know, he found your father right off. I don't know why the guy you hired him couldn't locate him."

Probably because I made that part up, I scream silently.

"You found my father?" My voice cracks on the word *father* and for a second my throat feels funny, like it's closing up on me.

Sam reaches over and hands me a piece of paper. "That's his address and phone number. Jeremy and Zoe are editing all day tomorrow, so they'll be working. There are no social activities on tomorrow's calendar, so you're free all day."

I look at him, not comprehending what he's trying to tell me.

"I can take you up there, if you'd like," he says. "It's a little less than an hour away. It's a real nice little town—a lot of celebrities have their mountain get-away cabins in the hills around Carlito."

The world is moving too fast now. It's one thing to know about my father, but confronting him is quite another. What if he doesn't want to see me? What if he really is a horrible person and not at all the laughing man of my memories? Furthermore, I have a job to do. I have to stay close to Jeremy. I can't go running off to see my long lost father!

I jump up and Marlena almost bounces off my neck. She digs her little claws into my cashmere Mizrahi shrug and emits a series of frightened squeaks.

"Thank you," I say, in a voice that doesn't even resemble me. "I believe Andrea said she's booked us in at Skin Spa, so tomorrow's looking kind of full."

Sam is watching my hands and when I look down, I see that I have twisted the piece of paper he's given me into a tight coil.

"If you change your mind," he says, "just let me know. My apartment is above the stables, or you can call on the house extension." When I forget to acknowledge this, he continues. "I hope I haven't upset you. I guess I was thinking you'd be glad to know he isn't really lost."

I try and snap back into some semblance of composure. I straighten up and smile politely. "Of course you haven't upset me," I say. "I'm just surprised that's all. I never thought you would…" And to my absolute horror, my voice fails and I burst into tears!

Sam is up and out of his chair. He moves to touch my arm, and Marlena apparently remembers my instructions because she strikes, sinking her needle-sharp little teeth right into Sam's wrist.

"Ouch!" Sam pulls his arm back and is shaking it vigorously.

"Are you all right?" I cry and try to step toward him but he sees Marlena, still hissing, and backs away.

Lights go on in the bar area as the French doors to the dining room are suddenly flung open. Jeremy, Zoe, Mark, Andrea and an assortment of other guests spill out onto the patio just in time to catch Sam hopping around like a lunatic. Everyone stops and just stares, watching as I pursue Sam and he tries to get away.

"Is that blood?" I hear Zoe ask. "Oh, my God, he's bleeding!"

"What is going on?" Mark asks. "Someone get the man a towel."

A woman shrieks. "She's got a rat around her neck! Help her!"

This stops me. I step back and Sam stops twirling. We both look at the horrified faces of the small crowd around us and after a long moment of absolute silence, Sam begins laughing. It is not the hysteria of a terrified victim. It is a genuine laugh of deep amusement, and when I realize this, I begin to laugh, too. So, of course, we look like two absolute loons.

Jeremy is the one who saves the situation. He laughs and keeps right on walking over to the bar where he begins pulling out bottles and lining up glasses.

"Obviously we have some catching up to do!" he cries, and begins asking for drink orders. The others follow Jeremy in a swarm, leaving Sam and me to compose ourselves. Consuela materializes silently from her hiding place in the kitchen, a white towel and first-aid kit in her plump, sturdy hands.

"Marlena's had all of her shots," I say tentatively. "I don't think she really meant to bite you. Ferrets are very smart creatures. She apparently thought you meant me harm and so she was trying to defend me. I feel just awful!"

Sam shifts his attention to Marlena, who still isn't at all sure about our situation. "Is that how it was, weasel?" he asks softly. "You're a trained attack-rodent?"

"Ferrets are not rodents," I correct. "They are from the Mustelidae family—genus Mustela. Their relatives are the badger, otter, mink and…" I don't finish the family roster, because I suddenly remember the weasel is included and do not want Sam calling my precious a weasel.

"So," Sam says, nodding, "another example of what pedigree can do for you, huh?"

I know he is maligning my privileged background and ignore his attempt to bait me.

"I'd better take Marlena back to her cage," I say. "We really are sorry." I turn away, but not before Sam notices that once again my eyes have started leaking. Honestly, it must be a hormonal thing, I reason. There is absolutely no reason to be this upset. I've seen Sam's wrist and Marlena barely broke the skin. Okay, well, at least he doesn't need stitches!

"Porsche," he says. "Wait!"

But I don't wait. I can't stand here another second feeling like a pimple-faced wallflower at a school dance. I just need to be alone. I need to think and I need to figure out what I'm going to do with the piece of white paper that I have managed to hang on to throughout the crazy events of the last few minutes.

I reach the guest cottage, put Marlena in her cage, walk back outside and try to calm down. I am sitting on the cottage patio for the longest time, but I feel as if I'm going to jump out of my skin. I stare out at the starlit sky in front of me.

"Porsche?" Andrea's voice startles me and I jump.

"Sorry," I say. "I didn't hear you come up."

Andrea gives me a funny look and sits down in the Adirondack chair next to mine. She is holding a champagne flute and takes a long sip before she starts talking.

"So, what's with you and Sam?" she asks quietly.

"Nothing!" I say a bit too loudly.

"Porsche," Andrea admonishes. "Don't go Hollywood on me. What is it?"

I shake my head. "It's not what you think."

"I'm not thinking anything," she says. "There's this… current between the two of you. I mean, it's obvious—something's going on…"

She lets her voice trail off and I could swear she looks almost, well, wounded. I feel torn between spilling my guts and playing it cool. This lasts for about three seconds and then I feel the words welling up inside me. I'm like the Crespi fountain in Italy, spilling over with every drop of information and unable to stop myself.

"I mean, I suppose it's wonderful that he's found my father, but I don't know if I want to…I mean, something like that is sort of…well, private. What if…"

"What if he's a complete loss and there you are with Sam, a relative stranger, albeit an attractive one, and you feel exposed?" she finishes.

"Exactly! And then there's Jeremy," I add. "I am not here to take care of my personal business. I am here to find out…"

"Whether Jeremy's pulling a stunt or not, and I think you've done that," Andrea finishes. "I mean, didn't the last few nights rule that out for you?"

I can't tell her I want to find out who's behind all of this. What if she calls Renee? Renee would have my head if she thought I were not waiting for Emma and instead doing more than my assigned task.

"Right," I say and feel very uncomfortable lying to my new friend.

Andrea pushes her hand deep into her pocket, pulls out her car keys and hands them to me.

"Here. I won't need my car tomorrow. Take the keys." When I frown, she adds, "Don't worry that something will happen and you'll miss it. Scott's got the place crawling with extra security and the cops have been here off and on all day, completing their investigation. Only a fool would try something now."

Maybe her reassurance is what makes me reach for the key and slip it inside the pocket of my black Armani jeans. After all, Andrea is right, a person would have to be insane to try and attack Jeremy with the estate so well-guarded.

Besides, Carlito is only an hour away. I'd only be gone for three hours and I'll leave early, before the others are even up. What could happen in three short hours?

Chapter 9

Marlena and I are so sleepy! Actually, I am the one who's tired, but Marlena feels my pain. She is sitting beside me in Andrea's green Jaguar convertible, wearing her dark glasses, too. I pick up my cup of Starbucks Café Verona and bring it slowly to my lips. The entire night was filled with anxieties. I couldn't seem to shut my mind off. I worried about Jeremy, sorting through the list of suspects endlessly. I got stuck when I reached Sam's name and obsessed about my feelings for him until dawn, it seemed. Then I worried about meeting my father after so many years. What was I going to say, "Hello, what's new?" I take another sip of coffee. Ahead of me, at the end of a dusty cul-de-sac, up a winding, tree-lined driveway, sits my father's trailer.

I turn to Marlena and whisper. "You know, I've always thought trailers to be quite romantic. Like tree houses for grown-ups, or paper plates instead of china. It's all so…disposable, you know? You pick them up and plop them down and when you're done, you just toss them out! And so cozy, too!"

Marlena sighs and nuzzles the leather seat.

"You know they've got almost everything in them these days," I add, "even fireplaces and Jacuzzi tubs." I chew my bottom lip and look at Marlena. "I know what you're thinking, you know, and you're quite wrong. I am not stalling. I'm just waiting to make sure he's up."

The sun is directly overhead making the early awakening theory just a tad lame, but I am desperate. I want some sort of sign that what I'm about to do is right. After all, I know about psychological trauma, and being rejected by two fathers, one biological and one a stepfather, couldn't bode well for my mental health.

"We must keep our expectations low," I warn Marlena.

She isn't paying a bit of attention to my case of nerves. She has jumped up onto the dash and is quivering with ill-concealed excitement. Standing in the middle of the gravel driveway is a huge, long-necked, white fur ball on four spindly legs. I squint, then pull my sunglasses down and squint harder. Too small to be a camel.

"Why, Marlena, I think that's a llama! Oh, look, baby! He's the same color as you!"

The voice inside my head wakes up and takes over. *There's your sign, princess,* it squawks. *Now let's get going and get this over with!*

I slip the car into Drive and begin to slowly edge my way up the driveway. The llama watches us with a disinterested expression on its face, apparently not inclined to move out of our way. I stop a few yards away from the animal and turn to Marlena.

"Now what?" I say. "Do you speak llama?"

Marlena begins chattering and squeaking away, running from her seat to my lap and back to the dashboard again in a frenzy of excitement. She's spotted something else. A huge white duck waddles out to join the llama, followed by what appears to be her entire brood. As we watch, a large mutt appears and joins the crowd of onlookers. The menagerie is just standing there, unmoving, and I am feeling distinctly nervous. There is absolutely no sign that any human is in charge of this zoo.

"I think maybe we should blow the horn or something," I tell Marlena. I actually get ready to press the heel of my hand to the midsection of the steering wheel before second-guessing myself and letting my hand fall back onto the gearshift.

We are at an impasse. I pick up my Starbucks cup and take a sip to reassure myself that I have not left civilization as we know it. I find myself smiling nervously at the stone-faced llama and have to stop myself from waving a little "hello" wave.

Finally I can wait no longer.

"Marlena, baby, I want you to stay here like a good girl. In fact—" I lean down and open the door to her kitty carrier "—I want you to wait in here, just to be safe."

Marlena needs a little shove of encouragement to crawl into her carrier and tells me, in no uncertain terms, that she thinks I'm being unfair, but I only have her best interest at heart. The dog looks hungry.

I cut the engine, slip the keys into my jeans pocket and open the driver's side door.

"They're just animals," I tell myself. "Sweet, little animals."

Another dog picks this moment to wander out from behind the trailer, breaking into a trot as it realizes there's action on the front drive. This dog doesn't look hungry. It looks
like a crazed maniac. It is three times the size of the shaggy-
haired mutt and I am certain that it is at least half wolf.

"Nice doggie," I say softly.

The big dog joins the others. It doesn't bark or growl
or do anything other than sit down beside the duck family and pant.

I take one slow step toward the crowd of animals.

"Hi," I say, using my best "Mommy" voice. "I'm here
to see Lambert Hughes, your, um, owner? Master? Dad?"
I smile and take another step. "Hey," I say. "If he's your
dad then that must make us…well, family or something.
He's my dad."

"Porsche?"

I gape, open-mouthed, at the llama.

"Damn! You talk?" This is too amazing!

There is a chuckle, which I realize has not come from
the llama but rather from the branches of the tree lining the
driveway nearest to the animal. The branches rustle and a
man drops softly down to the ground.

I gasp and then bite down hard on the inside of my
lower lip. My father could be George Carlin's identical
twin, dressed in combat fatigues. He sports a long, gray
ponytail despite the large bald spot atop his head. His face
is weathered and short gray stubble covers his reddened
cheeks. His eyes are blue, like mine, and when he smiles,
it is the face I remember from childhood.

"It's you," I hear myself say. "I remember you!"

He is staring at me as if seeing a mirage. He passes his
hand across his eyes, shakes his head, and when he takes

his hand away, I see tears welling up and spilling over onto his cheeks.

"Porsche," he whispers again. "I knew you'd come. One day, I told myself, she will come."

I smile at him and take a hesitant step forward, but my father rushes to close the gap between us. He reaches out, pulling me into a crushing embrace that smells of wood smoke and animals.

I am hugging him as hard as he is hugging me and I am filled with such joy and sadness, all at once, and both feelings overwhelm me as I realize I am holding my father.

When he finally takes a step back, he is still holding me by my arms, as if afraid to let go, afraid I'll vanish. I know I don't want him to let go, for the very same reason. I am amazed to be standing so close to my father after all these years. What should I say to him? Where do we go from here?

"What were you doing up in that tree?" I hear myself say. Oh, you idiot!

What was I going to say? "Why did you leave me?" or "Did you really sign your rights away?" It is too soon for those big questions.

"The tree?" He looks puzzled for a nanosecond. "Oh, the tree!" He looks over his shoulder. "That's my post."

A slight chill brushes my skin and I feel the tiniest shiver of goose bumps.

"Your post?"

My father's eyes cloud and he frowns. "They'll be back, Porsche," he says in a low mumble. "And when they come, they will try to kill us all!"

Oh, great! My father is a paranoid schizophrenic!

"Who is coming?" I look at the animals, hoping he means them, but knowing he doesn't.

"Gooks. They've been breeding. Soon there will be enough to overrun us."

I sigh silently and a little flicker of hope is extinguished deep inside my heart. I had so hoped for one normal parent. You were right, Mom, I think. This was a bad plan.

My father is watching me intently and when I don't change my facial expression to reflect my inner disbelief, he grins. It is a crooked smile, tilting up one corner of his mouth, making the crow's feet around his eyes crinkle. It makes him look so likeable and merry, not at all like a lunatic, which of course he is. He waves one hand dismissively.

"I know, I shouldn't have started with that one, but really, I just couldn't help myself," my father says, cackling. "And the little people will be with them!"

I make a very concerted effort to remain rooted to the spot where I stand and to look politely interested. I nod, like I understand and agree with him.

My father suddenly looks very sad. "Oh, Porsche," he says mournfully. "What have they done to you?"

"Who, Dad?" I ask. I don't even realize I've called him "Dad" until the word is out of my mouth, but he just seems to grow more distressed.

"Porsche, did your mother tell you I'm crazy?"

"No, Dad, she didn't…"

He takes a step back, letting go of my arms and stands regarding me with a doleful expression. He nods his head like he understands.

"I know, honey," he says. "She's your mother. I was up in the tree because I'm fostering a nest of vireos." He cocks his head and smiles softly. "Contrary to what you may have been told, I am not a card-carrying lunatic or drug-addicted monster. I don't think I ever was, but I understand

other people have their stories and they'll stick to 'em, I
suppose."

"They said you signed away your parental rights," I say.
I didn't plan to blurt it out like this, but there it is and I feel
an overwhelming need to know exactly what is what.

My father nods. "It was all I could do at the time. Your
stepfather had me penned in with lawyers and your mother
was going along with anything he said. They were threatening me with criminal charges, too." He runs one weathered hand across the top of his head, and sighs. "I'm not
gonna lie to you, baby. I was pretty messed up back then.
I came back from the service hurtin' turkey—strung out on
drugs, alcohol, anything that would wipe out that time."

I study my father thoughtfully. "Mother said you were
in the Green Berets in Vietnam," I say, hoping this will lead
to more information.

He nods, but his eyes do a funny thing; they darken and
seem instantly less accessible.

"Where did you serve?"

He is about to answer me when my cell phone goes off.
The shrill tone startles both of us, but it sends the animals
into paroxysms of barking, quacking, braying anxiety. My
father turns to them, soothing and shushing, while I pull
the offending phone from my hip holster and study the
number. The area code is the only thing I recognize, but
it's enough to tell me something's wrong.

"Hello?"

"You've got to get back here," Andrea says without preamble. "Right now!"

She hangs up. I hit a button and try to call her back, but
her phone goes straight to voice mail.

"Something wrong?" my father asks.

"I've got to go," I say, torn between the urgency in Andrea's voice and wanting to be sure I'll see this man again. "The friend who loaned me the car I'm driving has some sort of crisis. I need to get back to San Jacinta." He's nodding like he understands, but I add, "Let me get a piece of paper. I want you to have my number. I'd like to come back and talk more, if that's all right."

He smiles and I dash to the car, grabbing the first pen and piece of paper I find.

I scrawl my number on the back of a gas receipt and give it to him, then just stand there, not certain of how to end things. I want to hug him, but something holds me back. I don't want to presume too much. He might not long for me the way I have longed for him, but I hope he does.

He takes a step forward and gives me a strong hug. I am surprised to feel him trembling beneath his camouflage jacket, surprised to discover that he is thinner and weaker than I at first thought. I wonder if he has been ill or too poor to buy the food he needs. I am swamped with questions I want to ask and feelings that keep washing over me like tidal waves.

When I let go of him, he frowns and pretends to see something in my hair. He reaches behind my ear, and just as I remembered, steps back holding a quarter between his thumb and forefinger.

"Lose something, honey?" he asks with a grin.

A weight seems to lift off my shoulders and I feel lighter, as if perhaps there is a chance to have something I've always longed for, a normal life even if it's with an abnormal father with only a quarter to his name.

"What do I call you?" I ask him.

He leans back a little to look at me and I see the sparkle is back in his blue eyes.

"Hell, honey, you can call me whatever you want—Dad, Daddy, Pa, Shithead. Hell, it don't matter what you choose to call me. The thing that matters is, I'll always answer."

I carry the way those words make me feel all the way back to San Jacinta and the wrought-iron gates of the Paradise Ranch. I drive the winding canyon roads as fast as I dare, worrying about Andrea and wondering what has happened to make her call me back, but I don't lose the warm, peaceful feeling seeing my father has given me. It is like a life jacket and I feel invincible.

When I pull through the entrance gates to Paradise, I spot Andrea standing by the fountain in the courtyard, a grim expression on her face. She doesn't smile as I pull up or offer any greeting at all. She just stands beside the fountain, waiting until I step out onto the cobblestone driveway, carrying Marlena, and walk briskly toward her.

"What's wrong?"

Andrea looks over her shoulder, as if worried about eavesdroppers, then begins speaking rapidly in a low voice.

"They weren't going to be filming today," she says. "I thought they were going to be looking at the dailies while Mark and I went over some of the pre-publicity releases."

"So, that's not what happened?"

Andrea shakes her head. "No, those idiots! Jeremy announced he and Zoe were planning to do their own stunt work on tomorrow's fight scene. I don't think Mark even knew about it, because he seemed pretty pissed that they weren't using the doubles. Anyway, Mark insisted on calling the stunt coordinator. But before Randy could make it out here, Jeremy was insisting on blocking the scene. He said Scott and Dave could help since Scott was former military and Dave's almost as experienced."

"I thought Dave was in the hospital?"

Andrea shakes her head. "That was just an overnight observation. He got out the following morning. Other than a few burns on his hands, he's fine. At least, that's what he says. Given this morning's events, I'm not so sure."

I'm trying to follow her, but I can't see how Scott and Dave would fit into a stunt rehearsal. I say this and Andrea grimaces.

"Jeremy wasn't thinking. He wanted to play with Scott, his new boy toy. He's worse than a schoolgirl with a crush and this time Dave saw right through it."

"What happened?"

"Dave handed Zoe the gun. It was supposed to be unloaded. In fact, Dave said he'd checked."

"Oh, my God, did someone get hurt?"

"Zoe could've killed Jeremy," Andrea says. "He's just lucky she's a piss-poor shot."

She is about to say more when the sound of raised voices carries out onto the courtyard from inside the house.

"It's insane," she says. "They're all at each other's throats. Mark is trying to calm them down, but…"

We are interrupted by the front door swinging open behind us. Dave stands there, his back to us, facing Scott and Jeremy. On either side of him are two of Scott's newly hired security guards.

"This is stupid! I checked that gun. I swear to God it was empty! It's not my fault! Somebody must've…"

"Shut up, Dave!" Scott roars. "You fucked the dog on this one. It's a done deal. We're calling the police."

"Mr. Reins, I…" I hear Dave say, but Jeremy's expression is stony and cold.

"It's over, Dave," Scott says. "You're going to the bunk-house and waiting for the cops to get here!"

Dave turns and I see his face, red with anger and wounded confusion. The guards start to lead him through the doorway but before they can leave, Dave breaks free and whirls back around.

"You think I don't see what this is, Scott?" he says, no longer pleading. He's angry now and knows there's no point in trying to salvage the situation. "You set me up! You're chasing the rich dick. You think I don't know that? You think I don't see you're just fucking him for his money?"

"That's enough, Dave," Scott says. He has moved just slightly to take a stance between Dave and Jeremy.

Dave's entire body radiates rage and hurt. His bald head is fire-engine red, almost purple and I am afraid for him because he seems so out of control. Beside me, Andrea seems to read this and moves a step closer to the front door.

"You think you can just ruin people's lives and there are no consequences?" Dave yells. He tries to push past Scott and get to Jeremy but the two guards grab him. "Well, there's always a price to be paid and yours is coming!"

Scott moves then, pushing his former partner backward, out the doorway and into the courtyard.

"That does it," Scott says. "I'm taking you to the cops myself!"

His hand is on Dave's shoulder and even from where I stand I can see Scott's knuckles are white from the pressure he is exerting on Dave's collarbone. Dave doesn't wince, but he moves in the direction Scott leads him. The two security guards follow them and the four disappear behind the stables. A minute later the white panel van throbs to life and drives off.

"Christ, Jeremy!" Mark says, emerging from the shadows behind his client. "Do you just have a death wish?"

Jeremy seems dazed or, I think, high. He stares off after the van, almost as if he can't quite comprehend what has taken place. After a long moment he looks at Mark, as if seeing him for the first time.

"I think the current fried his brain, you know?" Then, as if the entire episode were forgotten, he cranes to look past Mark. "Where's Zoe? We've got work to do."

For a moment, Andrea and I just stand in the courtyard, staring after Jeremy and Mark as they walk away from us into the house. Mark is following Jeremy and continuing to berate him with questions, but Jeremy doesn't answer. I hear him calling out for Zoe and realize he isn't even attempting to answer Mark. Mark is getting angrier, if the volume and tone of his voice is any indication, and I am certain another conflict is about to erupt.

"Jeremy is insane," I murmur. "Either that, or he's using. Andrea, someone's trying to kill him and he doesn't seem to get it. I don't understand. What is it with him? I know he's scared. Is he just trying to act tough or what?"

Andrea nods. "I've never known him to be this bad," she says. "Usually, when he's doing a picture, he stays as straight as an arrow, but for some reason this project is different. I think it's Zoe. I think Jeremy's sorry he ever agreed to do the film with her."

"So, he's self-medicating." This is common with addictive personalities; I remember this from my abnormal psych course. Jeremy probably would benefit from an antidepressant, or better yet, another film project that didn't involve an ex-girlfriend.

We round the corner into the great room and find Jeremy faced off against Sam, with Zoe and a tall red-headed man I've never seen before watching the two argue.

"It wasn't an accident and Detective Saunders should know that," Sam is insisting. "You need to press charges. I can't believe this! I leave you all alone for ten minutes and look what happens!"

Jeremy shakes his head, but Sam dials anyway and waits to be connected. When he is, he turns his back on the rest of us, walking away as he tells the detective what has just happened.

Jeremy raises one eyebrow and looks at Zoe, who seems unable to meet his appraising glance.

"Do you want to continue running lines, lovey?" he asks her.

After a long pause, Zoe mumbles something that I swear sounds like, "Whatever you want, Master."

"Come on, Jeremy," Sam says stepping between the two actors. "You pay me to be your manager, so I'm managing. Go study your lines, rest, do something, but call it a day with the stunt planning. Detective Saunders said he'll be here soon. It's been a long day already."

Jeremy looks as if he wants to argue with Sam, he is frowning and opens his mouth as if about to protest, but I am surprised by what he says next.

"I can't rest, Sam. This whole thing has upset my karma. Let's saddle the horses and take Porsche here out to see the ranch. It'll be like old times, me and you." Jeremy isn't waiting to hear what Sam says, he's leaving the room and heading for the stables before either of us can say a word. Gone is the slurred speech. Jeremy seems perfectly sober now, which makes me wonder if this is something he does frequently, and if so, why?

Zoe starts after him. "I want to go!" she cries.

Jeremy either doesn't hear her, or is ignoring her.

Sam looks at me, takes in my high-heeled Dolce & Gabbana sandals and raises an eyebrow. "You know how to ride?" he asks.

I toss my head and try to look superior. I just hate it when Sam acts like I'm an incompetent child. "Of course," I say.

"Western saddle, not English?"

I swallow. "Well, sure!"

Okay, so I have never ridden Western, but how hard can that be? There's a little horn thingy to hang on to. So what if I haven't ridden since that one brief summer in fourth grade? It's like a bicycle. You don't forget how to ride a horse, do you? I just have no appropriate hat or shoes for riding. I sigh silently; accessories are just so essential!

I realize Sam is still watching me, a smirk tickling the edge of his mouth. He, of course, is perfectly attired for riding. I look at his black, lizard-skin boots with a distinct feeling of envy. Oh well, I'll show him.

"I don't suppose you brought riding boots in all those suitcases?" he asks, baiting me.

"No, but I'm sure I have something that'll do." I don't sound at all sure, even to myself.

"Don't worry about it," he says. "We'll check the tack room."

Oh, I can just imagine the plethora of dusty, cobweb-covered footwear waiting for me in the stable. I am so-o grateful!

I follow him outside into the brilliant sunlight of another late February afternoon in California. The weather is perfect, breezy and close to 70. It is truly spring. The grass inside the paddock is a brilliant emerald, flowers are in bloom and here I am, feeling like a prisoner sentenced to hard labor. I can't afford to let Sam and Jeremy know that I haven't ridden in years. I have to go with them. What if they say something important and I miss it? I want to know if they think he's behind all of the sabotage or just this particular incident.

We step into the stable and Sam leads me into an immaculate room covered in leather reins and harnesses. A shelf runs around the perimeter of the room above my head and it is lined with riding boots, flawlessly polished, shiny cowboy boots of every imaginable size and vintage. I suck in my breath and feel the little tickle of elation I always feel when I score a retail hit. I am in the Saks Fifth Avenue of western footwear.

"What size?" Sam asks.

"Seven, narrow." *Ha! Find that!* I think. I am further amazed when he reaches up and plucks down a pair of cordovan, lizard-skin boots from the middle of the shelf. He peers inside the shaft, nods to himself, and hands them to me. Dan Post, women's size seven, narrow. Well, I'll be damned!

"Did Jeremy buy out a shoe store, or did he happen to have a size seven narrow girlfriend?"

Sam shrugs. "The boy likes to be prepared, I suppose. Too much money and too little time. If the urge hits him, he likes to go. Jeremy's not one for being held up by inconvenience."

I don't even need to ask for boot socks. Sam opens a drawer, pulls out a pair of brand-new wool socks and hands them to me.

"You'll need a hat, too," Sam says and pushes a white straw hat firmly down onto my head. "Blondes like you burn in the desert sun."

"I don't, I tan."

Sam smirks. "Not a real blonde, either, huh?"

I glare at him. "I am, too!"

Jeremy arrives, looking like a pirate in cowboy's clothing, wild and dark, his long, curly hair springing out from beneath the brim of his well-worn, straw hat. Jeremy has a mischievous grin but now it seems as if it might bubble over into peals of hearty laughter. His dark eyes glisten with anticipation and for once Jeremy seems truly alive.

Sam walks toward me leading a large brown mare. "This is Daisy," he announces. "I figure you two might be a match. Daisy'd rather walk than trot and if it were all the same, she'd rather eat than walk."

I regarded the huge animal with a skeptical eye. Daisy casts a baleful look back toward her stall, and I feel instantly relieved. She's old and tired, I think. She's perfect, but I can't let Sam know this. "So, you're saying you think I need something tame?"

His grin is answer enough. I feel my face growing hot as he steps closer, handing me the reins. "Well, never having seen you in the saddle," he says, "I just thought you might like to start out slow."

I can't even think of a reply, but it wouldn't matter anyway because Sam isn't waiting around for an answer. He is walking away, leaving me standing there with Daisy's reins in my hand and no earthly idea what to do with the two-thousand-pound animal.

"Would you like a leg up, miss?" the groom says, materializing out of nowhere to stand behind me.

Sam and Jeremy are saddling their horses and in a few moments we will all be heading out. I look at Daisy and feel the first real twinge of fear licking at my self-confidence.

"So," I say, feigning nonchalance, "are there any little tricks or tips I should know about Daisy?"

The groom is an older man, with dingy white hair and a well-lined face that crinkles when he smiles at my question.

"Daisy? Tricks? Humph! This ole girl don't give nobody a moment's bother. She's as gentle as a lamb, Miss Daisy is. All's you gotta do is climb up on her back and she'll do the rest."

I nod and put a toe in the stirrup. The groom grabs the reins from me and steadies Daisy as I hurl myself up onto her broad back. I sit astride the huge horse and try to remember anything at all from my brief fiasco as an equestrian student.

"Just keep the ball of your foot in the stirrups, miss. You don't want to go shoving your whole foot into it, might wind up stuck."

I nod and move my foot just as Sam and Jeremy walk their horses up to join us. Sam's horse is brown and white and a bit broader than Jeremy's black stallion. Jeremy's horse suits him. It dances impatiently, snorting and forcing Jeremy to pay attention or else lose control.

"Ready?" Sam asks, riding up beside me.

When I nod, he nudges his horse and we fall into a single-file line—Sam, Jeremy, and me, only Daisy doesn't take the cue. The men move out of the stable and Daisy is still standing stock-still.

"Come on, horse!" I cry softly. "Let's go!" I give her flanks the same gentle nudge I'd seen Sam give his horse, and nothing happens.

"Oh, God!"

"Daisy, git!" the groom says sharply and slaps old Daisy on the hindquarters.

With an irritated snort, Daisy begins to slowly plod after Jeremy and Sam. As we leave the shelter of the dimly lit stable and emerge into the bright sunlight, I find myself scouring the nearby bluffs and undergrowth for paparazzi. All I need at a moment like this is to know that a picture of me and this fat, has-been, glue-factory reject will grace the cover of *The Entertainer.* I am so not liking this part of my job!

"Come on, Matilda," I say, kicking Daisy's belly. "Try and stay within the same county as the others!"

Daisy pays me back by expelling a long, loud blast of gas as she picks up the pace to join the others reluctantly.

"Did you say something, lovey?" Jeremy turns around in his saddle and laughs as the two of us slouch up behind him.

"Having fun, Porsche?" Sam calls.

I give him a pained smile and sit up straighter in my saddle, ignoring them to look out at the trail ahead. I find I have relaxed into Daisy's comfortable walk and am enjoying the leisurely ride around Jeremy's estate. I am lost in thought, replaying the morning's meeting with my father when I hear the two men speaking and realize I need to be paying attention.

"You can't play with people's relationships," Sam is saying. "You're lucky he didn't kill you."

Jeremy and Sam are riding side by side with Daisy and me only a few yards behind them.

"Sam, I wasn't playing this time. You've gotta trust me on this one. At first I was, sure, but there's something about Scott. I think this could be the real thing this time."

Jeremy seems to be pleading with Sam but I don't think it's having the desired effect because Sam turns in the saddle and lifts a mocking eyebrow. "The real thing, is that what you call it? Please. You wouldn't know the real thing. To you, any relationship that goes beyond a brief roll in the sack is the real thing."

Jeremy's eyes darken and his scowl looks dangerous, but he doesn't dispute the matter. I think he must be remembering Sam's wife and daughter and knowing better than to fight Sam for that point.

"Okay, okay," Jeremy says, sounding resigned. "Maybe I'm wrong about Scott, but damn it, Sam, I didn't just waltz into it trying to ruin his relationship with Dave. I didn't even know they were hooked up!"

Sam shakes his head and looks away for a brief moment before turning back to his protégé. "Did you ever think you might need to be more aware of what's going on around you, Jeremy? Or are you so used to being the star, you've forgotten that anybody else might count, or have feelings, or even have a different opinion from yours?" Sam examines Jeremy's face as if searching for some missing piece of a puzzle. "Have you forgotten who you are and where you come from?"

I realize that the two men have forgotten me. Surely Sam wouldn't be saying these things if he realized I could overhear them. I pull up on Daisy's reins gently and give the two men a little more space, but the wind carries their words back to me and I can't help but listen.

"No," Jeremy says and I hear the thin barrier that keeps his anger from showing begin to crumble in that one word. "I haven't forgotten my fucking life! You know I haven't!" Jeremy's eyes are liquid fire as he stares at Sam. "How do you forget a father too drunk to take care of his wife and kids, so drunk he runs his car into a snowbank on the way home from the bar and fucking freezes to death! How do you forget your mom crying herself to sleep every night because she misses the goddamned bastard even though she has to work two jobs to feed the kids he left behind? You know I haven't forgotten that fucking cesspool of a town, Sam. You, of all people, know I haven't forgotten, but damn I've tried and Scott made me forget, even if it was just for a moment. I had fun. I felt good and I fucking forgot about it!"

Sam isn't saying a word. He's riding along beside Jeremy, listening, which appears to be all Jeremy really needs right now because he can't seem to stop talking.

"Why don't you just say it, Sam? You think I'm a fucking phony. Well, I am. Every day I make myself over into someone else because I don't even know who I am anymore."

Sam frowns at him. "Why can't you be who you are, Jeremy? What's wrong with that?"

Jeremy looks at him, as if Sam's not getting it. His eyebrows lift and he shakes his head slightly.

"Who I am? Who I am didn't get me here. Who I am didn't get make me enough money to make sure my family never has to take another handout or wonder how the bills are going to get paid. It's who I'm *not* that buys my future. I don't ever want to be who I was!" Jeremy's voice cracks on the last word and I look away, certain he is going to cry and knowing he wouldn't want a relative stranger to witness him losing his composure.

I keep pulling back on Daisy's reins, trying to fall farther behind, but no so far behind I can't convince Daisy to keep moving along the path. I barely hear Sam when he answers Jeremy.

"Who you were is a tough, committed boy who had to grow up before he even had a chance to have a childhood.

Who you are is a man with enormous talent and too little self-confidence to believe in himself. You need to step up to the plate, boy. You can't hide behind your past anymore. You have to move forward."

I look at the man talking and know he hasn't taken his own advice. I look at Jeremy and wonder if he is tempted to say something like this to his mentor, but then I see the way Jeremy is looking at Sam and realize he would never say anything to hurt him. Jeremy loves Sam. He looks up to him. He needs him. It is all there in Jeremy's eyes, pure and unconditional. It doesn't matter that Sam confronts Jeremy, because Jeremy trusts him.

I lean forward and pat the side of Daisy's neck, wishing I had a relationship like the one between Jeremy and Sam. For some reason I think of my newfound father and a yearning wells up in my chest that surpasses any homesickness I have ever felt before. If things had been different for us, if my parents had never divorced, maybe he would have been that person in my life.

I hear Sam talking to Jeremy again and when I hear Dave's name, I nudge Daisy and urge her closer to the two men.

"I think you should let Scott go," he's saying. "If you're serious about him, you can't expect the man to stay objective about his job. And if you're not serious, he's not going to be objective about that, either."

"I don't think..."

Sam holds up his hand, stopping Jeremy from finishing. "Exactly, you don't think. You live in the moment. That's good for your career, but bad for your health. I think Dave was serious. I wouldn't be at all surprised if he came back looking for you. You've got to be objective about this, Jeremy. You've got to put your immediate wants aside and think about the bigger picture. You're not just one person operating alone, kid. You're a business. You have employees, co-workers and your family to think about."

I wonder if Sam ever stops thinking about the big picture. I listen to him lecturing Jeremy on responsibility and the big picture, and while I know it's true, I can't help but wonder if the man ever loosens up enough to live in the moment. Don't get me wrong, I realize the man has a point; Jeremy's life is in danger, but does Sam ever loosen up?

I feel guilty instantly for thinking like this. The man has lost his family. I wouldn't be surprised if he never loosened up again, but will he ever live again? Will he ever allow himself to care for another human being other than Jeremy Reins?

The trail is rounding a stand of trees and in the distance I see the outbuildings of the estate. We are beginning to head home. I shift in the saddle, grateful to know the ride will eventually be over. My thighs ache from gripping Daisy's wide body. My back is stiff, but my bony bottom is taking the worse part of the beating, pummeled over and over again against the hard, leather saddle.

Jeremy points to a riding ring set up with barrels and jumps, then turns his horse's head to lead the three of us toward it.

"Come on, Sam, for old time's sake!"

I start to remind them I'm still there, When Jeremy kicks his horse hard and takes off with Sam in close pursuit. Daisy walks a little bit faster, but shows absolutely no inclination to move any faster and for the first time, I wish she would. Jeremy and Sam are in heaven. They ride through the open gate into the ring and immediately race toward the first set of jumps. I envision a rodeo and think of long-haired girls in western outfits, riding into the rink carrying flags or banners. I wish for one moment that I could be a fearless barrel racer, flying in and passing Sam as I raced toward the other end of the arena. I wonder if this would capture the cowboy's attention long enough to pique his interest.

I kick at Daisy's flank with no visible results. She continues to trot complacently to the edge of the ring and then she stops, unwilling to cross the threshold into real horse territory.

"Damn mule!" I say softly.

Daisy lowers her head and begins to nibble at a tuft of grass. Inside the ring, Jeremy and Sam are having the time of their lives, yelling out, laughing, all while racing their horses around the course. I push my hat back on my head and wipe sticky sweat from my forehead.

Suddenly, Daisy the Half-dead rears her head, whinnies violently and turns into a whirling dervish. I barely have time to grip the saddle horn and hang on, forgetting completely about the reins as Daisy begins bucking.

I know I scream, but the sound is lost in the frenzy of the moment. I grab for the reins but they are flying loose and Daisy is moving too fast for me to do anything but hang on for dear life. She kicks, she spins, and in an instant she is running flat out, faster than I could've believed possible, away from the riding ring, heading straight for the cliffs that border the drop down into the rocky shore of the Pacific Ocean.

Chapter 10

I grab Daisy's mane and the saddle horn, hanging on with every ounce of strength I have, but knowing that if Daisy stays on her current course, the two of us will plunge over the cliffs and fall to our deaths. I have a brief second where I wonder if she knows where she's going and what will happen if she doesn't turn, but then I remember that a horse's brain is roughly the size of a walnut.

I scream, but the wind carries the sound away from me and all I hear is the pounding of Daisy's hooves. They sound like thunder, growing louder and louder, the sound magnifying as Daisy runs. I think of Jeremy and Sam, stupidly chasing each other around a set of jumps set up to mimic nature while I am actually out here facing the real thing, my own impending demise.

"Daisy, stop!" I scream. "Whoa!"

It is like trying to direct a tornado. My suicidal horse is

going out in style. Her heart will probably explode from exertion as we hurtle to our deaths. She will be too stupid to realize she's even killed herself!

The hoof beats grow louder. I smell the salt water and see the bright blue sky beyond the cliff's edge.

"Porsche, hang on!"

Sam and Jeremy, their horses straining with the effort to catch Daisy, flank either side of the crazed animal. Sam shouts something, a quick cry, and cuts his horse into Daisy, forcing her away from the cliff. Daisy, momentarily distracted, slows just a bit but it is enough for Jeremy, who reaches out and grabs her reins. Sam, still herding Daisy away from the cliffs, leans toward me, one arm outstretched, and yells, "Take your feet out of the stirrups and hang on to me!"

There isn't time to tell him that I have long since lost track of the stirrups. He pulls me and I am aware of lifting up and off of Daisy. I grip Sam's arm and shoulder and somehow wind up in the saddle with him, my legs straddling his horse, our bodies molded chest to chest, as he slows his horse and brings him to a standstill.

Jeremy and his stallion rein Daisy in, eventually bringing her to a halt and then turning to wait as Sam brings his horse even with the stallion.

I am certain that next they will check to make sure I am not dead before they shoot my mentally defective animal, but no. Instead they start whooping like a couple of high school boys and high-fiving each other.

"Damn!" Jeremy crows. "That was fucking awesome!"

"Whoo-hoo!" Sam cries. "What a rush!"

I push back away from Sam's chest and look from one man to the other in frank amazement. They can't be serious. But they are. They are laughing and congratulating themselves and completely oblivious to the fact that I could've died just now!

Sam is the first to realize that I do not find this situation amusing and certainly do not consider my near death experience to have been fun. He lifts my chin with one finger and bends his head slightly to inspect my face.

"Hey," he says softly. "You all right? You weren't hurt, were you?"

Every nerve in my body screams "Of course I'm not all right!"

I manage not to say this, but he sees something in my face because his eyes soften and the smile fades away.

"I'm fine." Of course my voice squeaks the words out an entire octave above my normal speaking range, but I hold myself erect and try to look him in the eye.

Sam nods. "Of course you are," he says. In a louder voice he calls to Jeremy. "Hey, she says she thinks we should work this up into an act and do it again!"

My pride is salvaged and I completely get why Jeremy loves him.

"Bloody hell, lovey!" Jeremy cries. "Wouldn't Lloyd's of London love that! I bet the policy premiums would jump a million dollars! Let's do it!"

Sam laughs. "I thought you said you wanted a drink?" he says, and thus distracts his friend from all thought of another run.

"Well I, for one, need a long soak in a tub," I manage to say.

Sam squeezes me, then gently lifts me so that I face forward, my back cradled against his chest, and urges his horse on toward the stables. I relax back against him and close my eyes, inhaling the spicy scent of his cologne and letting my mind drift with possibilities.

I must have dozed off, because suddenly we are riding into the courtyard, the horses' hooves waking me as they clop across the cobblestones and stop just short of the fountain. I open my eyes and see Andrea standing there, her eyes wide with concern.

"What happened?" she asks. "Did Porsche get hurt? Is she all right?"

I grin at her. "I'm fine. My horse got jealous of the other two and decided to show them how fast she could run."

Sam's voice rumbles through my chest as he gives Andrea the more accurate picture.

"Daisy got bit by a horsefly and took off on her."

Andrea nods, but I see a speculative look in her eye as she takes in the way I sit cradled by Sam's arms. I sigh inwardly and begin the process of untangling myself from my warm sanctuary. The rules are different for people like me. We can't just run off and fling ourselves into the arms of the first handsome stranger we meet without serious repercussions.

I mean, a woman of my financial stature and pedigree can't indulge herself in physical chemistry. Don't get me wrong. I dally occasionally, but it's always with forethought and the appropriate knowledge born of a good private investigator on permanent retainer. All my friends use P.I.'s for background investigations. We have to; otherwise, we could become the victims of kidnappings, scams or other nasty little vignettes. It's just easier to stick to our own kind. I'm not being snotty about it, just factual. As much as I might find myself attracted to Sam, I couldn't really act on it, could I?

This realization is making me feel really sad, probably

because I'm tired and I must be feeling sorry for myself. Still, the reality that my fantasies can never come to fruition is just altogether too, too...well, I just don't know the word for it, but it isn't at all a nice feeling and I *so* hate unpleasantness!

I hop down with Sam's assistance and hear Jeremy chuckle as my knees buckle under me and I nearly collapse.

"A bit off our game, are we, lovey?" he calls. "Good thing we didn't do anymore trick riding today, eh?"

I roll my eyes at Andrea, who steps forward to grab my arm, and turn back to give Jeremy a contemptuous look. Need I remind the little twit that we have been riding for a good...I glance at my watch and thump it with my forefinger. It must've stopped because it says we've only been gone for an hour. I am just sure we've been riding for four. Well anyway, I almost *died* out there!

"There's a stone in my boot," I say haughtily.

"Really, lovey? Let's see?"

I toss my head and dismiss his smart-ass attitude by turning my back on him and smiling widely at Andrea. "Let's go back to my cottage," I say brightly. "I am just parched!"

Andrea nods and walks beside me, not obviously assisting me, but I know she's there and ready to catch me should my shaky legs give way again. I love this woman. We walk off slowly and Andrea waits until we're absolutely out of earshot before she says a word.

"Did Daisy really take off, or did you do that to stir Sam up?" she asks.

"No, Daisy really ran and there is nothing between me and that cowboy. I mean, honestly, you don't really think he's my type, do you?"

What I meant to say was, "Don't be ridiculous! He's not

my type. He's a cowboy, for God's sake, and I'm an heiress!" But it comes out all wrong which is peculiar, especially as the father of psychoanalytic theory, Sigmund Freud, says there are no accidents. He would say I must have unconsciously been wishing to have Andrea tell me that the cowboy is exactly my type and therefore made the Freudian slip of asking the wrong question.

Andrea plays by Freud's rules when she answers me. "Why not?"

Answer a question with a question. You'd make a great therapist!

"Because, Andrea, he works for Jeremy. He's just an out-of-work high school drama teacher. What on earth would we have in common?"

We are walking into the cottage when Andrea answers. "I don't know how to answer you, exactly, except to say that you fit. When I look at you two, you fit, like you belong together. There's just something there."

I laugh, but inside my stomach flips over hard. "Yeah," I say, heading straight for the kitchen and the refrigerator. "Hormones. Our hormones fit together. It's all chemical."

I can't look at her. My heart is suddenly banging around inside my chest like an irate prisoner overdue for release and I realize I'm burning up it's so hot inside the tiny kitchen. I busy myself pulling open the freezer door and filling two glasses with ice while behind me I hear nothing at all.

I am opening a Diet Coke when I hear Andrea say, "No, I think there's more than chemistry between you two, but it really doesn't matter, I suppose. You two will never act on it."

I nod and feel a dull ache start up somewhere behind my ribs. "Of course not," I say, plopping two straws into the glasses. "He would never fit into my world and I'm sure he knows that."

"Oh, that wasn't what I was thinking," she says, stepping closer to the counter where I stand with my back to her.

"Oh?"

"No, Sam's the kind of man who would fit into any situation. Any situation of his choosing, that is. No, I was really thinking you wouldn't fit into his world."

I spin around without thinking and find myself face-to-face with a softly smiling Andrea. It is too late to stop myself from taking the bait, even though I now see the trap.

"*I* couldn't fit into *his* world?"

Andrea shrugs and reaches over to take one of the glasses of soda.

"I don't mean the cowboy part," she says. "I'm sure you could eventually learn to do a little of that. I mean, you'd have to get into shape, but…"

"Get into shape?" This is too unbelievable for words! "I'm in great shape!"

Andrea's smile grows. "For the red carpet, yes, but for ranch life? No way!"

I walk past her out onto the patio, where I take my time settling into a chaise lounge.

"So if my physical conditioning isn't the reason I wouldn't fit into Sam's little world, what is?"

Andrea takes a sip and frowns. "You know, I'm out of line here," she says. "I spoke without thinking. Let's talk about tomorrow night."

The woman is maddening. Now she's patronizing me!

"No, I insist," I say. "I want to know why you think I wouldn't fit into Sam's world. Really. You won't offend me. I'm a big girl. I can take it."

Andrea sighs. "Well, Porsche, now, you are very young and Sam is a little bit older."

Relief washes over me. So *that's* it! He's older. I can live with that one!

"It's not just the age thing, Porsche," she is saying. "Sam's only in his mid-thirties. It's a matter of maturity and life experience."

She's saying I'm immature and inexperienced? "Andrea, I may be twenty-four but I haven't exactly led a sheltered life, you know. I've lived all over the world."

Andrea nods. "I know, but I'm talking about what's important as you mature. Sam isn't dazzled by money and status. He's more..." She hesitates. "Well, given the losses he's experienced and the way he's lived his life—he's just more...well...grounded. You're not mad at me for saying that, are you?"

I am, but saying so would brand me everything she's just accused me of being, so I smile and murmur, "Oh, honey, of course not!"

The phone on the kitchen counter rings, startling us both and breaking the moment that was about to build into uncomfortable silence or worse, an argument. I mean, how could the woman think that I am not grounded? I know what I want, don't I?

I pick up the receiver gratefully and say, "Hello?"

The cowboy's voice answers me. "You've got a guest at the front gate. Says her name's Emma Bosworth. Is she for real, or should I have her sent away?"

Emma! I thought Renee was going to call me before she arrived! I frown at the phone suspiciously.

"What does she look like?"

The cowboy chuckles. "I love this celebrity paranoia,"

he says. "Well, from the looks of her, she's a pretty young thing, couldn't be much more than twenty-two."

In the background I hear the little minx giggle. Damn that cowboy, he's got Emma suckered already!

"She smells right nice, too," he adds. "Let's see here…beautiful green eyes, blond hair and a real lovely figure. Good dresser, too—real sharp, sophisticated tastes. We don't see a whole lot of her type around these parts, no sirree, Bob!"

I hold the phone away from my body, stare at it as if it has been suddenly inhabited by aliens and wonder who in the world has taken over Sam's body. He has never laid it on this thick before.

"Great!" I say. "I guess I forgot to tell anyone that she was coming. She's working on a project with me and will be staying for a day or two. I trust that won't be a problem, will it?"

"No, ma'am," he says. He is changing his tone now, sounding more formal and reserved. "We live to accommodate," he adds, but I don't take Sam for a fool. I know he'll run a background check on her just as soon as he can.

"Whatever. Can you show her to the cottage?"

What bee flew up his nose, I wonder as I hang up the phone.

"What's up?" Andrea asks.

I shrug. "Oh, my best friend's here. Renee thought it might be best if we had a little backup, only I wasn't expecting her to arrive so quickly. Do you think you can help me concoct something to tell Jeremy? Something to explain why I'm suddenly inviting a guest to come stay when I'm a guest myself."

Andrea takes a thoughtful sip of her soda and nods her head. "Sure. We'll think of something by dinnertime."

"Dinner?" I'd forgotten all about dinner.

Andrea finishes her drink and puts her glass down on the kitchen table. "It's at eight. Jeremy's got quite a few of the principals staying over to work on tomorrow's scenes, and of course, Mark and I will be there. I'll figure out something to tell him by the time you two get up to the house."

That is a huge relief! Andrea and I walk to the door and when I open it, I see Sam and Emma riding across the turf-like lawn in a golf cart, laughing hysterically, as Emma stands up, gestures wildly with her right hand, and belts out in her high, clear soprano voice "Amaz-ing Grace, how sweet the sound!"

Oh, dear God, someone please tell me this is not happening! Emma is not—could not, would not under pain of death, but surely *is*—telling the cowboy about the night we ran away from boarding school and got arrested for under-aged drinking in the city's outdoor amphitheater! When the police responded to the call, they surrounded the granite benches, switched on a powerful spotlight and found me, alone on stage, leading an imaginary choir in a rousting chorus of…yes, "Amazing Grace." Dear Mother in Heaven, will I ever be allowed to forget that night and move on?

One look at Sam's face tells me the answer to that question. Not a chance.

How have these two managed to become this familiar in such a short time? How has dear, innocent-faced little Emma managed to coax the surliest man alive into eating out of her hand? It just blows my mind!

"Well," Sam says, pulling right up in front of us. "Here we are!"

"Oh, Sam, you are such a delight!" Emma coos. "Thank you so very much!"

I swear I'm going to vomit.

"My pleasure, little lady!" he answers. "I can't believe you've never met a cowboy. You just seem like you're right at home out here."

Emma laughs her golden, wind-chime chuckle and tosses her hair back carelessly. "Oh, Sam, you sweet-talker you! How could any girl not feel at home around you! I just can't believe it! All my life I've wanted to meet a cowboy and there you were, just waiting by the gate!"

She makes it look so easy. Even the unflappable Andrea is smiling at her, utterly charmed.

"You headin' up to the house, cowboy?" she asks, falling right into Sam and Emma's act.

Sam is tipping his hat to her and gesturing to Emma's recently vacated seat. "Why, sure, little lady! Just take a seat and my trusty steed and I will be glad to chauffer you up the hill."

I am going to gag. And Andrea thinks I am not mature enough for Sam?

When I have Emma safely inside, I close the door and study her more closely. There are huge, dark circles under her eyes and her clothes practically hang on her normally curvy figure. The Chanel suit jacket is a soft peach tweed and I notice a tiny tear on the top part of her left sleeve, something my normally fastidious friend would never abide, let alone allow to be seen in public.

"All right," I say, tugging her into the kitchen and pushing her gently into a chair. "Now tell me what's wrong."

Emma sighs. "Oh, it was such a long flight," she says. "I'm just absolutely worn to a nub!"

I pour her a soda, turn to hand it to her and Emma, my sweet, dear, best friend, flinches! It is a tiny move, but unmistakable.

"Emma, dear God, what happened to you?"

She avoids looking at me, takes the drink and practically chokes on the first large swallow.

"I can't tell you," she says quietly. "I don't mean to be rude, but you know, I can't say."

Now this is new. I thought we were a team, we Roses. I thought if you were in the Inner Circle, you were In, not Out!

"Emma," I coax. "Come on, I'm one of you now!"

At least, I think I am. Maybe they're not so sure! Maybe I have to pass the test first.

"Really, Buggie, I can't. We don't…"

"All right. Okay." She is obviously close to becoming overwrought. I won't push her for details now. You don't push when the patient is traumatized. Dr. Porter told us this in abnormal psych class. It retraumatizes the victim. So I settle for, "Are you in danger?"

I am not expecting the reply.

"I don't know. I don't think so."

What happened to plain old, "No, I'm fine now"? I feel a shiver of anxiety run down my spine. She's obviously run to me thinking to kill two birds with one stone. She'll protect Jeremy and hide from whomever or whatever, only, what about the after-Oscar party? That's a high-profile event. The media will be all over us. It's been publicized absolutely everywhere. What then? How do I protect Emma if I can't even get her to tell me who's after her?

"What can I do to help?" I ask, knowing exactly what she'll say. I practically say the words with her.

"Nothing. I'll be fine."

Right. Sure you will. And I'll be the next Queen of England.

Marlena has had enough of our dramatics. She squeals, stands on her hind legs inside her crate and falls over backward, landing neatly in her hammock.

"What's wrong with her?" Emma asks, more worried about my ferret than about herself.

"She's saying she's lonely and her Aunt Em is ignoring her," I answer, letting the little fur-ball out of her cage.

"Oh, baby!" Emma coos, and wins my temperamental pet over as easily as she stole the cowboy's sour mood.

I leave Emma to take a shower and compose myself. After all, I almost died today! I return to find Marlena cuddled up in Emma's lap. I sit down beside my friend only to have Emma lean back in her chair and try to turn the tables on me.

"He's very handsome," she says.

I pretend I have no idea what she's talking about. "Who?"

"Sam, you idiot, and don't play me!"

I feel my face heating up and know I'm turning telltale red. Damn!

"He's Jeremy's manager," I say.

"So?"

I am certain now that Emma is seriously preoccupied with the danger she's in, otherwise she'd never need to ask such a question.

"Emma, he's a high school drama teacher."

She cocks her head and frowns. "Yeah, and the guide at the dude ranch was a college student. That didn't stop you from wanting to romp with him!"

"This is different," I say, not certain myself what I mean.

"Really?" Emma says with a smug little grin. "I thought so."

Marlena sighs contentedly and snuggles deeper into her aunt's lap but I realize I am beginning to feel just slightly irritated. Does no one get it? I can't have Sam. I don't want just a "romp." I want more. I want…oh, everything! Why can't I find a man of my standing who makes me feel the way the cowboy does? Surely they exist, don't they?

"Emma, wake up! Sam isn't one of us. He's handsome and smart and very loyal to Jeremy, but he's just not like us. He would never fit into our world. Come on, you know that matters."

Emma nods slowly. "So, he has no money and he's not in-bred. He's smart, loyal and devastatingly gorgeous. Yes, that does make sense. Of course you can't get involved with him!"

Great. Now she's being sarcastic.

I hear the sound of voices out by the pool and look out the kitchen window. Jeremy, Zoe, Mark, Andrea and Sam have gathered at the bar for cocktails. The sun is beginning to set and the sky glows a vivid purple and orange. Sam has showered and changed into a pair of worn, boot-cut jeans and a faded denim shirt fitted to his lean, muscular body. I watch him prepare a drink for Zoe and find myself studying his hands, mesmerized.

I don't hear Emma step up behind me until it's too late and she has followed my focused gaze out to the poolside bar.

"Yes, I can certainly see how you wouldn't possibly be interested in becoming involved with that stunning specimen of the best the male gender has to offer!"

Before I can protest, her attention is drawn to Jeremy.

"So, that's Jeremy Reins in the flesh, eh? I thought he'd be taller!"

I giggle. "I thought he'd be smarter, nicer, more mature, forceful and, well, charismatic, but oh well!"

"And that's Zoe Feller!" she breathes. "Why, she's a tiny rail of a thing!"

I roll my eyes. Emma is starstruck. Go figure.

"Zoe is an absolute nutcase. She follows Jeremy around, mooning over him, and all because she believes she has to become her character."

Emma frowns, nose wrinkling. "What's the movie about?"

"I don't know. It's a sequel to some horror thing. They're witches or vampires or something. I don't know. I'm not into that sort of film."

Emma's mouth drops open. "*Hill People?* They're making a sequel to *Hill People?*"

I shrug and stare back out at the little group by the pool. "I guess. They're wearing black robes and moaning a lot."

"Bug, it's not a horror movie! *Hill People* was amazing! A schooner leaves England around the same time the Pilgrims leave for America, but they get lost during a storm. They wreck on this island that's inhabited by this primitive tribe of cave-dwelling cannibals…."

"And that's not a horror film?"

Emma's eyes are round and huge. "No! They don't really focus on the eating part. They only eat people during their rituals. It's about the blending of the two cultures—the development of their new, blended culture and religion. It's amazing. It's so…" Emma pauses, struggling for the right word. "Primal," she says finally. "It's spiritual and earthy and so, so deep. You know, Zoe actually wrote the script. It won an Academy Award for Best Picture. Anyway, back to the movie. Jeremy is the tribal leader who takes Zoe from the Englishmen. At first she resists him, but the ship's captain gives her to Jeremy! Oh, my God, when they finally have sex it's…" Emma stops, falling silent as she once again stares out the window. "He may be short, but he can take me anytime!"

"Emma! He's a drug-using nymphomaniac! And I think he's stopped playing for your team anyway, so give it up! He's screwing his bodyguard. See the big, no-necked guy standing by the gate? That's him."

"Shut up!" Emma cries. "You're spoiling it for me!" She watches for another long moment, then bites her lower lip and frowns harder. "It doesn't matter anyway," she says, turning back to me with a soft sigh. "That's not why we're here, is it? Let's talk about who's trying to kill him."

Oh, God, I think. It's finally happened, the moment we used to talk about late at night in our dorm room. We are full-fledged grown-ups. No one's going to ride in and do it for us. We're in charge of making sure nothing happens to bad boy Jeremy Reins, just the two of us. This is actually sort of thrilling. For the first time in my life, I am really and truly needed.

I look over at Emma and think, we are invincible. I look back out the window at the group by the pool and think maybe, just maybe, I could even think about getting to know the cowboy a little bit better. I could crack that tough exterior and heal the broken heart I know is somewhere buried inside the man.

Yep, and right after that I'll take care of that little world peace issue and maybe even run for president.

Chapter 11

Marlena is crushed. She cannot believe she'll be missing the Oscars. I try to tell her that Emma's missing them, too, and that they'll both be attending CeCe Goldberg's big bash, but she is still hissing and snarling as I prepare to leave.

"You look simply stunning," Emma cries when I join her and the others in the living room of Jeremy's downtown L.A. penthouse.

I pause in the entryway to the living room and consciously take my moment. I know Sam is watching me. I have already seen him turn away from his conversation with Mark to stare in my direction, but I avoid meeting his eyes. I don't want him to know that it matters what he thinks.

"Ralph won," I tell her.

"Oh, I just know Vera's heartbroken," Emma says, grinning.

I am wearing a Ralph Lauren beaded black lace strapless gown with a train. It clings to my body just enough to hug my waistline and then billow out into a soft swirl of chiffon and lace. My hair is pulled up in a French twist. I carry a matching black lace and crystal Daniel Swarovski Paris evening bag and wear Fred Leighton simple diamond drop earrings and a matching diamond choker. I have written mental thank you notes to Kristy Burke a thousand times in the past few hours, thanking her for somehow knowing my style better than I ever could.

"Vera will live," I say. "You're wearing her."

Emma looks down at her gown and says, "This old thang?" in a deep southern belle accent. "I'm only going to the after-ball. It's not like I'll be attending the main event!"

But she smiles because she knows she looks absolutely radiant in her pale pink Vera Wang off the shoulder satin gown. She is wearing Harry Winston pink diamond chandelier earrings, a matching necklace and a beautiful pink diamond and emerald bracelet. Her auburn shoulder-length hair has been pinned up loosely by the studio hairstylist that Andrea arranged to have sent to the penthouse, and delicate tendrils escape to frame her face and huge green eyes.

Andrea crosses the room to join us, elegant in her Atelier Versace gold lace over champagne colored chiffon gown. I nod approvingly at her choice of the Fred Leighton diamond briolette necklace and cannot help but stare at the huge diamond ring on her left hand.

Andrea follows my gaze and murmurs, "Guilt," quietly. She looks up, meets Mark's gaze, and smiles at him before turning to take a flute of champagne from the waiter who hovers at her elbow.

"Love is grand, isn't it?" she says. Her husband is very much still in the dog house, it seems, and I am surprised.

I thought they'd made up after the Diana incident. Has something happened?

I am distracted by Jeremy's arrival. He walks into the room and takes my breath with his overwhelming presence. This is "star quality." It is more than the three piece Dunhill tuxedo in midnight blue. It is the regal bearing and charismatic élan with which Jeremy moves through his world. He will step out of our limo and own the red carpet. He seems taller somehow but I know he is not. It is all in his manner. He has transformed himself from the bratty, inebriated louse and become the icon.

He smiles at the three of us, clearly feeling the effect he is having and enjoying it far more than I enjoyed my brief moment with Sam.

"So, lovey," he says, voice husky, eyes liquid darkness. "I take it you didn't expect me to clean up well enough to escort an heiress?"

I will not be starstruck! Emma is doing enough of that for both of us.

"No, Jeremy," I say. "I'm just surprised you were able to knot your bowtie all by yourself."

Sam coughs, turns away and busies himself at the bar.

"Bug!" Emma protests. "He looks simply adorable, don't you think?" She is looking at Jeremy like he's a slice of key lime pie and she's starving. "Bug, I mean Porsche, doesn't really think that, Jeremy! She thinks you look amazing—*don't* you, Bug?"

"Bug?" Jeremy raises an inquiring eyebrow when he hears Emma's pet name for me and I am not about to go into it with him.

"It's a long story and I'm sure it would bore you," I say. "Anyway, aren't we late?"

Andrea looks at Mark and he fairly leaps into action. "We'd better get moving," he announces. "The car is waiting downstairs."

Sam steps forward, coming into my line of vision so that I am forced to notice him. The high school teacher has been transformed. He is wearing a Billy Martin Western-style black tuxedo. I know this because Val Kilmer wore one to Cannes and I remember talking with him about vintage Billy Martin. Sam is wearing a black satin bolo tie with his white wingtip collar dress shirt and a black vest that hugs the contours of his muscular torso. The crowning touch though are his black ostrich skin boots—elegant, understated and very sexy.

He knows I'm studying him and is watching me as my gaze travels the length of his body and meets his eyes. He is not at all uncomfortable with my perusal and I find myself suddenly ill at ease. He is smiling, all the way up to his eyes—a mischievous, devil-may-care, challenging smile. The man knows the effect he is having on me and is completely comfortable with that knowledge. Damn, this is exactly the kind of man who could sweep an unaware woman right off her Manolos.

"Emma will you…" I start to say, but Sam reads my mind and answers the question before it is asked.

"Emma and I will meet everyone at the Wilshire," he says, looking at me. "Don't worry, I'll take very good care of Emma and the little weasel."

"Ferret," I correct. "Marlena is a ferret and I have promised CeCe that I'll be bringing her, so…"

"You're taking your ferret to CeCe Goldberg's party?" Emma asks, clearly incredulous.

"It's for the children," I say. "Marlena loves children and there will be quite a few attending."

A tiny muscle in Sam's jaw begins to twitch. Either he's irritated or he's trying not to laugh; I really can't tell.

"Oh, all right!" Emma says grudgingly. "I'll bring her, but you do have a leash, don't you?"

I produce the rhinestone encrusted harness and matching leash and hand them to Emma. "Pink. They match your outfit," I say, hoping this will sweeten the pot a bit.

Emma grins. "You are so nuts!"

"But you love me anyway!"

"Are you coming, lovey?" Jeremy says from the doorway, and we're off. My first Oscar ceremony and I'll be front and center with an actor destined to walk away with at least one of the little icons.

Once we're settled in the limo, sipping champagne, Mark takes over, becoming "The Agent."

"Porsche," he begins. "This is your first time attending the Oscars, isn't it?"

When I nod, Jeremy laughs. "A virgin," he crows. "I didn't think there were any left!"

Mark ignores this and begins his lecture. "This is a very important night for Jeremy. I'm sure I don't have to tell you that you will be in the public eye and in front of the camera every second…"

"Oh, for heaven's sake, Mark," Andrea murmurs. "This is Porsche Rothschild you're talking to. She certainly knows…"

I lean forward and put one hand on Mark's knee. "Don't worry," I say. "There isn't going to be one wasted frame. Jeremy and I are *so-o-o* into each other, isn't that right, *baby?*" I move back in my seat, snuggling into the warm crux of Jeremy's ready embrace.

"Oh, you are the player, aren't you, lovey," Jeremy whispers in my ear.

The limo eases to a stop, the back door opens and we are blinded by the lights of a thousand cameras all swinging into action. Jeremy hops out easily, turns back and extends a hand to help me out onto the red carpet. For just one moment, I am completely overwhelmed and frozen in place.

I don't know how Jeremy senses this, but he does. He grins at me, slides one arm around my waist, and when I don't move, bends to kiss me tenderly.

"Just follow my lead until you feel comfortable," he whispers.

He never lets go of my hand, but I manage to hang back just enough to allow him his showcase interviews. Gradually, I remember who I am and where we are and the importance of becoming Jeremy Reins's girlfriend.

When I link my fingers with his and move into his body, he reads the signal and says, "Perhaps Porsche would be the best one to answer that."

The blonde in front of us sticks the microphone in front of my mouth and says, "So, how did you two meet?"

The carefully rehearsed answer pops into my head and out of my mouth without hesitation.

"In Greece," I say casually. I look at Jeremy adoringly. "On the Onassis yacht, wasn't it? I believe Danni was hosting a little get-together, and well, we just saw each other…"

"Across a crowded boat," he finishes, laughing. "I couldn't take my eyes off of her." He gives me a brief peck, smiles, and we're past that hurdle and on to the next.

It is amazingly easy, and by the time we enter the Kodak Theater lobby, I am enjoying myself. The lobby walls sparkle with a thousand beads of twinkling light, but they go almost unnoticed due to the glitz and glamour of the attendees and the celebratory pageantry.

We step inside the auditorium and I catch my breath. Boxes line the walls, jutting out like balconies, complementing a tiaralike silver-leafed oval and smaller ovals that crisscross the ceiling of the three-story theater and stage. Techs are everywhere, moving around the perimeter of the huge room, dangling from catwalks, adjusting lighting and preparing to bring the ceremony live to millions of starstruck viewers.

I sneak a peek at Jeremy and realize that he is completely in his element among these people and in this larger-than-life pomp and ceremony. Clint Eastwood sits behind us with his entourage. Sofia Coppola is three rows back, talking animatedly to Gwyneth Paltrow. Kate Hudson waves at Jeremy as she walks past us, taking her seat directly behind Tom Cruise. I take a deep breath and feel momentarily out-of-place and talentless.

Jeremy has his arm resting across my shoulders as the house lights begin to flicker, signaling the final approach to the beginning of the ceremony. Sarah Jessica Parker is rushing in, but sees me and waves. Finally, someone who knows me, even if our friendship is a casual one born of living, at least part of the year, in the same city and attending all the same parties and events. I feel better now.

Finally the lights go down, the music begins and I am completely swept up in the flood of excitement and magic that is all-consuming now that I am actually in the audience. It is affecting Jeremy, too. His hand tightens on my shoulder, his body tenses and I feel how much this evening means to him. It is not pretense that makes me turn my head and kiss him on the cheek.

"Do you have a speech prepared?" I murmur.

He chuckles. "No. I've been nominated three times and never won. I wrote out speeches then and I think it jinxed me. So, no speech for *Time Apart*, just…" He doesn't finish and the unspoken wish floats between us as we watch and wait for the Best Actor category to come up.

Later, in the limousine riding from our obligatory fifteen-minute appearance at the Governor's Ball to CeCe Goldberg's gala, I toast him with my champagne flute.

"I did not know it was possible to hold one's breath for longer than three minutes," I say. "But I swear, you didn't breathe throughout the reading of the nominees."

Jeremy smiles and I want to say, "Remember this feeling. Your stupid white powder can't touch this." But of course, he must know that. He holds the heavy statuette in one hand and beams at the little figure.

"I don't recall breathing, or walking up the steps to the stage, or even taking the statue in my hand. I remember Clint saying, 'Congratulations,' but nothing until then."

"Well, your speech was brilliant. Lovely and touching. I, for one, am very thankful you didn't read it off an index card!"

Andrea's smile seems to reflect the way I am feeling about Jeremy at this moment. It is a tender smile, full of warmth and genuine fond regard for the man who is so often an immature brat of a boy. But right now, in this moment, he is realizing his potential and aware of the possibilities before him. It is a beautiful, golden moment and I, for one, am hoping he seizes the opportunity to grow beyond his bad behavior.

I catch myself thinking these things and wonder what in the world has come over me? Perhaps it's all the psychology coursework.

I take a big swig of Cristal and try to adjust the settings in my obviously screwy brain. Sure, I need to be on the lookout for any threat to Jeremy, but let's get real here, this is the party night of the Hollywood year. The town is swarming with rent-a-cops as well as the real deal. Scott's brought in an elite team just for the evening. What am I worried about? Let's have some fun!

We pull up to the Wilshire hotel, host to CeCe Goldberg's extravaganza, and I realize I have only adjusted my interior thermostat down a couple of notches, from prison guard to hall monitor. An overactive superego is terribly hard to tame, that is, until I walk into the ballroom of the Beverly Wilshire and see Emma Bosworth in Sam the cowboy's arms.

Andrea misses this because she is doing her job. She has my elbow in a death grip and is forcefully steering us through the crowd to the receiving line. CeCe Goldberg and a host of luminaries all involved with the fund-raising for Miller Children's Home are standing in front of me, fake smiles plastered across their faces as they greet each arriving guest. I am quite sure they're putting the benevolent pinch on each newcomer for a deep pocket donation. I know that's what I would do and will be doing just as soon as Andrea's deposited me at CeCe's side.

"Porsche!" CeCe cries, seeing me for the first time. "I thought you were lost!"

CeCe Goldberg is thinking no such thing. She is issuing a reprimand for my late arrival and I am ignoring it. CeCe didn't work her way up the network ladder to become the Goddess of Investigative News Reporting by being unaware of anyone important's comings and goings. She knew Jeremy had won Best Actor and she knew it would mean he had interviews and stops to make first before arriving at the gala. CeCe Goldberg was also savvy enough not to raise a stink because Jeremy Reins's presence at her party would more than make up for my arrival in both donations and goodwill.

However, now that CeCe has set the snippy tone for the evening, I am disinclined to think kindly of her. I take my place beside her, noting the unmistakable signs of yet another face-lift and the careful way in which she'd applied makeup to disguise the imperfections of her almost seventy-year-old face. At least she is tastefully attired in an Armani midnight blue silk gown and Harry Winston jewels. Overdressing always screams insecurity, I think.

But enough about her; I am craning my neck to try and see Emma and Sam on the dance floor and failing miserably because of the huge, fat man standing right in front of me.

"Ms. Rothschild," CeCe's assistant coos ingratiatingly, "this is Harry Bonds from…"

I take my cue, smile warmly at the man in the Gucci tuxedo, and launch right into my pitch about the needy children served at the Miller Home. I know I will do this until the bulk of the guests have arrived, and while I am totally aware of what a good cause it is, I could just scream from wanting to find out what that damned Emma has up her sleeve with my cowboy!

Jeremy is content to stand by my side for a little while, but eventually he allows Andrea and Mark to lead him off to a table where Kim Cattrall is holding court. I shift my weight from one high-heeled foot to another and force my attention back to garnering money for the needy orphans. At one point the line thins and I spot Sam, his head thrown back as he laughs at something Andrea and Emma are telling him. As if feeling my gaze on him, he abruptly turns and our eyes meet. Emma reaches up to tell him something else and this time all three of them turn to look at me. They are laughing!

"What?" I mouth silently to my traitorous best friend.

She pretends not to notice. The three of them turn back to their conversation and I can't help but see the way Sam is smiling at the two women. He smiled that way at me too, before we left for the Oscars. With a sinking feeling I realize he probably smiles this way at all women and that it really doesn't mean anything at all special. After all, isn't this the man who taught Jeremy Reins, the consummate actor, everything he knows about high drama?

As if summoned, Jeremy appears at my elbow, closely tailed by a quite morose Mark.

"Dance with me," Jeremy murmurs in my ear. "Mark's driving me insane and you are such a lovely antidote to boredom." He leans past me and lays his hand and a considerable amount of charm on CeCe. "You don't mind if I steal her, do you, lovey?"

CeCe's too sharp to let opportunity pass her by. "Well, dear, of course," she says, all smiles. "If you'll think about giving me that interview I've been dying for!"

Jeremy plays her well. He smiles, bows just enough to be courtly and then winks at the piranha.

"Do you think your viewers can take me live and unfiltered?"

Without waiting for an answer, he leads me out onto the floor and sweeps me into his arms in a grand and very public display of attention. I hear the clicking of a million shutters and wonder where Emma has stashed Marlena. Marlena has little patience with flashing lights.

"Lovey," Jeremy whispers in my ear, "you're being very obvious. That's why I came to get you."

I start to pull back but Jeremy's hand tightens on the small of my back.

I relax into him but manage to mutter against his chest. "What are you talking about? Of course I'm being obvious. Isn't that the point?"

Jeremy kissed my temple softly. "Obvious about Sam. You're practically falling off your heels trying to follow his every move, lovey. I had no idea you fancied him so." The English accent is broad and thick and completely put on.

"I don't know what you're talking about!" But the protest sounds weak even to me.

"Lovey," Jeremy cautions. "Don't try and bullshit the best. I know the look and frankly, I am delighted you appreciate the man as much as I do, but I must warn you, I don't want him hurt. He's had enough pain, Porsche. Don't trifle with that man. He's not the kind. He's too raw. If it's sex you want…"

He's not strong enough to keep me from rearing back to frown at him now. I barely register the whir of shutters as I rush to defend myself.

"Unlike most of your lady acquaintances, I am not the kind to go looking for a casual fuck. And while I do find your friend somewhat attractive, I have absolutely no intentions of pursuing anything other than polite conversation. Furthermore, I was not looking at Sam, I was watching my friend, Emma. After all, I'm the only one she knows here."

Jeremy chuckles. "Well, now, that's not exactly so. It seems to me she and Sam are getting along right well."

The music is slow and seductive with a pulsating, Latin rhythm that should lull even the most staid couple into a steamy dance floor encounter, but I am making us look like wax figures. I am becoming more agitated and would like nothing more than to push Jeremy aside and leave, but I can't. Jeremy underscores this by smiling indulgently and kissing me on the forehead.

"Remember where we are, lovey," he directs.

I force myself to smile and mold my body into his as he expertly guides me around the floor. Jeremy has worked his way under my skin and now all I can think about is Emma and Sam.

"Why is it you have a problem with me hypothetically liking your buddy, but Emma appears not to bother you. She's almost as wealthy and well-traveled as I am. What's the difference?"

Jeremy's answering whisper burns through my chest and singes my very heart.

"Lovey, the money has nothing to do with it. Emma's not a player. You are. She's looking for love and you're running from it."

I keep my face safely hidden in the hollow of Jeremy's neck, fighting back tears that seem to have materialized out of nowhere and now threaten my suddenly shaky composure.

She's looking for love and you're running from it, echoes like a mantra inside my head and it is all I can do to keep breathing. Am I truly like that? Do I run from love? I mentally review every love affair—well, serious love affair—of my adult life and realize there haven't been any. Not really. No relationship that's lasted more than nine months. My longest love affair was with an Italian million-aire, Milos, and it only lasted a year because it was a con-tinental relationship. The longest we ever spent together was on a two-week cruise in the southern Caribbean.

The music ends and Jeremy makes no move to leave the dance floor. He stands still, his arms cradling me from the prying eyes of the paparazzi cameras. When the next song begins with a rapid dance beat, he makes no effort to change position.

"I've upset you, Porsche. I'm sorry," he says.

That is all it takes for me to pull myself back together. Pity. I don't do pity. I raise my head and smile brilliantly at him.

"I am fine," I say. "Let's have more champagne, shall we?"

Inside I feel like ice, hard and cold. Impenetrable. I don't know why I allowed myself to get so upset. It's not as if I actually care about the cowboy. It's not like he mat-ters. I must be tired, that's why I suddenly found myself feeling so absolutely yucky.

Jeremy looks at me strangely, then seems to get it, be-cause he takes my hand and leads me off the dance floor, right to the table where Andrea, Mark, Sam and Emma are all sitting.

"We are parched," he announces as he arrives. "Poor Bug has been glad-handing the wealthy public forever and I have talked to reporters until I'm hoarse. Let's have some champagne!"

"Where's Marlena?" I ask Emma.

Emma looks at Sam, as if seeking permission to answer, and he is the one who answers for her. What in the hell is it with those two anyway?

"When we got here the police stopped us. I had no idea but there's a law in California that prohibits having ferrets for pets. They were going to call Animal Control until I made a few phone calls. We took her back to the penthouse. I thought it would be safer."

"A law against having ferrets as pets?" I can feel the frown lines creasing my forehead at the same moment Andrea pokes me and gestures toward a photographer. I throw my head back and laugh. He snaps his picture and I turn to Sam again.

"You're telling the truth, there really is a law?"

Sam's eyes darken. "I would never lie to you about something as important as your pet rodent." The words are uttered like a solemn vow, but his jaw twitches and I realize he's teasing me.

I take a sip from my newly filled flute of Cristal and feel Jeremy slip his arm across my shoulders again. I lean back against him and play the smitten socialite to the hilt, but I am really wishing I could throw Emma off Sam's scent. The minx! I'll have her ass if she's chasing Sam. I mean, he is vulnerable, and while Jeremy thinks he reads Emma, I know her to be a conniving schemer.

I lean back into Jeremy and look up at his face, following his line of vision to the doorway. Great. Zoe, Diane and Zoe's entourage are entering the ballroom. What in the hell are they doing here? The Governor's Ball is the biggest party in town. Why have they left?

"Oh, shit!" Jeremy swears under his breath as Zoe approaches our table. "Let's dance." He starts to get up, tugging at my hand, and I seize my opportunity to get Sam to myself. "Oh, Jeremy, I've got to run to the ladies' room, ask Emma, she's dying to dance with you."

Jeremy sees this, grabs Emma's hand and says, "Shall we?" The two are on the floor before Zoe can utter a word.

Andrea and Mark are up and gone, too. I look at Diane's triumphant smile and realize this is just what she enjoys most, upsetting the peaceful lives of others. I am fantasizing about slapping the woman silly, seeing myself wiping the smile right off the homewrecker's overly made-up face.

"Come on," Sam says in my ear. "You look dangerous."

A little frisson of anticipation runs the length of my spine as I stand up and allow him to escort me to the dance floor. When we turn to face each other and he places his hand on the small of my back, I feel the heat from his hand radiate through my body.

"So, you prefer to dance with dangerous-looking women, do you?"

He chuckles, pulling me into him with a practiced air and I hope he doesn't feel my heart beating as I relax against his chest.

"Usually? No. But you looked like you were about to start a catfight, and I try to avoid those at all costs. You're unpredictable."

"Unpredictable?" I coax.

"Well, you have a history of fountain jumping and…"

"Now, wait, that was only one incident. I'm quite…" I stop, not certain what to say next. I can't say that I'm predictable, staid, conservative or anything even approaching this because I'm not and I don't want to be.

"What about the skydiving?" he says.

I have to laugh now. "That was done for charity," I say. "And I was totally terrified."

"Really?"

My God, he smells good! I love the feel of his starched

dress shirt against my cheek. "Well, maybe a little, but mainly I was thrilled. It gave me an excuse to do something that scared me a little bit."

"Un-huh." I am certain he doesn't understand me. "So, you like to feel challenged, a little bit scared? I guess routine bores you."

His tone has changed, becoming more serious, and I don't give him the flip answer I think he's expecting.

"I love the excitement of pushing myself beyond what I think I can do, so in that respect, I suppose I love a challenge but routine has its place. There wasn't really a place for routine in my life before I went away to boarding school, and by then I suppose I felt obligated to rebel against it. But to tell you the truth, I yearned for it. I wanted limits and boundaries. I wanted someone to care enough to impose them and protect me from myself."

"And did they?"

"The school? Hell, yes. My family? No."

Sam is quiet for a moment, spinning me slowly around, his hand gently guiding me through familiar moves and steps. I forget about the questions and focus instead on feeling this one moment, memorizing it to savor later.

"Andrea told me you went to see your father," he says abruptly. "How'd it go?"

I look up at him and grin. "He's a lunatic. Maybe that's where I get it from. He was in Vietnam, and to talk to him, I think he believes he's still there."

Sam frowns. "I'm sorry."

I cock my head and inspect him for signs of pity. When I find none, I answer. "Don't be. I like him. I'm glad I went. I needed that…closure."

The song comes to an end and instead of leading me back to our table, Sam heads for a side exit.

"Where are you going?"

He doesn't look back as he's answering me. "Outside. I think we could both use a little fresh air."

We walk down a thickly carpeted hallway, past security guards and uniformed police officers, out a doorway that leads to the pool and down the sidewalk that dances with eerie colored lights from the water's reflection. He doesn't break stride, in fact he seems to walk faster and with increased purpose, until we round the poolside cabana and escape into a dimly lit garden.

Without warning or preamble, Sam stops. I bounce into him, scramble to disentangle myself, and find that his arms have encircled me, preventing my escape. I look up, about to ask him what in the world he's doing, and find him staring down into my face, his expression completely unreadable.

"See any photographers?" he asks.

I frown and look carefully at the surrounding bushes. "No, why?"

Sam smiles softly. "I wouldn't want them wondering about Jeremy and this." He cups my chin with one finger and lifts my mouth to meet his. His lips brush mine and as I move my hand to grip his waist, the kiss deepens. He kisses me with an intensity that is both intimidating and breathtaking. His tongue explores my mouth and his hands pull me closer, into his embrace. I want this moment to go on forever. I feel the heat of his body catching mine like dry timber and suddenly wanting him consumes me.

When he breaks the kiss, he is smiling. "Scared yet?" he asks.

My heart thuds against my rib cage and my knees are completely unreliable.

"I don't know if I'm scared," I say. "Maybe you should do that again so I can be certain. Or maybe you're the one who's…"

There is no finishing my sentences with this man. When he kisses me this time there is no doubt about his intent. Sam the cowboy wants me every bit as much as I want him. His fingers trace their way across my back, leaving the silk of my gown and finding bare skin. I hear a soft moan—mine—and feel my fingers clutch his waist, imploring him not to stop.

The sound of voices growing closer breaks the intensity of the moment and we move apart just as a couple emerges from the pool area, arguing.

"I don't care what you have to do. I just don't want her around. She's everywhere!" It is Andrea's voice, angry and desperate.

"Babe, we're in the middle of a project. She's not a star, but she's a key secondary actor. I can't just tell Zoe to cut her. The project's already over-budget. It will cost too much." Mark's voice echoes off the garden walls, pleading with his wife for understanding.

"Keep her around and it may cost you your marriage," Andrea answers quietly.

"Babe, you know I'd do anything…"

"Almost anything, it seems," she answers coolly.

Sam pulls me deeper into the shadows of a palm tree, hiding us both behind its broad trunk. Andrea and Mark pass by without noticing us.

"Babe, I just won't go to the studio unless there's a crisis. You can come with me, if you want. Honey, please, this is business."

Andrea's response is drowned out by the sound of a loud explosion. The ground beneath us rumbles, sirens and alarms sound everywhere as car alarms and security systems are triggered.

Sam and I run toward the hotel's interior, both of us worried that Jeremy is in terrible danger.

Chapter 12

I am the first through the doors, the first to stumble to a halt amidst the carnage that once was the elegant lobby of the Beverly Wilshire Hotel. People are everywhere, evening gowns mix with security uniforms. Tuxedo-clad men lift pieces of furniture and debris off injured party-goers.

"Emma!" I scream. The sound of my voice is swallowed in the panicked cacophony that surrounds us.

Sam grabs my arm, pointing outside as he pushes me forward. "Jeremy."

We make our way slowly through the swell of people exiting the shell that once was the Wilshire's magnificent entryway, emerging into the cool night air as more ambulances and emergency vehicles rush into the rectangular drive and attempt to draw closer to the scene. Firefighters have surrounded the burnt-out hulk of a vehicle and continue to coat it with chemical spray even though the flames have apparently been extinguished.

Jeremy is standing flanked by Scott, uniformed police officers and plainclothes security men on a manicured square of lawn across from the front entrance. He is holding a blood-soaked white handkerchief to his forehead and doesn't see us approach. He and the others are clustered around a body lying on the ground, a body that is mostly obscured by kneeling EMTs.

I start to run, when one of the medics shifts his position and I catch a glimpse of a slender foot clad in a lavender metallic Rene Caovilla sandal. It is Emma.

I push past anyone in my way, almost unaware that Sam is helping me or that Jeremy is telling the others to let me through. I stop when I see the emergency techs working furiously to stop the flow of blood from Emma's right arm. She is unconscious but breathing. Another medic is starting an IV in her left arm as a third relays information into a cell phone. I have a moment of ridiculous relief that she is not dead, not dying, followed by the horrible realization that, for Emma, she is critically wounded. Emma is a pianist, a classically-trained composer.

I look up and around the courtyard, the hairs on the back of my neck rising as I remember the fear in Emma's eyes when she arrived at Jeremy's estate. She was running from something or someone. Had they discovered her, followed her to the Oscars and tried to kill her? Or was this the first serious attempt on Jeremy's life? What were they doing outside?

Emma is so pale, so still. When an EMT returns with a gurney and the others prepare to move her, Emma moans and her eyelids flutter.

I elbow my way past one of the medics who is standing

by Emma's side and kneel down by her head. I reach out, stroking the blood-matted hair away from her face and waiting for another sign that Emma is regaining consciousness.

"We need to move her, miss," someone says.

I nod. "Well, go ahead. Just be careful!"

Still, when they lift her, Emma cries out sharply and this time her eyes open. Disoriented and in pain, she stares up, wild-eyed. "Bug!"

I am by her side, rushing to keep up with the fast-moving gurney. "I'm here, honey."

"What happened? Jeremy?" Her face clouds, then she struggles to sit up, finds herself restrained by the stretcher's transport straps and struggles harder, panicked. "Did you see him?"

"Who, honey—Jeremy?"

Emma's struggles are growing weaker and she sinks back against the gurney.

"Emma, I'm coming with you. You'll be fine." We reach the ambulance and when I attempt to follow the EMTs inside stop me.

"You'll have to follow us," she says. "We can't take you." This alarms Emma, who again begins to struggle.

"No, no! He's coming! I saw him!"

I look into my best friend's terrified face, willing her to stay with me. "Who's coming, Emma? Who?"

"Ray…" She doesn't finish. Instead she sinks back against the stretcher with a soft moan and falls silent as another medic closes the back doors to the ambulance, leaving me to watch the departing vehicle.

I feel crazy inside. Every nerve cell, every fiber of my body screams with frustration and worry. I need to be with Emma. I turn back toward Jeremy, Sam and the others and stop, remembering that I do have help available, maybe. I pull my cell phone out of my purse and punch in Renee's number. When she answers I am momentarily overcome, but something inside me takes over, sealing off the panic I feel and transforming it into a removed and analytical reporter of fact and supposition.

"Emma's been hurt." I scan the area behind me. The police are widening the cordoned-off area as a huge gray van with the words "LAPD Bomb Squad" on the side is slowly making its way forward. "We were at CeCe Goldberg's function at the Beverly Wilshire when there was an explosion outside. I see the shell of a burnt-out car and I'm pretty sure it's our limousine. The last three numbers on the tag are all I can read and they're the same as the limo that picked us up this evening."

I say a mental thank you to my photographic memory, take a deep breath and continue.

"Jeremy's okay, but Emma's just left in an ambulance for the Century City Hospital, at least that's what the patch read on the EMTs uniform. She's fading in and out of consciousness and her right arm was bleeding heavily."

I hear Renee's breath quicken and the scratch of a pen as she writes.

"Century City, you say?" she asks. "Okay, now don't worry. I'll have protection in place within the next thirty minutes."

Renee must realize Emma is in danger, but she doesn't offer any information about this. Instead she asks more questions.

"Was she able to say anything to you? Did she see anything?"

"She said, 'He's here. Did you see him?' and I could tell

she was very frightened. When I asked who she saw, she started to say Ray something but the morphine kicked in and she passed out."

"Good girl," Renee says. "What about the limo driver, was he killed?"

I look over at the burnt-out shell of a car and shudder. Where was the driver? Shouldn't he have been with the car?

"I don't know. I'll find out."

I hear the muffled sound of Renee's voice, instructing someone in the background and then she turns her attention back to me. "Is Jeremy safe?"

I look for him and see him standing with Sam, still surrounded by police and security guards. The anger that suddenly surges up inside me surprises me until I realize that he could possibly have been the intended victim and, therefore, the reason Emma is now lying in a hospital.

"He's fine. That's the thing about Jeremy Reins—he always lands on his feet."

"Porsche, are you thinking this explosion was aimed at him or at Emma?"

I look at the remains of our limo and try to think logically. "I would think it was aimed at Jeremy, because his limo is the one that blew. In order to plant a bomb under or inside the limo, someone would have needed to get close enough to do it. That requires forethought and planning. I would assume maybe someone who had access to the vehicle would have been a key element if not a perpetrator. Emma hasn't been in L.A. that long. The thing that keeps me from being sure this attack was aimed at Jeremy is that Emma was obviously scared when she arrived."

Renee sighs softly. "I see. All right, here's what I need you to do. I want you to stick with Mr. Reins…"

"But, Emma…"

"Porsche." Renee's voice hardens. "You must trust me and do as I say on this one. Emma will be fine. She will be watched and her safety insured. In all likelihood this attack was aimed at the man you and Emma are to protect. I will send you backup as soon as possible, but it may take a little longer to put in place. Emma's safety involves a matter of national security. Jeremy's does not, therefore I can't utilize the same resources that I will use to cover Emma. That means, Porsche, that you have to do the best you can until I can find and send you help. I know you haven't been trained for this and what little training you have had won't be enough if his situation turns any uglier, so don't place yourself in imminent danger. Call the police, rely on Jeremy's security guards, and try to be the first alert to danger and not the first responder."

"So you want me to baby-sit Jeremy Reins while my best friend is actually in danger and in the hospital?" The entire Gotham Rose deal is starting to lose its appeal as I realize loyalty doesn't rank higher than duty to one's job. It doesn't make sense. Let Jeremy find his own babysitter!

Renee sounds as if she's fighting for patience when she answers me. "Porsche, I know you don't understand and I am not at liberty to tell you anything further but perhaps this will help. If you follow Emma, you could very well be signing her death certificate. If this was an attack on Jeremy and you cause further publicity by visiting your friend in the hospital, then the people interested in finding her will have a neon sign leading them right to their target. We don't want that, now do we?"

I shake my head, realize she can't see through the phone, and say, "No."

"Good! Remember this, too, Porsche—Jeremy Reins is in grave danger. He needs you. You are not his moral judge and jury. You are his lifeline."

"Yes, ma'am," I answer and hang up, feeling numb and cold inside. What in the world have I gotten myself into? The reality of the Gotham Rose assignment seems to permeate my entire being in a way that it hasn't before. I look at Jeremy and Sam standing a few yards away and remember Renee's instructions. Jeremy Reins needs me.

How many people can I say that of in my little corner of the world? I have no children, no siblings, no spouse and, other than Emma, no one who really needs me. Now that someone does, how can I walk away? Okay, fine. It's Porsche Rothschild to the rescue.

I am experiencing displaced aggression, I remind myself. The source of my anger, the attacker, is unknown and unavailable to me, so I irrationally take it out on Jeremy. I must be more objective. What sort of shrink will I be if I can't maintain a professional stance with my patients?

Oh, bite me! the voice inside my head rails. *You're not a shrink yet, anyway.*

I walk up to join Sam and Jeremy. Mark and Andrea are now with them but Zoe, Diane and the rest of their cadre are nowhere in sight. I scan the crowd, looking for other recognizable faces and see CeCe Goldberg standing right in front of the hotel's main doorway, microphone in hand, speaking earnestly to a camera that follows her as she steps out into the entryway of the hotel and gestures toward the limo. Good old CeCe, ever the intrepid reporter, is on the job. Never mind that the Miller's Children's Home event is a failure, by all means, CeCe, cover the news!

Sam moves to my side, draws me away from the others and speaks gently. "Is Emma all right? As soon as we're cleared to leave, I'll see Jeremy off and we can go to the hospital to see about her."

I stare at him, dumbfounded, and struggle for an answer. "Thanks," I manage finally, "but I need to make some calls first, you know, to her family."

Sam looks at me, frowning, confused by my hastily made-up answer. He's probably thinking that if Emma were *his* best friend, he'd be by her side.

"I was thinking we'd probably be in a hurry to leave town anyway. I mean, won't Jeremy be safer at Paradise than he is in town? I can always hire a driver and return in the morning. The EMTs think she'll be taken into surgery right away so I'll have a little time."

Now Sam is really thinking I've lost it because his frown deepens. Andrea saves me. She steps in between us and stares up at Sam with a concerned look on her face.

"I think Porsche's right," she says. "Jeremy needs to get away from here and I wouldn't let anyone stay at the penthouse tonight. It's too risky. I mean, it's not as secure as the ranch is, is it? Mark and I will come along as well and I'll drive Porsche back in to see Emma in the morning."

Scott has been in earnest consultation with a uniformed police officer, but joins us just as Andrea offers her opinion. He nods his approval and gestures toward the burnt out limo, his expression grim.

"He's upping the ante," he says. "I need to get Mr. Reins back to the estate as quick as possible. I've ordered an armored stretch Hummer for the ride, as well as a new driver.

The police want to talk to Reggie—the limo driver. I have it waiting around the corner. As soon as they can get some of these emergency vehicles out of the way, we'll get moving."

"Marlena!" I cry, suddenly remembering my baby. "Can we stop and pick her up?"

Scott gawks at me like I've suddenly taken leave of my senses.

"We can't take any chances," he says. "We've got to go straight to the ranch. I'll send someone after your…pet… later."

"He's right," Sam adds. "It's too dangerous." But the look on his face says he's having serious doubts about me. I'm sure he's thinking I care more about Marlena than I do Emma or Jeremy, and I can't correct him.

"I'll go to the condo and pick up Porsche's rat," Mark says, responding to a fierce jab Andrea's just delivered to his rib cage. "But Andrea, I want you to ride with the others. I don't want either of you coming to the penthouse. Scott's right, it's too risky."

Mark straightens his shoulders and stops slouching for the first time since his debacle with Diane. He is putting on a valiant show for Andrea and when she starts to protest, he is even firmer with her.

"Andrea, this isn't something I wish to debate. I'm going. I'll be fine and I'll join you at the estate."

Sam shakes his head, just enough for me to notice, and turns away to rejoin Jeremy. He thinks I'm spoiled, endangering Mark to protect Marlena. My heart sinks hopelessly, knowing I've lost any possibility of… Well, of what, a relationship? I stare after him, hardening myself and letting go of any illusions that his kisses might have brought. He is not like me. There was never any future to be had with him anyway. I have a job to do and the feelings I had about Sam are now luxuries I can't afford.

Scott nods to the officer he'd spoken to earlier and calls to Sam.

"We're clear. Let's go."

Jeremy lets Scott lead him down the drive toward the waiting Hummer. I realize, watching him walk, that he is unsteady on his feet and somewhat dazed. Andrea notices as well.

"I overheard the police briefing the bomb squad captain. Jeremy and Emma were out in the courtyard when the car exploded," she explains. "Apparently they had come out for some fresh air and then decided to take the limo and return to the penthouse. God knows why! But Emma was slightly in front of Jeremy when the car exploded. That's why her injuries were more extensive than his."

I wonder if somehow Emma knew, or became alarmed and had moved to shield Jeremy. I wonder why she'd suddenly convinced Jeremy to take the limo, abandoning the rest of us and just disappear like that. It doesn't sound like something Emma would do but then, lately, Emma did a lot of unexpected things. I mean, sure, she's a schemer, but she's never been one to abandon a friend, even for an enticing moment with a movie star. No, Emma must've been alarmed about something.

When we are all safely ensconced in the back of the stretch Hummer limousine, I listen as Jeremy talks to Scott. His words come fast, spilling out in a rapid-fire recounting of his moments before the explosion and the chaos that ensued afterward. Scott listens patiently, but with the patient air of having heard this from Jeremy already.

"I saw the driver leave the limo," he tells Scott. "He

must've gone inside to use the john or something. Then, a second later, the fucking thing explodes! It must've been a remote control detonation, don't you think?"

Before Scott can answer, Jeremy turns to Sam, wild-eyed. "How is she? Have you called the hospital?" He looks at me, his eyes suddenly sparkling with what appear to be unshed tears. "I'm sorry, Porsche, I'm sorry! I didn't know…Emma was…"

He breaks off, overcome, and I almost jump across the short distance between the two of us to demand, "What? She was what?"

Jeremy looks at me and shakes his head. "She was…" He frowns, perplexed. "I don't know. What was I saying?"

"You said Emma was something—what was it? Was she frightened?"

Jeremy frowns. "Frightened? Maybe that's it. I think so." He frowns, puzzled, and seems to stare off into space.

"Jeremy, did Emma see someone? Did she say anything to you?"

But Jeremy seems not to hear me. He just sits, staring at a spot on the carpet, and refuses to answer me. I force myself to lean back against the stiff leather seat of the Hummer and close my eyes. I have to organize my thoughts. I have to assume Jeremy was the target and develop a plan for finding Jeremy's attacker before more innocent people become victims. The key will be to discover which of the key players in Jeremy's life were nearby and able to have been a part of each act of sabotage.

"Zoe!" Jeremy cries suddenly. "What happened to Zoe?"

Scott's deep voice rumbles. "She wasn't hurt. Her security people got her group away from the hotel before the police even arrived. The only people hurt were the ones hit by flying glass and debris in the lobby, Ms. Bosworth and you."

I open my eyes and study Scott. Where had he been when the bomb went off? Wasn't it his job to insure Jeremy's safety?

Sam is apparently thinking the same thing and when he asks the question, his tone is sharp, almost accusatory.

"I gave them directions to give us a little space," Jeremy answers for him. "They were outside, but they were maintaining a discrete distance. Come on, Sam, that's how we always do it!"

But Scott is giving Sam a cold glare, which Sam returns with equal, though heated, venom. I close my eyes again and refocus my thoughts on narrowing the list of possible suspects within Jeremy's inner circle. Everyone close to Jeremy has had the opportunity to hurt him, but who among them has the motive?

Andrea's cell phone rings and I hear her answer it. "What? Are the police there? Oh, my God!" I open my eyes as Andrea covers the phone with one hand. "Mark's at the penthouse. Someone's been there and torn the place apart! He says the police and hotel security are both there, as well as a crime scene unit. They've interviewed the staff and apparently have no idea when or how the break-in occurred." She turns to me and says, "Marlena wasn't harmed apparently. Mark says her crate door was open and he found her under your bed, hiding."

Andrea hands the phone to Scott and for the rest of the trip to Paradise, he stays on with Mark to get updates from the police and hotel security.

I underscore Scott on my list of suspects. I don't know why he'd want to hurt Jeremy, but if there were continual risks to his safety, Scott's job security would certainly be assured. I see the look of hero worship in Jeremy's eyes and realize that he thinks Scott is keeping him safe. Perhaps this is Scott's plan; to become indispensable to Jeremy, to stick around long enough to make Jeremy fall in love or at least believe he needs Scott's protection to survive.

I am thinking about this when we arrive back at Paradise Ranch and quickly have my suspicions aroused further. There is now a uniformed guard manning the wrought-iron gate leading into the estate, and when Scott lowers his window to speak to him, the guard practically lunges through the window in his haste to report in.

"Sir," he says to Scott, "there was a breech of vector twelve at zero-twenty-one-thirty-eight. We responded with unit two and made visual contact with a suspect who then eluded our attempts to capture him."

Scott's face hardens and he nods briskly.

"Were you able to get him on the surveillance cameras?"

The guard shakes his head. "It was too dark to obtain a clear image, sir, but they were able to give us a description."

There is not a sound from the back seat of our limo. We are all completely riveted to the guard's recounting of the evening's activities, but when the man describes the intruder, Andrea gasps softly.

"That sounds like Dave, doesn't it?" she whispers to me.

I nod as the man's radio squawks loudly. "Unit One, respond!" a disembodied voice says.

Scott reaches out the window and takes the walkie-talkie from the guard's hand.

"Unit Two, this is Hawk. Go ahead."

"Sir, we've found something. I think you need to see this. We were patrolling the area where the intruder was last spotted and we've come upon what appear to be a series of weight-triggered incendiary devices on the putting green behind the guest house. I think you need to see this, sir. It's pretty incredible." The man's voice rings with barely contained excitement and I know I'll have to find a way to view the discovery without arousing too much curiosity.

The Hummer stops in the courtyard and when we all move to exit the vehicle, Scott stops us.

"I need everyone to wait here until we've cleared the area," he says.

Sam ignores this advice, saying, "I'm coming with you. I want to see for myself. The rest of you stay here and wait for the police to get here."

I know I need to go with them. I might miss out on valuable clues if I stay behind, but how will I get them to take me?

"I think we should all go," I say, but Jeremy cuts me off.

"Sam's right, lovey," Jeremy says. "No need to put ourselves in harm's way."

"Oh, give me a break, shorty," I start, but Andrea wisely takes over, intervening with a more peaceable approach.

"Sam, if it's all the same to you, we'd rather tag along. I mean, I'm sure the security people have gone over the house, but I just feel more secure out here with you. Maybe it's a safety in numbers thing, but after all that's happened, I just don't want to be alone."

You know, I have to admire a woman who can wrap a man around her little finger and bend him to her will so efficiently and with such an apparent economy of effort. Sam melts, as does Jeremy, and Scott—well, who could tell with him, but he isn't arguing with us anymore. I make a mental note. Next time I will bait my trap with honey.

We approach the putting green that lies off to the right,

behind the guest house, and stop when Scott holds both arms out like a crossing guard. In front of us two men stand under brilliant white spotlights, meticulously combing the emerald-green turf with a metal detector.

When they see Scott, they straighten, mark the area with a small orange cone and cross the green to debrief.

"It's not a very sophisticated device," a short, grey-haired man offers. "But it'll do the job. I'm thinking former military. Actually, anybody who knows where to look on the Internet could've built it. There are four of them scattered around this hole. The others are clear, but we're going to go over them again just to be absolutely certain."

Scott's lips form a thin, angry line and I wonder if he's thinking like I am, that Dave has returned to have his vengeance on Jeremy.

While the men examine the small explosives, I begin walking around the area, skirting the green itself, trying to determine how the intruder got past the security guards and into a fairly open and well-guarded part of Jeremy's home.

The spotlights illuminate the grass, highlighting the bumps and textures in the sod with eerie shadows and rough definition. Footprints rim the green and I examine them casually, trying not to appear too interested as I follow one set away from the others. I walk for about twenty feet, to the edge of the spotlight's circle of light, and stop, puzzled. The footsteps abruptly stop and the grass is unbent by any sign of a waiting golf cart or means of transportation. It is as if the intruder simply vanished into thin air.

I squat down beside the last set of footprints and carefully study the area, drawn by a thin line of bare soil that cuts into the surrounding sod. A two-foot square is clearly visible when I look closely.

"Lose something?" Sam stands over me, blocking out my light. I ignore the distain in his voice and answer the question.

"No, I think I've found something. Step out of my light and look at this."

He squats beside me and follows the outline of the square as I point it out to him.

"Footprints lead away from the putting green, see?" I point to the bent blades of grass clearly illuminated by the spotlight's slanted illumination. "And they end here. They just disappear, so I knelt down to try and see if there were any vehicle tracks or something to explain why they just end, and voilà!"

"No, shit, princess!" Sam says with a soft whistle. "I think you might've found something." He tugs at a piece of sod, and with a soft whoosh of air it lifts away, revealing a wooden trapdoor and a rusted metal pull.

A whiff of musty earth and salt air assails us and I begin to cough. Sam sniffs, looks beyond us to the cliffs that overlook the ocean and nods to himself.

"It's a tunnel. That's how our visitor's been getting onto the grounds. Hey, Scott, come take a look at this!" Sam calls. "Good work for a debutante," he says before Scott and the others can reach us.

But this is also his way of dismissing me. When Scott and the others arrive, I am shouldered aside as the men take over. Scott takes a flashlight from one of his men, makes a show of checking the gun inside the pancake holster he wears strapped to his waistband and cautiously begins his descent down a very ancient, wooden ladder into the tunnel.

"I've got the walkie," Scott says to the two guards. "If I get into trouble, I'll call."

They nod, grim-faced, and Jeremy says, "Be careful!" Andrea rubs her hands over her bare arms, shivering in the chilly night air. I step up beside her and watch Scott disappear below ground before speaking to her.

"Let's go back to the cottage and find warmer clothes," I say. "I think they'll be fine without us for a little while."

We walk the short distance back to my cottage in silence. Once inside though, Andrea lets loose. "You know what you found, don't you?" she asks, her face lit up with an excited glow that I hadn't noticed outside.

"Yeah, a tunnel." I am frankly more interested in kicking off my high heels and stepping out of my gown than I am in speculating on the obvious.

Andrea nods. "Yes, of course it's a tunnel, but do you know why it's there, or how it probably came to be on this estate?" She doesn't wait for me to answer her. "This estate was built right before prohibition. I know this because I'm the one who found the house for Jeremy. It belonged to a mobster who worked in Tony Cornero's rum-running operation. They smuggled liquor in from Canada in motorboats. I bet the tunnels were built then."

"Andrea, how do you know all this?"

She laughs softly. "I suppose I'm the eternal student," she says. "I just like to know things. I find California history to be fascinating."

I look out the kitchen window and see that Scott has returned from his journey into the tunnel and is standing surrounded by the others, shaking his head and swiping dirt off the shoulders of his tuxedo. As I figured, he's come back empty-handed.

Sam and Jeremy turn away from the tunnel opening and begin walking back toward the house as Andrea joins me to watch. She leans forward over my shoulder, raps sharply on the windowpane and motions them toward the guest cottage.

Jeremy is in the middle of pouring a second shot of tequila when Mark arrives with Marlena. It is almost 3:00 a.m. and Mark looks exhausted.

"Scott said to tell you the police are on their way back out," he tells us.

"I'm going back out to see what Detective Saunders will tell me," Sam says. His voice is husky with fatigue and the fine lines around his eyes and mouth have deepened with the tension of the night's events.

"Scott's with them, Sam," Jeremy says. "Why don't you call it a night?"

"I want to hear what they've found for myself," Sam answers. He doesn't need to tell any of us that he no longer trusts Scott to do his job. "The bomb squad's cleared the main house. It's safe to go back there. I figure everyone's pretty tired. Maybe you should all try and get some rest. I think we'll be pretty busy with the police investigation by morning."

Andrea and Mark are the first to leave, followed by Jeremy who trails behind them with tequila bottle in hand, humming nonchalantly under his breath.

"I don't buy that he's not scared to death," I say, watching Sam for his reaction. "He's a good actor, but I've noticed he hasn't stopped drinking since we got in the Hummer to leave L.A."

Sam doesn't answer this directly. "Your ear is bleeding," he says softly. "Stand still." With a practiced touch, he wipes the blood away from my earlobe, applying pressure to staunch the bleeding.

"Thank you."

Marlena sniffs Sam's hand, ever the curious ferret, and doesn't take a chunk out of his ministering fingers. I consider this a minor miracle and am even further amazed when she decides three's company and this new activity is boring. She leaps from my neck to Sam's shoulder and down onto the ground to seek more interesting opportunities, leaving me to stand there with the cowboy ministering to my wounded ear.

I am aware that every nerve ending in my body has suddenly gone on full alert. I feel him behind me, smell the scent peculiar to him and feel the heat that seems to radiate from his body into mine. It makes me jerk away abruptly, uncomfortable with my feelings and uncertain of how to handle them.

"I'd better get back out there," Sam says, turning toward the door with an abrupt spin that lets me know he's felt what I feel and is shoving it aside, just as I am. We have more important matters to take care of first.

"I'm coming with you." I grab my black cashmere Armani sweater from the back of an armchair and hurry to catch up.

"No." But it's a half-hearted denial. Maybe it's the determined look he sees on my face, or the fact that he's tired and arguing with me is pointless that makes him give a resigned shrug of his shoulders and start walking again. It doesn't matter. He couldn't stop me. I have to know who's trying to kill Jeremy Reins and not just because I'm a Gotham Rose working her first mission. It's personal now. My best friend is lying in a hospital.

Chapter 13

A thin gray shaft of light illuminates my bedroom window, but that is not what has awakened me. Marlena has lost her mind, at least that's what I think. It's to be expected. She spent the entire day and most of the night in her crate in Jeremy's penthouse condo. She's witnessed a break-in and hidden to avoid injury or perhaps death. Why should I be surprised to see her running along the windowsill beside my bed, chattering and scratching at the glass? It's not as if she can talk and get the trauma out of her system.

"Come here, baby," I moan, patting the pillow beside mine. "Tell Mommy."

I am impossibly tired. I raise my head to look at the clock and shudder when I realize I've only been asleep for a few hours. Marlena ignores my request and scratches again at the window, hissing and emitting a low growling sound I've never heard from her before. I may be exhausted, but I am also Marlena's mother and I know something is wrong now.

"What is it, baby?"

I walk on my knees across the bed to the window and cup my hands around my face to peer out into the darkness. Marlena jumps on top of my head and squeals. Orange flames lick at the far wall of the main house. Thick white smoke billows up into the sky. I hear sirens approaching in the distance and can make out figures running across the lawn.

I stare horrified at the sight before me and almost ignore a flicker of movement that just registers in my peripheral vision. A figure darts out from the pool house and moves to the shelter of a utility shed just yards from the guest house back patio. Someone is outside and from his crouching run, I can tell he doesn't belong on the estate.

I pick up the phone, punch in the main house number and hang up after only two rings. Everyone is already outside.

Marlena watches me struggle into jeans and throw on a T-shirt in the darkness. I don't bother with shoes. There isn't time.

For a moment I just stand there, trying to decide whether to run up to the house and signal the security people and police or try and follow the guy myself, hoping to at least give the police a description of the arsonist.

I hear a strange sound, like water hitting bricks, a splashing sound that seems to be coming from the right side of the guest cottage. A horrible thought suddenly occurs to me. What if he's pouring gasoline around the perimeter of my quarters, in preparation for torching it? I can't let him do this! Marlena's inside.

What're you gonna do, debutante, ask him how it makes

him feel? You're a shrink-in-training, not a superhero! My inner voice does wonders for my confidence. I'm going to have to take this up with my own therapist when I get back to New York, but not now!

I look around for something to use for a weapon, but of course, no one's left Mace or a gun lying out and there are no rocks. I slip quickly around the far side of the house and see an empty wine bottle sitting on the table along with two empty wineglasses. Bingo.

I grab it and ease back around the front of the cottage, listening and hoping to pinpoint my quarry's location. The splashing has stopped, replaced by something that sounds like a soft scratching. I have to make my move before the guy throws a lit match and blows the bungalow up.

I take a deep breath, sidle up to the corner and quickly peer around. I can't be seeing what I'm seeing. Dave stands with his back to me, apparently struggling to get something out of his pocket. A lighter or matches, I'm guessing. For a second I hesitate, uncertain. I don't even have any upper body strength. I could kick myself for not working out! But when I think of Marlena, trapped inside what may become an inferno, my motherly instincts take over and I am flying the length of the cottage, bottle raised high in the air.

I bring the green glass down hard on top of burly Dave's naked skull. For a terrible moment absolutely nothing happens. The bottle doesn't break and Dave doesn't drop like a rock. This is totally not like the movies, but I don't wait around, either. I go right for the instant replay, lifting my weapon with both hands and swinging it like a baseball bat this time, high and inside the strike zone.

The bottle connects with the side of Dave's head and makes a sickening crunch that turns my stomach. Dave sways, spins around on his heels and drops to the ground with a soft moan. It is then that I see what Dave had been trying to accomplish. His fly is half-open and the zipper is stuck on the fabric of his tidy-whities. Dave had been relieving himself against the wall of the cottage.

I look around, mainly from habit, and feel relieved that this will be one undocumented photo opportunity. I kneel beside my victim, grip his wrist and feel for a pulse, afraid that I may have unwittingly killed him. When I see the deep rise and fall of his chest, I drop the arm, relieved, and try to figure out what my next step should be.

Tie him up! Right. Tie him up. I scramble to my feet, run inside the bungalow and root furiously though my Gucci accessory bag until I produce two Fendi scarves and one Dior. Dave is still sleeping peacefully when I return and continues to breathe deeply even when I sit on his stocky back to get a better grip on his arms. He is hogtied, hand and foot, with beautiful silk scarves, and it only takes me five minutes to do it.

I stand up and survey my handiwork, proud of myself for making such short work of an obviously violent and dangerous man. Of course, he doesn't look particularly dangerous or violent at the moment, but that may have some thing to do with the brightly colored scarves.

I nudge him with my toe and when he doesn't move, decide it's all right to leave him long enough to summon help. I run across the lawn, skirting the pool area and head for the small group of people assembled by the stables, watching the firefighters put out the blaze that could have reduced Jeremy's palatial home to ash and cinder had it gone undiscovered.

Scott is standing beside one of the firefighters, his face

and body covered in grime and soot. He is talking into a walkie when I arrive, distracted and busy issuing orders to whoever he has listening at the other end, but Sam sees me running and moves out from the crowd to meet me.

"Oh, God, I was on my way to check on you," he says. "But I needed to make sure everyone was out of the house. I couldn't find Andrea." For the first time since I've known him, Sam appears rattled. "Did the sirens wake you up?"

"No I think the arsonist did. Marlena was scratching at the window and just going crazy, so I looked outside and saw the house was on fire. Then I saw someone run out from behind the pool area and thought maybe it was the fire-setter."

"You didn't happen to get a good look at him, did you?" He asks the question, but is so sure he knows the answer that he doesn't even wait to hear it, just turns his head to watch the fire and only half listens to my response.

"Oh, better than that—I actually caught him, knocked him unconscious and tied him up with three of my very best silk scarves. I personally like Dave in the pink Fendi, but then we all know how partial I am to pink."

"Oh, well, I suppose it was dark…"

"Porsche, what did you just say?" Andrea appears at my side, tugging Mark along with her. "Did you say Dave did this and you like him best in pink? I thought he was in jail."

Finally. It takes another woman to actually pay attention.

"Yes, I thought so, too, but there he was. And when I came up behind him I thought he was pouring accelerant around the guest cottage. I knew I had to do something, so I grabbed an empty bottle of pinot grigio and hit him over the head. There wasn't anything else to tie him up with but three of my scarves. I don't know for certain that he started the fire…."

Now Sam's on full alert. "Did you say Dave was pouring accelerant around the cottage?"

I shake my head, frowning. "No, I *thought* he was pouring accelerant around the bungalow. Actually, he was peeing and when his zipper got stuck, I bashed him over the head. He's tied up behind the guest house."

Andrea, Mark, Sam and two firemen are all staring at me, open-mouthed, eyes wide, clearly not sure they should believe what I'm telling them, but Sam is the first to break away and summon Scott and a nearby police officer. I can see Scott looking at me, then back at Sam, and know he's having a hard time believing I could take down a seasoned security professional, but something apparently makes them decide to check out my story. They hop in a golf cart and go flying across the yard toward the cottage, leaving me to follow on foot. By the time I arrive, the cop and Sam are both trying to pull Scott off his helpless ex-boyfriend.

"Why?" Scott yells. "Why the fuck did you do that? You could've killed me, man! And the meds on the putting green, what in the hell were you thinking? You're gonna kill me over this stupid shit?"

Dave is struggling and somewhat disoriented, but he manages to gasp out a barely intelligible defense.

"I didn't," he says. "I was here, but I wouldn't do that to you, I swear to God! I posted bail and I wanted to talk to you, so I was waiting for you to come back to your quarters. You never came and then there was this explosion and I saw somebody running. It wasn't me!"

"Dave," Scott roars, losing complete control, "you were a fucking munitions expert in the army. What do you mean, you didn't do this? Be a man. At least admit what you did to my face."

But Dave just glares at Scott and looks away without saying another word. I hear the cop tell Sam that they can test Dave's hands for any signs that he's handled accelerant or explosives, so it doesn't really matter what Dave says now. The tests will remove all doubt.

I look at Dave and wonder if he is telling the truth. My head is spinning with fatigue and for a moment I wonder if I'm going to pass out, but instead I sink down onto the low fieldstone retaining wall that borders the flower beds beside the cottage entrance. At some point I decide I might even try lying along the wall, just for a few minutes....

There is a big gap in my memory because Sam is suddenly shaking my shoulder and the others are no longer standing where they were. In fact, everyone has disappeared except for Sam.

"Porsche, bedtime," he says softly.

I think bedtime was many hours ago but who can argue the point? I was, after all, sleeping and now here I am outside with people just vanishing into the night like ghosts.

"Where's Dave? Where'd everyone go?" The questions come out of my mouth in a sleep-filled slur that makes Sam bend his head close to mine.

"Dave? They took him to the police station. The others went back up to the house a while ago. You've probably been asleep for a couple of hours."

"My scarves! I wanted to get my scarves back!"

He dangles them before my eyes. "The least I could do, given that I didn't believe you when you told me."

I smile sleepily and close my eyes, shivering as my cheek touches the cold stone wall. "Yeah, I'm good," I whisper. "Night-night."

I am asleep before the last syllable escapes, dreaming

blissfully until Sam interrupts again by scooping me up into his arms and walking toward the cottage. He stops in front of the door and gently kicks it open with one foot, steps inside and kicks the door closed with his heel.

I lean my head against his chest, enjoying the feel and smell of him and knowing I shouldn't. My head is simply too heavy to lift away from his body, and besides, I don't want to. I want him to let me sleep where I am, in his arms, until at least late afternoon. When he lowers me to the bed my mind rebels, but my body sinks down into the feather mattress and instinctively curls into a ball.

I feel him slip the shoes off my feet then pull the covers up over my body. At least, this is how I remember it, but when I wake up hours later I am shocked to find I am sleeping in my camisole and panties! I sit upright in bed and stare around the room, trying to piece together my last few minutes of consciousness before I fell asleep.

I spot my jeans and shirt neatly folded on a chair, my sandals lined up on the floor below them, and feel my face growing very hot. I do not remember taking off my clothes and I certainly do not remember Sam removing them!

Marlena is sleeping on the pillow next to mine and when I move she opens one sleepy eye and squeaks.

"Okay, then you tell me," I say. "Did that cowboy do this?"

Marlena sighs softly and goes back to sleep. I am thinking about it, but my cell phone interrupts that fantasy.

"Porsche?" Renee's voice sounds different, perhaps a little tense but who can tell with her? "Is Haley with you?"

"Haley?" I say, but I'm wondering, who in the hell is Haley?

"She didn't come home from the Hewitt School yesterday. The Governess called this morning and said her sources think a young girl matching my daughter's description boarded one of your family jets this morning. The flight plan logged with the airport shows her destination as Los Angeles."

"There's no way. She doesn't know…"

Renee breaks in. "I'm afraid there is. I keep a duplicate key to my private office in my bedside table drawer. It's gone and the file I have with your personal information is missing as well."

"You keep a file on me?"

"Of course I do! We have to do a background investigation and maintain any information we can on you girls in case…" Renee doesn't finish this thought before she hastens to add more. "The files are designed to look like every other file I have on the members of the club, so Haley doesn't know about the Roses or your mission."

I am out of bed and moving now, snatching jeans and a Stella McCartney top out of a suitcase and trying to dress as Renee talks. That little shit, Haley! I should've known she wouldn't be content to wait at home for me to send her a souvenir of my trip.

"So she'd know how to order a plane? She'd have the number, the pass code, everything?"

Renee sounds defeated when she answers. "I'm afraid so."

I look in the mirror and decide bed head will just have to remain au courant because I won't have time to do anything to it, let alone take a shower or apply makeup.

"When is she due to land?"

"If it's her, she should be arriving at LAX in about an hour and twenty minutes."

I look at the clock on the kitchen counter—1:56 p.m. Even if we left now, there would be no way to meet the plane on time. The trip to the airport couldn't possibly be made in less than an hour and a half.

"What do you want me to do?" I walk to the front door, open it and stare up at the main house. I don't even know who's around or if there's a car I can borrow. I see no sign of life from the mansion, but I hear the sound of a bulldozer or some other piece of heavy equipment down by the burnt-out bunkhouse.

"Olivia is on her way to the airport where I have a plane waiting. You remember her don't you, my assistant?" Renee hurries on. "She won't be landing until seven your time. I need you to get to Haley and keep her with you until Olivia arrives and can bring her home."

I am silent; thinking how I can accomplish this when there will be at least a thirty-minute gap between Haley's landing and my arrival.

"Porsche, I must warn you that there is someone who would do anything to hurt the effectiveness of our organization. He may be behind this. He may realize Haley is vulnerable and go after her."

"You're talking about the Duke, aren't you?" I ask. "Emma told me about him. She says you think he runs a high-society crime ring or something, that is, if he even exists. He's the one trying to undo all the good the Governess has done in forming the Gotham Roses."

"I don't think we can afford not to look at him as having a hand in my daughter's disappearance. It could be as simple as a schoolgirl lark, but I just feel you should be warned, it may be much more than that. She may be thinking she's meeting someone, perhaps she received a message that you were even sending for her. I have no idea. I just want her back, safe."

"Don't worry," I assure Renee. "I'll take care of her."

But I hang up wondering how I'll reach her in time and what I'll find to keep the little brat occupied for the five hours it will take for her "nanny" to arrive.

I am out the door and sprinting up to the mansion as soon as I sever the connection with Renee. I have no story concocted for my sudden emergency trip to the airport or for Haley's identity. I suppose that's why I like a good crisis; it forces me to use my imagination and creativity. I would be hell at a job where I was required to do long-range planning. Nothing ever seems to hold my interest for that long. No, I prefer chaos and crisis. Perhaps I should consider doing emergency work when I graduate. *Focus, Porsche!* I remind myself. *This is no time for daydreaming!*

Andrea is sitting in the dining room drinking coffee when I arrive. Immaculate as always, she takes in my disheveled appearance and laughs as I come running into the room.

"Let me guess," she says. "You ran out of coffee in the guest house and the maid forgot to refill the canister."

"Where is everyone? Where's Sam?"

Andrea stops smiling and frowns. "Sam took Jeremy into the studio about two hours ago. Why, is something wrong, Porsche?"

"I need to get to the airport. Someone's flying in and I must meet her plane."

Andrea pushes her coffee cup aside. "Well, I can take you."

"No! I mean, thanks, but she's landing in an hour and fifteen minutes and we wouldn't reach her in time. You see," I say, struggling for just the right amount but not too much information to give my ally. "It's Renee's daughter. She's probably trying to follow me out here so she can meet Jeremy."

Andrea smiles and shakes her head. "Kids, can't live with 'em, can't rip their heads off! Okay, we can call the airport and have an airline employee meet the plane and tell her to wait."

"No good. Renee's afraid she'll run." I don't mention the potential for danger. "Sam's right in L.A. and a lot closer to the airport than we are. Do you think he'd go out to the airport, I mean just long enough to meet the plane and cover until we arrive?"

Andrea nods enthusiastically. "Of course. Perfect! I'll call him from the car."

Good—quick thinking, Andrea. She'll call from the car, certain Sam will do her bidding and yet, not wasting time by hanging around the house to call. Ten minutes later Andrea, Marlena and I are in her Jaguar just outside the city limits of San Jacinta. Sam is already briefed and on his way to LAX. Could life's little crises be handled with any less stress? I seriously doubt it.

Andrea looks over at Marlena, sleeping peacefully in my lap with her tiny black silk nightshade covering her eyes. "Does she go everywhere with you?"

I stroke Marlena's soft fur and smile as she utters a soft little ferret snort. "Just about. She's my baby. I got her when I was studying theories of attachment and I'd just finished reading Harlow's monkey study. See, there were two groups of baby monkeys. One got petted and rocked for fifteen minutes a day while the other had no human or animal contact, just a wire bottle holder at feeding time."

Andrea frowns. "And the animal cruelty people didn't stop that?"

That stops me. I hadn't ever thought to ask. "I don't know. That's a good question, but anyway, the group that got loved grew up to be happy little loving monkeys, while the other group…" Oh, hell. Where were the animal control officers for this study? "Well, they were pretty sad little monkeys. Some of them even died."

"Porsche, that is awful! I mean, why do a study like that when it's just common sense that anyone will die without love!"

Good damned question again. What was I doing in this field anyway?

"Well, I don't know, but it sure made me love my little ferret all the more, and look how she's turned out! She's perfect."

Andrea is still frowning over Harlow's cruelty and I can't blame her, so I change the subject quickly.

"What happened to Dave?"

Andrea's attention shifts as she focuses on the terrible end to last night's festivities.

"Oh, don't worry about him," she says. "They took him right off to jail and I doubt they'll set bail at any amount he could afford this time! You know, this really threw Scott. After the police left, Scott just fell apart."

"Fell apart?" No matter how hard I try, I just can't imagine the tough guy losing his composure. I didn't think Scott was capable of that depth of emotion. To me, he is more of a machine, but when I say this Andrea disagrees.

"You know how those ex-military types are," she says. "It takes a lot to set them off, but once you do, they make up for all the times when we think they are inhuman robots."

I don't see men like Scott melting into a pool of salty tears and needing solace. "You mean he was mad or was he upset?"

Andrea's face is unreadable. She is wearing dark Ralph

Lauren glasses and keeping her attention carefully focused on the freeway, but her opinion about the matter is unmistakable.

"Oh, no, his heart was broken, especially when he began thinking about the other attacks on Jeremy and how they always seemed to happen in places that were thought to be impenetrable to outsiders. And then there was the timing. Scott finally admitted to Sam that he and Jeremy began their…flirtation, several months ago. Three weeks later, the trouble started."

I am feeling like such a naive fool. Why didn't I see any of this? Aren't the simplest reasons usually the most logical ones? If the attacks looked like inside work, why didn't I suspect Dave, he had the best reason for wanting to hurt Jeremy. And yet, Jeremy was never injured. Why? Was it poor work on Dave's part or reluctance to actually do harm? Was he afraid that Scott might become an accidental victim? If that were true, why booby-trap the pool and then jump into it? Surely he wasn't foolish enough to do that in an effort to throw everyone off his track; no one suspected him.

Andrea listens to my doubts but dismisses them. "Porsche, not everything in life works out in a perfectly logical and linear fashion. Sometimes people mess up. Dave was drunk when he jumped in the pool. He probably forgot he'd rigged the diving board."

I think hard on that one. I think about the absolute sorrow and hurt in Dave's eyes when Scott refused to believe he hadn't set the house on fire. I just didn't think Dave was ready to kill Scott. The anger wasn't there for Dave. Hurt, yes, but anger, no.

"I can't believe that Zoe scheduled a shoot today," Andrea

says, changing the subject. "The woman is obsessed with this film. It has to be just perfect. I bet it's close to a million dollars over budget already and the thing isn't half-finished."

"Does the studio even care about the budget with stars like Jeremy and Zoe?" I ask idly.

"Oh, you bet your ass they care, but this isn't their project entirely. Zoe's found a backer to fund almost all of it. She's so rabid about the whole thing—she's even guaranteed the overage cost. The studio won't be out a dime."

The woman really is a fruitloop. "Is she going to make anything out of it? I mean, if she's this over budget, what happens to the profits? And where'd she get that much money to piss away? Do they all just have more money than sense?"

Andrea's all-knowing smile readies me for a lecture on the facts and foibles of Hollywood reality. This is fine with me. I look at my watch and realize Haley's plane is scheduled to land in five minutes. I force myself to listen as she goes on about movies and money and the movers and shakers behind the scenes; thinking all the while about how I'll entertain the brat from hell without running into any bad men looking to harm her.

"Zoe's backer funded this project," Andrea is saying, "not Zoe. Films all have backers as do most of the production companies. I'm sure Zoe's got money in it, but not enough to worry her."

I fantasize about funding a movie and start thinking of plots. They all seem to be romances set in the Old West, with cowboy heroes who sweep the heroine off her feet. Why can't I get that damned cowboy out of my head? And did he really undress me?

"Porsche?"

"What?" Andrea's voice startles me out of my daydream.

"You weren't even listening to me, were you? I said, the airport's up ahead, next exit."

I am surprised by the amount of relief I feel washing over me. Up ahead low-flying planes land and take off, the roar of their engines reassuring me that I will reach Haley and Sam before anything can go wrong.

Andrea finds the private hangar where she has arranged to meet Sam without any trouble.

"I've been here a thousand times," she says breezily. "Mark is constantly flying in and out of town. They should be right up there." She points to a low-slung glass and steel building similar to the one where she and I first met only a few days ago.

I look, staring intently, and see Sam emerge onto the concrete sidewalk. My stomach does a little butterfly dance as the image of him kissing me the night before suddenly pops into my head. I force my attention back to the present and see that he indeed is escorting someone toward the car but the girl he has in tow is not Haley Dalton-Sinclair. She resembles Haley in basic build, but she doesn't have long blond hair. This girl's hair is very short, cut into edgy wisps of black that frame her pixie-like face. She is wearing ripped and faded jeans that sport multiple appliquéd patches, a worn leather biker jacket and hideous-looking black Doc Marten boots.

Andrea's placid jaw drops. "You know, I've never met Renee face-to-face, but I just expected that her daughter…"

"That is not Haley," I say, but as we pull up to the curb and Sam places his hand on the girl's shoulder to escort her to the car, I realize with a jolt that Haley is indeed buried under the atrocious disguise. When she takes a last drag on her cigarette before tossing it carelessly aside, I know for certain that Renee Dalton-Sinclair's daughter has found a way to set herself apart from her mother and all she represents.

I can't help myself. I open the door, step out onto the curb and look the little idiot over slowly from head to toe. "Well, as I live and breathe, you must be your sister, Haley's evil twin!"

Haley scowls. "Blow me, all right?" she says and scampers through the open back passenger door.

Sam is grinning. "Welcome to secondary education, Porsche," he says. "I figure you might want to sit back there with her."

Well, he figures wrong, but I can see he has no intention of sitting back there with her, so I climb in behind Little Mary Sunshine.

Haley's scowl has vanished as quickly as it appeared. She now becomes a new girl, a happy girl, a complete psychopath, if I don't miss my guess.

"Aren't you glad to see me?" she cries. "I can't believe your family! I mean, that was just so totally generous of your mom to offer a plane so I could come see you!"

So that's how the little brat did it. She snowed Mummy. Marlena stirs from her comfortable perch atop my shoulders and I pull the sleep mask off her face.

"Hi, cutie!" Haley says, wiggling one finger. "Remember me?"

Marlena, no fool, hisses dangerously.

"What's the matter with her?" Haley asks, putting on a hurt face that I don't for one minute believe.

"Marlena can smell a con a mile away," I answer. "Speaking of stinking, your mom called. Olivia's flying in from New York in a few hours to pick you up."

The storm clouds gather in the little monster's face. Gone is the win-you-over attempt.

"Shit! Then let's get the hell out of here and let the old douche bag wonder what happened!"

I feel both eyebrows raise up to a point somewhere above my hairline and know I'll pay for this moment with Botox in a few years. My mouth drops open, mirroring Andrea's and I shake my head in amazed disbelief.

"What drugs are you on?" I ask. "We will be right here waiting at the concourse when that plane lands and you will be going right back where you came from!"

Back comes the little princess. "Oh, come on, Porsche, please? I only wanted to meet Jeremy. I mean—" now she's playing to the front seat audience "—it's always been a dream of mine to meet Mr. Reins. He's such a dedicated artist and I want to study drama at Yale one day."

"Yale?" Sam says, interested now. "Really?"

No, Sam, she's blowing smoke up your pants leg. Ms. Thing is playing you.

"Please, please, please let me stay out here with you and Jeremy for a couple of days," she whines. "I won't be any trouble, really I won't. I'm sure he won't mind if you ask him. I was just so worried, you know, about the attempt on his life last night and all."

"No." I look at Andrea. "Is there a little lunch place or something where we could get her a snack before she flies back?"

Andrea looks over the rim of her dark glasses, studying the new arrival like she's just flown in from Mars.

"Um…Chicken and Waffle…uh…Rocco's Burgers…" She is running through her list of eating establishments, but Haley isn't interested.

"No. I want to meet Jeremy." She leans back against the plush leather seat, folds her arms over her chest and sticks her lower lip out like a complete two-year-old.

Sam is absolutely in love. His grin grows with Haley's resistance and I can't imagine why in the world he finds the girl so amusing.

"Maybe we should go have someone attempt to repair your hair," I say. "What did you do, chop it off with nail scissors and dunk your head in black ink?"

Haley glowers at me, juts out her chin, and gives a miffed little sniff in my direction.

Sam glances at his watch, then back at me. "Well, we could always run her out to the studio. I need to check in with security and update Jeremy on the police investigation. There's time enough for her to see a bit of this afternoon's filming. Of course," he says, his eyes never leaving mine, "she would have to swear on her mother's grave she'd then go peacefully with her escort back to New York."

"I'll do it!" Haley says, levitating off the seat with joy and leaning forward to grip Sam's face in her two hands. She smushes his cheeks together and cries, "I just love you! You so get me!"

I'm going to so get her, but it won't be pleasant and she won't forget it!

"You're sure it's safe?" I ask Sam.

"I think last night's arrest put an end to that worry. I think we've got our man right where he belongs. Dave's not getting out anytime soon."

"All right, I guess we can go. But only if you promise to behave," I say, turning my attention to Haley and grudgingly relenting. "But we're going to be right back here three hours from now. And you have to call your mother on the way over to the studio and tell her you're okay and you're coming home. She's absolutely sick from worrying about you."

I give Sam a wicked look. "You know, Sam is Jeremy's manager, Haley. He taught Jeremy everything he knows about acting."

That is all it takes. Haley gloms onto Sam, plying him with questions until we arrive at the studio gates. When Andrea rolls onto the lot, Haley becomes even more of a starstruck fan. Her eyes widen and as we climb out of the Jaguar and enter the hangarlike building, she stops talking completely and just stares.

Zoe and Jeremy are standing beside the set, talking in low, angry tones as we approach them.

"I don't care if it's a little thing," she is saying. "We'll have to shoot it over again."

Jeremy looks tired. "There's no point in it. We're all tired, at least wait until tomorrow."

Zoe is adamant. "No. You don't believe in this, you never have!" When Jeremy's face darkens into a hostile scowl, she backs off and instead begins to plead. "It's important to me," she begs. "Can we just call Diane out and have her do the last bit of it with you again?"

Jeremy gives in. "Fine, but you'll have to tell her. I just left her in your trailer a few minutes ago, she said she was too tired to even get up off the couch and go to her own trailer. She wants to go home and go to bed, but she wanted to talk to you first."

"This is her last scene. After we shoot it she can sleep forever if she wants, just not yet!"

"Fine. We'll do it over, but you get to be the one to break the news to her. I'm done playing the heavy. And when Ray wants to know why you've gone over budget again, you can be the one to kiss his ass about that, too!"

Jeremy's face reddens and he seems ready to unload on Zoe, but Sam steps forward between the two.

"Jeremy, I'd like you to meet a new friend of mine," he says. There is a slight elevation to his voice, a quality that must alert Jeremy to be on his best behavior because the star's features smooth into a smile almost instantly. He smiles at Haley as he answers Sam.

"Any friend of yours is a friend of mine, pard." The jovial western accent Jeremy uses with Sam has returned. "Actually, Haley here is a friend of your beloved Porsche's. She borrowed a Learjet and arrived unexpectedly because she was concerned about your recent close encounter with death."

"Smashing!" Jeremy cries. His eyes sparkle. "A bit of the hell-raiser, are we then, lovey? S'pose you'd have to be, hanging with the likes of Porsche!" Jeremy seeks me out, smiles adoringly, and shakes his head. "Ah, a woman of beauty," he sighs. "I am not surprised to learn your friend here is every bit the rosebud of earthly delight that you are, lovey."

Oh, he's laying it on thick. I roll my eyes behind Haley's back and stick my forefinger in my mouth, feigning a gagging motion.

"Oh, honey, really," I coo. "You're too, too much!"

Jeremy smiles and is about to say something when a woman's blood-chilling screams interrupt the relative quiet of the working set. Everyone within earshot freezes, listening to pinpoint the direction of the scream. The sound echoes through the open bay doors leading outside to the trailers. Andrea and Mark come running from the recesses of the building to join the rest of us, along with almost everyone who hears the wailing terror in the screaming woman's voice.

We reach the outdoor trailers as the door to one silver motor home bursts open and Zoe emerges to stand, screaming, on the top step. When she sees Jeremy her face is transfixed with a combination of horror and rage.

"You killed her! You never were true to us and now you've killed the only person I ever loved. Oh, God, Diane!" She looks completely insane, her eyes are wild, her long red curls fly out like Medusa's snakes and she flails her arms with maniacal abandon, overwrought with grief and shock.

Jeremy, stricken, attempts to go to her, but she lunges for him, forcing Sam to restrain her and motion Jeremy back.

"Call security," Mark yells, but they are already on the scene and pass the hysterical woman as they run up the steps and into the trailer.

Zoe can't seem to look away from Jeremy and struggles to escape Sam's strong grasp. Finally, she is able to loosen one arm which she extends in a grasping, clawlike motion toward Jeremy.

"You will never be safe from me," she says in a dull, leaden voice. "I will hunt you down and I will kill you."

Chapter 14

Renee doesn't care about Diane. I call to report in and Renee is only concerned about Haley. The girl is safely back in New York, so I don't see what the big deal is, but when Renee asks for details, she seems more interested in what Haley witnessed than the actual crime itself. I can't believe Renee is allowing herself to be so distracted from my mission. I mean, after all, the brat is safe and if you're asking me, that kid could witness wholesale slaughter without turning a hair. She was more interested in seeing a dead body than she was afraid because a killer was on the loose.

"The initial examination by the coroner leads the police to think Diane overdosed on some unusually strong cocaine, almost pure."

"Was Haley there when the coroner arrived?"

I sigh silently and take a calming breath before I answer no.

"Listen, do you think Diane's death could be tied to the attacks on Jeremy?" I ask. "I'm not as convinced as the cops are that Dave was the only one trying to hurt Jeremy. I'm just wondering if…"

Renee interrupts me. "Emma's getting out of the hospital in a few days. I've got two agents with her at all times and I want to be sure you know not to go see her before I can make sure she's safe. I don't want any possible slipups at the last moment."

I am lying on the bed in my room in Jeremy's Beverly Hills penthouse, staring up at the ceiling and praying for patience. It has been killing me not to call Emma, of course I remember! After Diane died and after I safely escorted Haley back to LAX, all I wanted was the comfort of my best friend and an ice cold Cosmopolitan.

"What do you want me to do?"

A huge part of me longs to hear her say, "Come on back to New York." But she doesn't. Instead she says, "I doubt seriously that Mr. Reins is in any further danger, I think the police have their man. However, I do think perhaps you could stretch your visit out a few more days." She pauses for a long moment before finishing. "Perhaps you could accompany Emma home on my private jet. I think she could use a little cheering up after all she's been through."

My heart sinks when she says "the police have their man." Renee obviously doesn't think I was much help and she certainly doesn't seem to want to hear my theory about Dave's innocence. But I am overjoyed at the prospect of seeing Emma and flying home with her.

"All right, I'll talk to Andrea and come up with a plausible reason to hang around. Maybe I'll go visit my father."

"That's fine, dear," Renee says, but it's clear that I have been dismissed and her attention is already elsewhere.

After we hang up, I drag around the room, playing with Marlena until I can't take my own mood any longer and wander out into the living room looking for the distraction of company.

Sam and Jeremy are standing by the huge plate-glass windows, drinks in hand, staring down at the sunset over the hills that surround our corner of Beverly Hills. When I walk into the room, Sam turns, sees me and smiles.

"You look like you could use one of those fancy cocktails you seem to like so much," he says. "What'll it be?"

The doorbell to the suite rings, interrupting my response and Sam looks questioningly at Jeremy. "You expecting anyone?"

Jeremy grins. "Relax, guard dog, it's just Mark and Andrea. I'll get it."

He crosses the thickly carpeted room and is at the door before Sam can beat him to it. His body hides the identity of the newcomer, but her voice is unmistakable.

"Jeremy," Zoe says. "I'm so sorry for the things I said. I was just…" She stops, her voice clogged with sobs, and walks into his arms.

"Oh, lovey," Jeremy murmurs gently. "I know. I know."

He ushers her into the foyer and the two of them stand locked in an embrace for a long time. Zoe is crying and Jeremy is stroking her hair gently.

"I loved her so much," Zoe says in a soft, broken voice. "She completed me. She fit after you and me, after we…"

"Shhh, lovey, it's all right," Jeremy soothes. "I know. She was there when I wasn't any longer. It's okay."

Sam and I exchange glances and he motions toward the hallway leading away from the living room.

"We'll be in the study," Sam says. Zoe seems not to hear him, but Jeremy meets Sam's gaze with a brief nod and the two of us disappear.

"Is Zoe just insane?"

Sam turns away from the table where he is pouring bourbon into two glasses and seems to be considering my question. "I don't know. I'd have to see her sober for more than a few hours at a time to tell you that and even then, who knows with Hollywood people? There are times I'm pretty sure Jeremy's gone round the bend, but when he's sober I can still reach inside and find the boy I knew back in Butte."

Sam hands me a tumbler with an inch of Wild Turkey in it and smiles apologetically. "I know, it's not a fancy frozen drink with an umbrella, but we're a bit short on supplies in here." He takes a long swallow from his glass.

I attempt to sip my bourbon like he does, without coughing and wincing at the acrid, unfamiliar taste. Sam is polite enough to pretend he doesn't notice when my eyes water and my face turns red with the effort. I can't stop thinking about last night but he seems not to even remember kissing me. We fall into an uncomfortable silence, which makes me nervous, so I drink more of the bourbon. I am beginning to like the warmth that spreads through my body with each sip and think perhaps it's time to let the cowboy know I'll be leaving in a few days. The ringing of the suite doorbell interrupts me.

When it rings again, Sam sighs and puts down his glass. "Jeremy must be in the middle of something with Zoe. I'll get it."

When he doesn't return my curiosity gets the better of me and I venture out into the hallway. When I hear Andrea and Mark's voices I relax and walk toward them. I look at my watch and realize we must all be going to dinner together. Good, I can ditch the bourbon and have a margarita with Andrea. Somehow, when Andrea's around, everything seems to flow more easily between me and the others. It's as if she's my social translator of all things Hollywood.

Mark and Andrea are in the hallway alone. Sam, Jeremy and Zoe are nowhere to be seen. The living room is empty.

"I'm so glad you're here!" I give Andrea a hug and turn to include Mark, but he has walked off into the living room and appears to be headed for the kitchen.

"What's going on? Is something wrong?"

Andrea's smile is worried. "I don't know. Sam thought Jeremy was in here with Zoe, but apparently not. He went off to look for them and now he's gone, too."

Sam returns, walking away from the hallway leading to my guest room, looking equally perplexed.

"I've searched the suite. Jeremy and Zoe must've gone off."

"But I have reservations at Koi. Jeremy's the one who asked me to make them, said he was dying to go. Do you know how hard it is to get a table there?"

Andrea strokes his arm reassuringly. "Darling, for other people perhaps, but not you."

Mark is like a well-trained dog, calming immediately under her touch. "Well, I know, but still it took some work." He peers at his diamond encrusted Rolex and frowns. "Well, should we wait or call his cell and have the two of them meet us there, or what?"

Sam holds up a small cell phone. "He didn't take his cell. Maybe he's just stepped down to the bar."

The two men leave to look downstairs, but an uneasy feeling is beginning to gnaw at my stomach.

"You think something's happened, don't you?" Andrea says quietly.

I meet her worried glance and nod. "Do you know where Zoe lives?"

Andrea is already moving toward the door, punching in a number on her cell as she stops to wait for me. "I'll let Mark know we're going to ride by Zoe's."

This is what I will miss most about Andrea, her ability to read my thoughts and stay fluid. She doesn't argue or panic, unless of course, her husband's under a dining table screwing a bimbo, but who wouldn't panic then?

"Let me grab my purse." I dart down the hallway, snatch up my little black Fendi clutch, turn to leave and almost squash poor Marlena. She is barring the door, hissing and chattering away, leaving no doubt that she intends to be taken along for the ride, or else!

"Honey, Mommy can't take you." When Marlena begins circling in and out of my legs, I give up. "All right, but you'll be bored out of your mind!"

Marlena snuggles across my shoulders and sighs, content just to be traveling with her mother. Andrea gives her a less than pleased once-over but doesn't say a word about Marlena's presence as we ride down the express elevator to the garage.

"We're probably overreacting," I say at some point along the ride to Zoe's. "They probably snuck back to her place to get high or get laid before dinner and they'll be really pissed to see we've followed them."

Andrea shakes her head. "I saw the way she looked at Jeremy after she found Diane's body. She meant every word she said."

"Why isn't Zoe blaming herself then? After all, Diane overdosed in Zoe's trailer on her cocaine. What does Jeremy have to do with it?"

Andrea just shakes her head as we head up the canyon road to the top of Mulholland Drive. "She told the police it wasn't her coke, of course, what else could she say?"

Andrea pulls into a short, brick drive and stops in front of a wrought-iron gate. She lowers the window and punches a code into a small metal box. The gates slowly begin to open.

"You have Zoe's pass code memorized?"

Andrea laughs softly. "It's no big deal. We're here so often lately I just do the code automatically. I even have a key, if we need it." When I look surprised, Andrea shrugs. "Zoe's needy. She's always asking Mark to come consult with her on one trumped-up excuse or another. Half the time he brings me along because he says I'm good with her. But trust me, this is the last time he encourages Jeremy to 'get in on the ground floor' of a project!"

Zoe lives in a low-slung, rambling Spanish style ranch that is rather plain looking from the outside. As we approach the front door, I catch a glimpse of the pool out behind the house and the view of L.A. from the top rim of the canyon wall. It is breathtakingly beautiful.

Andrea rings the doorbell and chews her lower lip, a worried expression on her face. "I don't see her car. Usually she leaves it in the drive, and there are no lights on, either."

Andrea walks back to her Jaguar and returns dangling a ring full of keys.

"So, Jeremy's not the only demanding actor Mark babysits?"

Andrea shakes her head as she searches for the right key, inserts it in the thick wooden door and we're inside within seconds. Andrea walks right past a flashing alarm pad on her way into Zoe's living room.

"Don't you need to disarm that?" I ask.

"She never arms it!" Andrea is disappearing down a hallway and I follow, trying not to lose her, but wanting to stop and study Zoe's home.

Andrea switches on lights as she goes, illuminating a home that could've come straight out of *Architectural Digest*. Zoe has a thing, it seems, for opulence. The oversize, overstuffed furniture is covered in rich gold and red brocades and velvets. Pictures hang on the walls in gold gilt frames. European antique pieces are placed in vantage points that showcase the patina of their well-polished finishes. Zoe's rooms could appear in any designer layout, but they are completely devoid of personality or warmth.

"Where are you going?" I call after Andrea.

Her voice floats back to me. "I'm just double-checking to make sure they're not here." She appears then, heading in my direction and stops to meet me midhallway.

"They're not here." She leans past me to open the door just behind me. "Come on, we'll check her office and then call Mark."

Zoe's office is the only room in her house that appears to have an owner. Her desk is a battered old monstrosity, dinged and scarred with use. Her laptop sits in the middle in front of a worn but comfortable cordovan leather desk chair. Papers sprawl across the desktop, along with watercolor paintings of costumes and sets. Photographs line the walls in simple black frames and I wander over to look at them.

One picture stops me and I lean in to examine it. Zoe is sitting at a table in a club along with three other people, two of them women, but it is the man sitting next to Zoe who catches my attention.

"Andrea, come here a second and look at this picture. I know I've seen this guy before, but I just can't place him. Do you know who it is?"

She walks up beside me and squints at the picture. "Oh, yeah, that's Raymond Estanza. He's the president of Octagon Enterprises."

Octagon Enterprises. The face and the name suddenly zip into focus. Emma and I met him at the Canal Room. I lifted his wallet right before his wife materialized and tried to kill Emma.

My heart is doing the cha-cha inside my rib cage. "How does he know Zoe?"

"I don't know how they met. They've known each other for a few years at least because I've seen him at a few of her parties and I believe they may even have dated for a short time. Anyway, they must be pretty close because he's got a lot of money invested in Zoe's picture."

"The one she's working on now?" The hairs on the back of my neck stand up and goose bumps are breaking out along my forearms.

Andrea nods and starts to walk back to Zoe's desk.

"Is Ray married?"

Andrea is rifling through Zoe's papers.

"I don't think so, why?"

"When I met him in New York, it seemed he had a woman he was serious about."

She almost killed Emma in the ladies' room, I want to add, but don't.

Andrea shrugs. "I've seen him around at social functions, but not with any one woman in particular. He's a venture capitalist. Some of his investments are in the entertainment field, but I don't know what else he does. To tell you the truth, I didn't like him. He seemed, well, sleazy to me."

Alarm bells are sounding in my head and yet, there is nothing concrete to back up my instincts. I fish my cell phone out of my pocket. When Renee answers, I take a deep breath and launch right in, hoping she'll at least trust me enough to tell me what I need to know.

"Okay," I say without preamble. "I need to give you an update. Zoe Harper came to Jeremy's penthouse about an hour ago. She said she wanted to apologize for saying the things she did when Diane died. But then they disappeared and it just didn't feel right, so Andrea Lowenstein brought me out to Zoe's house and there's a picture here of Raymond…" I close my eyes and will my memory to read the name on the driver's license in his wallet. "Estanza. The night I met you, Emma almost got killed by a woman whose picture was in his wallet. At the time I thought it was his wife. But you know all this. Now Jeremy's gone, there's a picture of that man here and he's backing Zoe's picture. I have no idea if the two are connected. What I do know is that my internal alarm bells are ringing and I need to find Zoe and Jeremy. What's the real deal with Ray Estanza? Emma didn't like him and I need to know why."

Renee is silent for a long moment and I assume she's considering whether or not to answer me.

"Raymond Estanza is the kingpin behind one of the

biggest cocaine operations in North America. The feds have never been able to make a case on him, in part because of his money and influential contacts. He has spent a lot of time and money establishing those connections and ensuring their loyalty. It has long been thought that he launders his drug money through Octagon Enterprises. That's why the Gotham Roses were called in and Emma was assigned to the case. Estanza has a weakness for very wealthy young women with good social standing. He takes perverse pleasure in addicting them to cocaine and then orchestrating their descent into forced prostitution."

I think of the beautiful woman in the ladies' room at the club and wonder what became of her.

"Lately, Estanza has broadened his circle of interest to young American women. Emma had no trouble infiltrating his organization and was getting very close to breaking it wide open when her cover got blown by another operative. If he's in L.A., or if you think he's made a connection between you and Emma, or Emma and Jeremy, then I would think one or all of you is in grave danger. Porsche, you must believe me, this is a very serious situation."

Renee pauses and I realize that Andrea has stopped searching Zoe's desk and has stopped to read a sheaf of papers she holds in her hands.

"I didn't want to tell you this," Renee continues, "but last night there was another attempt on Emma's life at the hospital. That's why I was so concerned that you not see her today. I was afraid not only for Emma, but for your sake as well. If Estanza thinks Emma or anyone else has incriminating evidence that could result in his arrest or the downfall of his drug smuggling operation, he will stop at nothing to eradicate that threat, even if it means taking innocent lives in the process. I want you to leave L.A. Now. Tonight. This is not a situation you can handle. I'll alert the Governess and we'll take…"

The cell phone loses the connection to New York and when I try it again, the line rings busy.

"Porsche," Andrea says, "I think I've found something."

I walk over to her, still hitting the redial button on my cell.

"Zoe changed the end of the script." Andrea's eyes are troubled when she looks up from the manuscript pages. "She's killed off Jeremy."

"What?"

"In the other version, the women of the cult take over, but they keep Jeremy's character, Reymundo, because he is the provider of the nectar these women need to stay alive. When I first read it, I thought they kept Jeremy's character as a sperm donor, you know, as the giver of life. But now they decide he's a false god when one of the characters dies. They decide to sacrifice him and anoint a new god, a newcomer to the tribe."

Reymundo. Nectar that gives life. Cocaine? My mind is scrambling to come up with interpretations.

"I think I know where she's taken him," Andrea says. "I think they've gone to her cabin in the mountains."

"Do you know where that is?" I ask. "We need to call the police and send them out there." I am moving out of the office at a run, hoping when I get outside my cell will work and I can reach Renee to notify the proper people.

"I won't be able to tell them." Andrea sounds panicked and defeated. "I only went there one time with Mark. Zoe loaned it to us for a weekend, but it was dark when we arrived so I'm not sure, but it's about an hour away in the hills near Carlito."

"Do you think you might recognize the road if we rode out there?"

"Maybe. I'll try."

Marlena is asleep in her carrier when Andrea and I return to the car, but she wakes up and crawls out to resume her nap in my lap. Andrea slips behind the wheel and drives like a madwoman, probably wondering, as I am, if we will arrive too late to save Jeremy.

She calls Mark from the car, hoping maybe he will remember, but he is as uncertain as she is.

"They're heading up there," she says, snapping her cell shut. "I guess they'll try, too. Mark says there's no way the cops would know because the cabin isn't even registered in her name, but he's going to call them anyway."

I stare out the window into the night sky and try as hard as I can to think of a way to find Jeremy faster. I think of all the tiny mountain roads that crisscross the hills above the small town and wonder if we will ever find him. I remember my father as we take the highway exit into Carlito. His number is still tucked safely inside my wallet and I dial with trembling fingers.

The phone seems to ring forever before he finally picks up.

"Porsche?"

"Hey, Daddy." I try and keep my voice bright and steady. "Listen, I'm kind of in your neighborhood on my way to a party and I was wondering if you could help me with the directions and maybe…babysit Marlena?"

Andrea follows my directions and we turn onto his street five minutes later. He is waiting at the foot of his long driveway, dressed in camouflage, his face blackened with grease paint so that only his eyes are clearly visible in the darkness.

"Jesus!" Andrea murmurs and stops abruptly in the middle of the cul-de-sac.

My father hops into the back seat of Andrea's car, smiles at the two of us and tips his black skullcap at Andrea. "Evening, ladies," he says. "Heading off to a little party, are you?" He leans forward, pulls a quarter from behind Andrea's ear, and laughs at her startled reaction. Marlena, apparently feeling left out, hops off of my shoulders and into my father's lap, an unheard of acceptance by my usually wary ferret. "Now, let's all relax a bit," he says, stroking Marlena's soft fur. "I've taken the liberty of making a few calls and I believe I know exactly where you're headed."

He points out a few landmarks on a hand-drawn map for Andrea then hops back out of the car with Marlena curled up around his neck.

"Don't do anything I wouldn't do," he says with a grin, but then I see a dark flash as his eyes meet mine. "But if you do, call me and I'll be right there."

He knows. I don't know how, but my father knows I'm headed into something dangerous. I shake off this feeling and fake a big smile back at him.

"Thanks, Dad! I should be back in an hour or two to get her."

My father nods without breaking eye contact and says in a low voice, "And if you're not?"

I stop smiling. "Then I might need a ride home," I answer softly.

He nods and without another word vanishes into the woods beside his driveway.

"Damn, Porsche," Andrea says. "That was interesting!"

Something hard and cold bumps up against my leg as

Andrea puts the car into gear. I look down and lying on the seat beside me is an ugly black gun. A little yellow scrap of paper is taped to the butt of the weapon.

Just in case. It's like a camera, all you do is point and shoot, no safety. Love, Dad.

"Damn, Andrea, look at this!" I pick the weapon up gingerly, avoiding the trigger and careful not to point it in her direction.

Andrea's eyes widen but she grins. "I'm liking that father of yours," she says. She pulls the car back out onto the road and starts driving in the direction my father pointed to while I study the little map. Two minutes later, I am rewarded by Andrea's triumphant cry, "There! That's the mailbox! We did it!"

"Pull the car over there," I direct and point to a spot farther down the road from Zoe's drive. "See if you can pull the car off the road and into the woods, facing back out so we can leave in a hurry if we have to."

Andrea does as I direct without another word and when she switches off the car's engine, the two of us sit for a long moment before I say anything.

"I vote we skirt the edge of her property and come in the back way. We'll get as close to the house as possible and if it looks like Jeremy's in trouble, we can call the cops."

Andrea nods but neither of us talks about the possibility that Jeremy may already be dead, and we certainly don't even entertain the possibility that Jeremy and Zoe have just run off for a little midnight rendezvous. After seeing the shrine Zoe has erected to Jeremy—or Reymundo, as she seems to prefer calling him—and reading the new ending to her movie, there is no doubt in my mind about Zoe's intentions.

We set off into the woods, following a narrow trail lit only by the available moonlight and walking single-file across what appears to be a narrow ridge that follows the hilltop. The sound of chanting and an accompanying drum-beat signals our approach to Zoe's mountain cabin. From this point on we drop to our knees and crawl the rest of the way to a vantage point just outside the clearing where Zoe is standing.

I press my lips together hard to avoid gasping out loud when I see Jeremy. He is naked and tied to a wooden pole that had been inserted in the bare ground of the clearing. Logs and sticks have been piled around the base of the pole, covering Jeremy's feet, and as we watch, Zoe slowly paces around Jeremy pouring liquid on the logs and chanting.

"Tell me this is all a movie scene and she isn't going to do what I think," Andrea whispers.

Zoe raises her arms high above her head and addresses the group of robed women in front of her.

"He has betrayed us, taken my lover to his cold grave and now he must follow," she says. "He is not our true leader. We must follow the will of Reymundo!"

Just as they did in the nightclub, the robed women chant, "Reymundo, Reymundo!" They begin to dance faster and faster around Jeremy and Zoe. Jeremy seems only half-conscious. His eyes flutter spasmodically and he attempts to speak, but the words come out in an unintelligible bab-ble. My heart is pounding almost louder than the drums beating below us as I pull my body up into a low crouch and look at Andrea.

"I want you to walk into the side of the circle farthest

away from Jeremy and create a distraction," I tell her.
"Think you can do that?"

Andrea nods nervously and looks back at the women below us while I start the count.

"What're you gonna do?" she asks.

"Well, while you're doing that, I'm gonna untie Jeremy
and get him away from these lunatics."

Andrea licks her lips nervously and glances back at me.
"You think about calling 9-1-1?"

Sarcasm, gotta love it.

"Yeah," I tell her, "but if you'll look closely, you'll see
Zoe is about to torch our boy hero and I don't think the local sheriff's gonna be able to make it in time to stop her.
I'll call, but I think we'd better plan on doing some of the
rescue work ourselves. Okay?"

Andrea sighs. "All right. I was just hoping. I mean, it's
basically gonna be just me against oh, I'd say, twenty
women. I was just thinking we might even up the odds
somehow."

I tug my father's gun out of my jacket pocket. "Don't
worry," I tell her. "If things get too crazy, I'll just shoot her!"

Zoe is moving dangerously close to Jeremy, a lit wand
in her hand.

I give Andrea a shove and say, "Now!" and watch as she
crawls off heading for the farthest point away from Jeremy.
A minute later there is a rustling across the clearing from
my hiding place and, as I watch, Andrea emerges from the
woods to stand at the edge of the clearing.

"Stop!" she yells. "I bring news from Reymundo!"

"Oh, now that is *so* lame," I mutter. "You think they're
gonna believe you?"

Andrea grins at a stunned Zoe and her friends. "Isn't

it wonderful that Zoe here is such pals with the Nectar Maker himself?" she says. "Why I think that's just grand!"

She takes a few more steps out of the woods to stand just at the edge of the circle. She flashes a look in my direction that seems to say, "All right, I've got their attention, now what?"

I start forward, moving very slowly up behind the stake where Jeremy is dangling. As I approach the edge of the clearing, I am aware that everyone else has stopped moving, including Zoe, and that they are all listening.

"I saw Ray earlier," Andrea says. "He says to send his regards, but he's moving on. It seems he's found a new plaything."

"This has nothing to do with you!" I hear Zoe say. "Leave us now or die with him."

"Zoe, honey," Andrea says as she steps closer into the circle. "I know you think Jeremy had something to do with…"

"Shut up!" Zoe cries.

I take advantage of this moment and dart forward, running the short distance to Jeremy and hastily beginning to untie the ropes that bind him to the pole.

I raise up, sheltered by the thick log and bring my lips close to his ear. "Can you hear me, Jeremy?" I whisper.

"Lovey?" he murmurs softly. "Is that you?"

"Yes. Listen to me. I'm going to untie you. Do you think you can walk?"

Jeremy nods slightly. "I think so. She gave me something. I feel weird, like this is all happening to someone else and I'm watching the movie." He giggles softly. "It's delightful, really, but not so much when you know it's you."

I want to slap him, but know how pointless *that* would

be. I fumble with the ropes, frantic to get the last knot undone, frantic to move him before we're discovered.

As the last rope falls free and Jeremy almost topples
from the stand of logs, I hear Andrea scream.

I push Jeremy behind me. "Run!" I say and shove my
cell phone into his hand. "Call 9-1-1 and run like hell!"

I don't know if he understands me or is even capable of
moving, but it doesn't matter. Two women are holding Andrea and Zoe has whipped around to face me, a maniacal
glint in her pale green eyes.

I pull the gun from my pocket, step forward and point
it right at Zoe's chest. Without taking my eyes off of her I
yell, "I will kill your redhaired leader if just one of you tries
to stop us!"

Zoe looks wild-eyed from me to the women behind her.
There is the smallest rustle from the group of women as
Andrea struggles to break away from her captors and they
try to decide whether to allow this or continue to hold her.

Zoe seems oblivious to this and the crazy smile returns
to her face. "And if you shoot me," she says softly, "we'll
kill Andrea."

I hesitate, uncertain, but realizing it's up to me to pull
this off.

"So, you shoot her," I say, forcing a smile. "I don't think
Ray would approve of that, do you, honey? If you kill Andrea, that's bad for business. She's married to one of the
top agents in Hollywood. He's got enough power to hurt
Ray's business."

Zoe's attention shifts, along with the others, to Andrea
and I see uncertainty in Zoe's expression. She's not sure.

"Killing Jeremy, now that was a brilliant idea," I say,
stepping a little closer. "That'll take care of those over-

budget woes. Jeremy will be the new Brandon Lee. People will flock to see the movie that killed Jeremy Reins. It'll make more money than *The Crow* did when Brandon got killed. That was brilliant."

Zoe is smiling now, almost lulled by my words and I move even closer because if she doesn't give me Andrea, I am going to have to kill her.

I make a mental note to take more courses in hypnosis and subliminal suggestion.

"I say, lovey, you know you've got it all wrong, really. I didn't give Diane that cocaine. If you want to blame someone, blame Ray. It was his stuff and you left it lying out. How was she supposed to know it was so strong?"

Jeremy's voice breaks my carefully woven spell and if I were not so intent upon killing Zoe and protecting Andrea, I swear I would just turn around, shoot the idiot and put him out of his misery!

"Liar!" Zoe wails. "I didn't leave anything lying out. I was waiting for…"

When Zoe doesn't finish her sentence, I finish it for her.

"You were waiting for Ray, weren't you?" I step right up in front of her so she can't look away. "Well, he came and left you a little present, only Diane found it first and now she's dead. Just think, sweetie, it could've been you."

"No-o-o!" Zoe sinks to her knees in the dirt, sobbing.

I squat down, keeping my face at her level, making the most of her weakened state. "You know what I think?" Zoe looks into my eyes and shakes her head no. "I think you must've pissed Ray off real bad, Zoe. You must've been a bad girl. I think you owe him lots of money on this film and you're in over your head. He gave you lots of money and lots of cocaine, and in return, you messed up. You were too busy stuffing coke up your nose to make a good picture. That's how come you decided to kill Jeremy, so your picture would make millions even if it sucked, which, I can tell you from looking at the script, it does!"

Zoe's face slowly fills with terror, her eyes are huge, her skin is ashen and she shakes her head slowly back and forth.

"He's crazy," she gasps. "I did what he said. I didn't talk to anybody about him. He thinks I'm talking to the feds. He thinks we're all against him. He's paranoid and he's going to kill me!"

"He saw you and Jeremy with my friend, Emma, didn't he?" I say softly.

"I don't know!" Zoe drops her head into her hands, sobbing. "He said if I ever told anyone what I know, he'd kill me—but I didn't! I swear to God, I didn't." She turns her head to look at Jeremy. "That's why I thought you…"

"Killed Diane," he finishes her sentence in a tired, weak voice. "No."

I glare back at him. "I thought you were leaving so you could make that important call for me."

Jeremy smiles softly. "Did it, lovey, but I couldn't leave you alone out here, now could I?"

Is everyone in Hollywood insane? I wonder.

I grab Zoe's arm and pull her to her feet, making sure her little band of devotees see the gun in my hand as I pull her back and away from the others.

"Let Andrea go," I say in a very firm tone. "Let her go and I will let the rest of you leave before the sheriff gets here."

That is all it takes. The women disburse in a chaotic scramble to elude the long arm of the law, abandoning their leader in a flurry of self-preservation. Zoe looks scared as I tighten my grip on her arm and I find this doesn't bother me. I want her to have a healthy respect for my abilities. As we start off back down the trail I let Andrea and Jeremy walk on a few yards ahead of us, before speaking.

"Zoe, I think if you go back to L.A., Estanza will kill you. You know too much and you're addicted to cocaine. You're unpredictable and Estanza can't have that."

Zoe makes a mewling sound, like a frightened kitten, and just stares at me, her eyes wild with fear.

"I'm going to talk to the police. They'll keep you safe until I can send some government agents to escort you to a safer facility. When Estanza's arrested, you'll need to testify. That's the only way you can get rid of him and the only way you can work out a plea bargain. Otherwise, you'll spend the rest of your life in jail."

"But he'll kill me!"

I shake my head. "He'll kill you if you don't. Testifying against him is your only chance to stay alive."

Andrea and Jeremy are just reaching the edge of the road when a pickup rounds the corner, illuminating them in its headlights.

"Get back out of the road!" I yell.

Andrea yanks Jeremy, who is now wearing one of Zoe's black robes, by the collar, pulling him safely out of the oncoming truck's path. The approaching vehicle looks like Sam's truck, but the flashing red light mounted on its hood is deceiving.

When Sam steps out of the driver's side, I almost run to him, but something stops me. His left arm is hanging limp at his side. He steps forward, shielding his eyes with his hand. A man steps out of the truck behind him and I catch my breath as I see the gun in his hand trained on Sam's body.

Raymond Estanza looks into the woods, his eyes resting on the spot where I know Andrea and Jeremy are hiding and says, "Where is she?"

Jeremy emerges from his hiding place, shields his eyes and smiles lazily at Sam. "Hey, pard! Where is who?"

Estanza motions Sam forward. I know what is coming and I am thinking as hard and fast as I can. Zoe's mouth opens and before she can shriek or say anything, I cover it with my hand and force her down onto the ground.

"Don't make a fucking sound!" I hiss in her ear. "If he sees you, he'll kill you. You stay here until I tell you to move." I don't tell her that I'm not certain I'll be alive to say anything. "I'm going to try and help the others. Stay right here. Understand?"

Zoe nods and I release her. I slip off my shoes and begin to creep quietly through the woods skirting the driveway, trying to get as close to the spot where the others stand as possible, but having absolutely no clue what I'll do when I reach them.

Estanza is slowly approaching Jeremy, the expression on his face grim.

"You don't want to play with me, boy," he says. "Where is Zoe?"

Jeremy looks puzzled, out of it and confused. "She left me," he says slowly, and I know he's playing the part and not as disoriented as he seems.

I see Andrea look in my direction, startled, and then swivel her head back to watch Estanza.

"Where is my husband?" she calls suddenly. She takes two steps forward to bring herself even with Jeremy, sheltering me from view, and talking loud enough to cover my slow creep toward the spot where Ray Estanza holds his gun on Sam.

"He's all right," Sam answers, but his voice is tight with pain. "We were about to leave the condo and come find you when this idiot…" Sam stops speaking with a grunt and I know Estanza has hurt him. I feel panic grip me with icy fingers and I know I have to do something.

Estanza nudges Sam forward but when he does, Sam doubles over in pain.

"What do you mean, where is Zoe?" Andrea asks loudly, still covering for me. "I thought she'd be with you. She ran off with the others."

Estanza slowly lifts the gun in his hand bringing it up toward Andrea and I know I can wait no longer. I level my gun at him, close my eyes and pull the trigger.

There is a horrible explosion, a cracking sound, and a scream that echoes into the darkness, followed by a loud crash.

I open my eyes in time to see a tree limb bounce off the top of Sam's truck and carom forward, bouncing off the truck's hood and striking a glancing blow at Raymond Estanza's back. I start running toward Estanza, but in the chaos of the moment he doesn't see me. He is trying to keep his gun trained on the three people closest to him. When I tackle him from the side, knocking him off balance, the guy doesn't even see it coming.

We crash to the ground, his gun goes flying, and I ride him like a mechanical bull.

I stick the gun into the base of his skull and lean forward to whisper in his ear.

"I, like, so totally have no clue how to use this thing, so you'd better not fucking move! Okay?"

Sam picks up Estanza's gun and holds it securely in his good hand.

"I don't know if I'd believe that, Ray," he says. "She's pretty good with a weapon. You saw how she just killed that tree branch. Hell, imagine what she'd have done if her eyes had been open!"

Chapter 15

The reflection of the underwater lights dances along the walls surrounding the pool area and adds to the festive air of the party Jeremy is hosting in my honor. Everyone who is anyone is in attendance—at least, everyone who is anyone in my life at this moment. Even Emma, who has been released from the hospital, is allowed to attend because of Raymond Estanza's arrest.

Emma is reclining against a chaise lounge and is being carefully waited on by a quite attentive Jeremy.

"Oh, lovey," Jeremy said earlier. "I was never serious about the man. He's so…well…military. I guess I didn't need quite that much rigidity in my life after all."

Jeremy doesn't say so, but I know he took it upon himself personally to facilitate Dave's release from jail and his reunion with Scott. Jeremy is not as bad as I'd thought him to be, or maybe the sordid business with Zoe and the near-death experiences that brought have caused him to mature. Whatever the reason, I have decided that I like the man, even if he is terribly spoiled.

My father and Sam have me wrapped around their little fingers. They sit, side by side, on matching lounge chairs and cast pitiful glances in my direction. They make a dangerous team.

"Porsche, honey, would you mind bringing us another shot of Wild Turkey? It's the only thing that eases Sam's pain, don't you know." My father has somehow adopted an Irish brogue and is laying it on thick. "I'd get it myself," he says, "but my arthritis is botherin' me lately."

"Porsche, if it's not too much trouble," Sam says, "a couple of beer chasers might hit the spot. I think I might be able to get them myself if it's too much for you...."

When I turn to do their bidding, Sam reaches out and catches my hand, stopping me.

"Come here," he demands, his voice low and husky with promise. I try to resist, but he pulls me down into his arms and kisses me thoroughly, something he's been doing ever since I killed the tree limb and became known as a dangerous sharpshooter.

I linger over Sam's kiss, feeling warmth spread throughout my body, and wanting more, much more than he can handle in his wounded state. I like to think of myself as a patient woman, but even a saint has her limits. Perhaps in a day or two...Sam kisses me again and I change my mind. Perhaps tonight...

"About those drinks, Porsche," my father calls impatiently.

"On your way, woman!" Sam says, pushing me up and onto my feet.

I walk away hearing their deep chuckles of amused delight echoing around me. They love their newfound power over the "little diva," as they've taken to calling me.

My cell phone rings and I stop to flip open the pink, crystal case. Renee, with perfect timing, as usual.

"Porsche? I'm calling to see how you're feeling. I'll wait and do the formal debriefing after you return to New York, but I thought I'd better check in today. You know, this was a stressful mission, even for a seasoned agent and not at all what I'd planned for your first time."

Hmmm. First time—does this imply the possibility of more missions? Is this Renee's way of saying she's pleased with me?

"I'm fine," I say, smiling back at my father and Sam. "I believe Jeremy is also fine, psychologically that is, I mean, considering that he displays narcissistic character traits which prevent him from having any truly accurate insight into the effects of his actions. And, as you may know by now, my father's Post Traumatic Stress Disorder could've been re-triggered, but I am fully confident that we have managed to avoid this complication by..."

"Porsche!" Renee sounds as if she is perhaps choking back a laugh, but I rather doubt this. "I really wanted to check on *you*. I'd hate to think we'd overload one of our newest agents so early in her career."

A little thrill of excitement runs through my body. *I'm in! I'm a member of the team! Porsche Rothschild is going to be a Gotham Rose!* Oh this is going to be so-o-o good for my self-esteem. I glance back at Sam and wink. I can't wait to tell my therapist the happy news.

Marlena scampers down off my father's chair and runs to join me as I say goodbye to Renee and start walking.

"Hurry up with those drinks!" my father yells.

I shoot the two men a dirty look over my shoulder as I go, but they only laugh harder. They know I don't mean it. They know they have each captured my heart, and they use this to their full advantage, the little bastards! I would sure like to know what I did to deserve this treatment, because whatever it is, I fully intend to keep it up for the rest of my life.

Marlena must read my mind because she stops in her tracks, rises up onto her hind legs and emits a long ferret scream. When I whirl around to see what's wrong, she topples over, playing "dead" on the slate patio floor.

I lean down to peer at her, she pops one eye open in a wild ferret wink and I could just swear the little minx is grinning!

Turn the page for an exclusive excerpt from the next
book in the exciting
THE IT GIRLS miniseries from Silhouette Bombshell.
MS. LONGSHOT
by Sylvie Kurtz
After the suspicious deaths of several top show
horses, the Gotham Rose spies called on socialite
Alexa Cheltingham to go undercover as a grubby groom.
Her riches-to-rags transition was easy—mucking
stables was a far cry from partying on Park Avenue.
She also had to protect the mayor's show-jumping
daughter, hunt for the horse killer, even dodge a
murder rap—all while resisting her chief
suspect's undeniable charms....
On sale December 2005
at your favorite retail outlet.

"The Governess has asked me to send you on an assignment." Renee added a slice of lemon to her tea.

I sat up a little straighter and anticipation shot through my veins. Thank you, Governess! At least *someone* had faith in me.

None of the agents had ever met the mysterious Governess, not even Renee. The only thing we could agree on was that, whoever she was, she was well-connected. And when the equally mysterious Duke entered the conversation, you'd think we were a book club discussing an old Victoria Holt gothic novel.

"Alexa, have you been keeping up with news of the show circuit?" Renee asked, reaching for a tea sandwich.

"No, not really." What was the point of salting a wound? I got my fix of horses through my foundation and my weekly trips to the estate in Darien, Connecticut, where I kept two horses. "Why?"

"A string of accidents have happened this winter on the Palm Beach show-jumping circuit. Canterbury Crown died of a heart attack while going over a jump and his rider was hurt from the fall. Drug testing showed cocaine in the horse's blood."

"Cocaine?" Who would do such a thing? Of course, some people would do anything to win—even hurt a defenseless animal. "What happened?"

"The police investigated, but came to no conclusion."

"You want me to look into it," I said hopefully. My heart fluttered against my ribs as I leaned ever so slightly forward.

"A few weeks later, a barn fire killed four horses, including the current National Horse Show champion, Total Eclipse."

Just thinking about the terror those poor animals had to endure raised my blood pressure and sparked my temper. But I bit my tongue. This was definitely my kind of assignment, but Renee was obviously not asking for my opinion.

"The latest victim is Monica Lightbourne, daughter of the media heiress," Renee continued. "Someone injected her horse, Blue Ribbon Belle, with a drug that caused a neurological reaction so violent the horse had to be put down."

"That's awful. How do you want me to help?"

"The Metropolitan Spring Classic Charity Horse Show begins in a week," Renee said.

"You want me to investigate at the show since I'll be there for my foundation's charity event." Yes! This I could do. No stretch at all.

"Not exactly." Renee sipped her tea, humor glinting in

her eyes. "As you know, the mayor's daughter participates in show jumping. He's afraid his daughter, who's the front-runner to win the Grand Prix, will be the next victim."

A small thrill spurred my pulse into a gallop. Finally a chance to do more than shuffle paper. Protecting the mayor's daughter was an elite assignment. Something I'd almost given up hope of getting because of Renee's attitude toward my leg.

Renee set her uneaten triangle of sandwich on her plate. "We want you to go undercover at the stable where she trains." She tilted her head. "As a groom."

"Excuse me?" I had to have heard wrong. Renee wanted *me,* heiress Alexa Cheltingham, to go undercover muck-ing out stalls? Just what had she put in her tea?

Renee studied me, then lifted both eyebrows and a shoulder in a gesture of dismissal. "I told the Governess this wasn't a good idea, with your leg and all. This will re-quire hard physical work, Alexa. Are you up to the job?"

I'd never let my "defective" leg stop me from achiev-ing my goals before. I certainly wouldn't now. If Renee wanted a groom, I could become a groom. "How hard can it be to shovel manure?"

Silhouette® BOMBSHELL™

BRINGS YOU THE LATEST IN
Vicki Hinze's
WAR GAMES
MINISERIES

Double Dare

December 2005

A plot to release the deadly DR-27
supervirus at a crowded mall? Not U.S.
Air Force captain Maggie Holt's idea of
Christmas cheer. Forget the mistletoe—
Maggie, with the help of scientist
Justin Crowe, has to stop a psycho
terrorist before she can even think of
enjoying Christmas kisses.

Available at your favorite retail outlet.

HOMICIDE DETECTIVE
MERRI WALTERS IS BACK IN

Silent Reckoning
by Debra Webb

December 2005

A serial killer was on the loose,
hunting the city's country singers.
Could deaf detective Merri Walters turn
her hearing loss to advantage and crack
the case before the music died?

Available at your favorite retail outlet.

If you enjoyed what you just read,
then we've got an offer you can't resist!

Take 2 bestselling love stories FREE!

Plus get a FREE surprise gift!

Clip this page and mail it to Silhouette Reader Service®

IN U.S.A.	IN CANADA
3010 Walden Ave.	P.O. Box 609
P.O. Box 1867	Fort Erie, Ontario
Buffalo, N.Y. 14240-1867	L2A 5X3

YES! Please send me 2 free Silhouette Bombshell™ novels and my free surprise gift. After receiving them, if I don't wish to receive any more, I can return the shipping statement marked cancel. If I don't cancel, I will receive 4 brand-new novels every month, before they're available in stores! In the U.S.A., bill me at the bargain price of $4.69 plus 25¢ shipping & handling per book and applicable sales tax, if any*. In Canada, bill me at the bargain price of $5.24 plus 25¢ shipping & handling per book and applicable taxes**. That's the complete price and a savings of 10% off the cover prices—what a great deal! I understand that accepting the 2 free books and gift places me under no obligation ever to buy any books. I can always return a shipment and cancel at any time. Even if I never buy another book from Silhouettte, the 2 free books and gift are mine to keep forever.

200 HDN D34H
300 HDN D34J

Name	(PLEASE PRINT)	
Address	Apt.#	
City	State/Prov.	Zip/Postal Code

Not valid to current Silhouette Bombshell™ subscribers.

Want to try another series?
Call 1-800-873-8635 or visit www.morefreebooks.com.

* Terms and prices subject to change without notice. Sales tax applicable in N.Y.
** Canadian residents will be charged applicable provincial taxes and GST.
All orders subject to approval. Offer limited to one per household.
® and ™ are registered trademarks owned and used by the trademark owner and
or its licensee.

BOMB04   ©2004 Harlequin Enterprises Limited

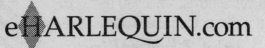

COMING NEXT MONTH

#69 DOUBLE DARE—Vicki Hinze
War Games

For U.S. Air Force Captain Maggie Holt, Christmas had always been about eggnog, mistletoe and holiday cheer...until the biowarfare expert discovered a plot to unleash the deadly DR-27 supervirus at a crowded mall on Christmas Eve. Now Maggie needed a double dose of daring—and the help of the DR-27 antidote's handsome inventor—to defuse certain tragedy.

#70 MS. LONGSHOT—Sylvie Kurtz
The It Girls

After the suspicious deaths of several top show horses, the Gotham Rose spies called on socialite Alexa Cheltingham to go undercover as a grubby groom. Her riches-to-rags transition wasn't easy—mucking stables was a far cry from partying on Park Avenue. She had to protect the mayor's show-jumping daughter, hunt for the horse killer, even dodge a murder rap— all while resisting her chief suspect's undeniable charms....

#71 THE CARDINAL RULE—Cate Dermody
The Strongbox Chronicles

Talk about mixed allegiances! Agent Alisha McAleer's latest assignment involved stealing the prototype of an artificial intelligence combat drone from her CIA handler's own son. And others wanted the drone—including a clandestine organization called the Sciarri and her former partner-turned-mercenary. With even her bosses proving untrustworthy, Alicia was on her own. Again.

#72 SILENT RECKONING—Debra Webb

Going deaf hadn't stopped Merri Walters from rising to the rank of homicide detective. But she had a new set of problems. Her old flame was now her boss, her new partner didn't want to work with a woman and a serial killer was on the loose, targeting country-music starlets. Posing as killer bait seemed suicidal, but Merri marched to her own tune, and wouldn't let anything—or anyone—stand in the way of nabbing her man....

SBCNM1105